An Archer's Crusade

3

An ARCHER'S CRUSADE

GRIFF HOSKER

LUME BOOKS

LUME BOOKS

Published in 2020 by Lume Books
30 Great Guildford Street,
Borough, SE1 0HS

ISBN 978-1-83901-215-0

Typeset using Atomik ePublisher from Easypress Technologies

www.lumebooks.co.uk

List of Historical Characters

Lord Edward (later King Edward I of England)
Princess Eleanor (later Queen Eleanor)
King Henry III (father of Lord Edward/King Edward I)
Richard of Cornwall (brother of King Henry III)
Henry Almain (Richard of Cornwall's son)
Baibars (former Egyptian commander of the Mamluks, who
came to lead all Turkish forces)
Eleanor (Countess of Leicester and the sister of King Henry III)
Simon de Montfort (the leader of the rebels in England and son
of the Earl of Leicester, Simon de Montfort)

PART 1

The Scouring of England

Map of 13th Century England

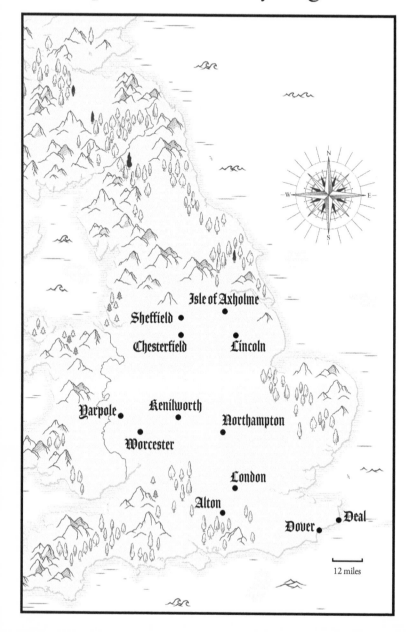

Chapter 1

I fought in the bloody battle that was Evesham, and my lord and master –
Lord Edward –rewarded me with a manor. Yarpole, however, did not
come with a knighthood, and that meant I was a tenant of Baron Roger
Mortimer and Lady Maud. Captain William had been knighted, but I
was merely an archer, and I knew of no archer who had spurs. Perhaps
we were considered too close to the peasantry of England.

I was not concerned about the lack of spurs. Having been an outlaw,
I had already risen far higher than my murdered father could ever have
expected. I was an outlaw because I slew my father's killer – if I had not
met Lord Edward in Aquitaine and become his archer, then I might
never have survived as long as I have. For that, I will always be grateful
to Lord Edward.

After the battle at Evesham, we set to clearing the dead. A huge funeral
pyre was built. Of course, we profited from that, and met other men at
arms and archers, for nobles did not sully their hands with such work.
The most interesting man I met, as we took our spoils from the dead
and then placed their bodies on pyres, was Hamo l'Estrange. I never
did find out whence he acquired his name, but he had been a sword for
hire for many years and had been on crusade with Simon de Montfort.

L'Estrange was a pragmatic man, and when he had realised that Lord Edward would win, he changed sides. Hamo was an entertaining man and I enjoyed his company. We spoke as we collected booty and bodies, and I learned much from him and the other swords for hire. The moment we met I could not help liking the huge man. He was a larger than life character and one of the few men at arms who still wore not just a full beard, but also long hair. He was a relic of an earlier time, a time when warriors cared less about the way that they looked and more about the way they fought.

The ongoing civil war, however, was far from over, and Lord Edward and his father, King Henry, had left the battlefield to join the siege of Kenilworth. That castle was almost impregnable, thus leading rebels had sought sanctuary there. I was grateful that I did not have to endure a siege, for they were messy affairs. No matter how few defenders, they always had the advantage. King Henry declared the land of the rebels to be forfeit and he wasted no time allocating it to those who had served the royal cause – like me.

I sent my men to the village ahead of me while I delivered Simon de Montfort's head to Lady Maud. My men and I were a good team; we had fought together for some time. John of Nottingham was my lieutenant and was the most loyal of men. I knew that whenever I was in danger, he had my back. The village should not have presented any threat, but I was aware that it belonged to someone before it became mine.

That done, I joined my men. I had left them to explore the village for I knew little about it, except that it was mine. As I rode into the huddle of houses and huts that made up the village, I used the vantage point of Eleanor's back to survey my new land and to see if a reeve came, cap in hand, to accept my authority. Eleanor was my horse and now as much a part of me as my war bow.

I saw there was a wooden church and that it had a separate bell tower. A church meant a priest – and if a reeve failed to come, then I would speak with the priest. There was a mill, too, but it looked neglected. The road down which I had travelled had not been paved; it was a greenway. The hall was the most imposing building to be seen, save the church, and I saw that Lord Edward's gift was less generous than it had at first appeared.

John of Nottingham led my men from the village to meet me. "Not exactly a welcome for heroes of the king, eh, Captain?"

"I care not, for it is now mine. Let us see if there is a stable. David, find me the priest and ask him to come to the hall."

My lieutenant, David the Welshman, spoke with a wry look on his face. "Ask?"

"Let us try kindness first. If you saw us riding into your village, I think you would fear the worst, eh?"

He laughed, for indeed we looked more like bandits than Lord Edward's archers.

I learned from my men that the previous owner was a supporter of de Montfort. Lord Edward was a ruthless man and he did not forgive rebellion easily. Matthew of Yarpole had died at Evesham, but I knew not if the village sympathised with the rebels. I also learned that the village had a reeve, who managed the manor for Matthew of Yarpole.

I dismounted and handed my reins to Tom, John's son. I had my sword and a dagger in my belt but doubted that I would need either. The hall looked less imposing the closer I got. It was wooden and it was old. The timbers and the lath had weathered, and both needed work. I did not mind hard work, but time was not something I had in abundance, for Lord Edward would summon me sooner rather than later – and if this was my reward, then I needed to make the most of it.

I opened the door and shouted, "Hello, the house?"

An old woman shuffled nervously in from a room at the back, presumably the kitchen. "Yes, sir, can I help you? The master is away, as is his reeve, Godfrey. I am Sarah and I run the house for his lordship."

Matthew of Yarpole had either given himself a title to which he was not entitled, or Lord Edward had been less than truthful about the meagreness of the manor. On reflection, it was probably the latter.

The old woman must not have heard the news, and so I informed her. "Matthew of Yarpole is dead: his head is with those of the other traitors who foolishly followed Simon de Montfort. If the reeve was with him, then he is dead, too."

She did not seem overly upset.

"I am Captain Gerald War Bow and I serve Lord Edward, the future King of England."

She bobbed a half-hearted attempt at a curtsy. It almost made me smile. "Welcome, sir."

"I have men with me, and they will need beds. How many chambers are there in the hall?"

"There is the master's chamber and four other rooms with beds in."

"And you, where is your home?"

She gestured with her head. "I have a hut by the stable. My husband," she made the sign of the cross, "God rest his soul, was the reeve before Godfrey was given his job."

Something in her words made me question her further. "Was your husband happy about that?"

She shook her head. "No, sir – and it broke his heart. I am sure that is what killed him. Is Godfrey dead?"

I shrugged. "I confess that I do not know him, but even if he is not, then he has lost all claim to his position. I will appoint a new reeve."

She nodded and looked to say something, but thought better of it.

I did not have time for dancing words.

"Speak, Sarah; you will find that I like honesty and plain speaking, for I am not noble born. What you see before you is an archer."

"It is just that my son, James, now works for the blacksmith but his father raised him to take over as reeve." She seemed to shrink as I stared at her. "It is no matter, Captain."

"Do not be afraid, I will meet him and consider him for the position. I am a warrior for hire and the nearest I have come to managing land is poaching from Sir Henry!" That made her smile and she looked less fearful as I continued. "Make the rooms ready. Is there food?"

"The rooms will not be a problem, but I am not sure there is enough food."

We had found food in the rebel camp at Evesham and had enough for a few days. "We have brought supplies with us."

"I will see to it, master." She left and I surveyed the room which was large enough to be used as a dining room and would suit me.

John of Nottingham came in and looked around. "This hall and the land need work, Captain."

"Aye they do but it is a home for us all, eh? Have our war gear and supplies brought in. We have a housekeeper, Sarah, she will cook. I will find this priest."

I stepped outside and immediately saw David the Welshman approaching with the priest. He was an older man, with flecks of grey in his beard. "This is Father Paul, he is the priest."

I nodded. "Go help John." David left us and I extended my hand.

"Father Paul, I am Captain Gerald, Lord Edward's archer and the new master of Yarpole."

His hand, when I grasped it, was rough. This was a priest unafraid of hard work. And he spoke plainly. "It seems we have a master who does *not* accord himself a false title."

My suspicions about Matthew of Yarpole had been right, then. "The manor, what can you tell me?"

"It was a wealthy one until Matthew of Yarpole came here. He was not a good lord and abused the village in every way imaginable. His reeve, Godfrey, had… appetites." He shuddered. "I am a man of God and do not understand such carnal desires." He glanced at me. "I suppose war does that to a man."

"Some men, priest, but not me and not my men." My tone of voice communicated that I would not brook insults to my men, who had served their king and prince well.

He smiled – he was not afraid of upsetting me and I liked that. "I believe you, and there is hope for Yarpole now!" He spread his arms. "You have twelve farms, but they do not produce the yield they should, for the former master sucked them dry. The mill has no miller, for not enough wheat and barley were grown to mill. There is a blacksmith, but he does not have enough work and I fear he will leave."

"Yet he took on the son of the former reeve."

"That is because the lad is his nephew."

That shone new light on the situation. "Could James be the new reeve?"

The priest looked at me in surprise. "You have learned much in a short time. Aye, he is a good lad and knows the land."

"I shall need your help, Father Paul, if I am to restore this village to its former glory – and I do not have much time."

"Then you shall have my help – but there is another problem you have yet to encounter."

"And what is that?"

"Baron Mortimer is the lord of all this land, but he does not bother overmuch with us. There are bandits eight miles from here, and they prey upon both the land and the people. In the greater scheme of things, it is not a threat to his lordship, but it weakens the people here and the surrounding villages. They leave the borderlands and head to the larger towns and cities. If men do not work the fields…"

I nodded. I could deal with bandits. "Then that will be my first task after I have spoken to the people of Yarpole."

It was night by the time I had spoken to every man in the village. There were still farmers I needed to see, but I had my reeve. Both James and his mother were grateful for my hasty decision and I never regretted it. I was a hunter of men and used to making split-second judgements. As an archer, you were either quick or you were dead. I was no fool, and I would use whatever time Lord Edward gave me to watch my people and make informed judgements as a landowner. James' uncle, Walter the Smith, was also happy when I came to an arrangement with him for weapons, arrowheads and horseshoes. Far from making money, this new venture was costing me, but we had profited from Evesham and I was philosophical. If I followed Lord Edward's banner, then there would be more coin forthcoming.

As we sat around the table eating our supplies, I reflected on the changes in my life. I was still young, yet I led my own company of archers and I knew I had yet to achieve my full potential. I had a home and I had land. My father had possessed a home, but it was merely a hut. I had achieved more than him, and I knew that, in heaven, he would be pleased.

Our conversations with the villagers confirmed the priest's words: the bandits, whilst not a serious danger to life, were an annoyance, for cattle were stolen as were sheep. Travellers were robbed and maidens could not walk abroad without men to guard them. John of Nottingham and many of my men had been outlaws and understood a man's life outside the law, but they had all changed and now regretted being forced down that path.

"Captain, perhaps we could speak to these men and persuade them to move elsewhere?" Jack of Lincoln had been a leader of bandits and understood them better than any. When I first encountered him, he was an outlaw. He had forgotten more about archery than I would ever learn, but he was getting older and I wondered when he would decide to give up the road.

I had a different view. My life as an outlaw was far briefer and now that I was a landowner, I had a changed perspective. "And you would inflict these bandits on other villages?" I saw on his face that he had not thought it through. "When you were an outlaw, if a man had come into the forest and asked you to give up – what would you have done?" I was talking to all of those who had been outlaws. I saw their shamefaced looks. "I do not wish to kill these men and I will try to speak to them, but I will not risk any of your lives. Tomorrow, we ride to this wood – which is eight miles hence – and we will treat it as though they are Lord Edward's enemies and we need to eliminate them. Tom will watch the horses and John of Nottingham will lead half of you. I will take the other half. My aim is to surround them and use our bows as a threat. Then I will speak. If they choose to fight, we try to wound them, but come what may, by this time tomorrow night, the bandits of Worsley Wood will be no more."

Jack of Lincoln nodded. "I can see that Lord Edward has made you a stronger man. I believe what you do is right, but if I led this company, I might not have taken this route."

John of Nottingham said, "And that is why Gerald War Bow is the captain of our company."

I used more of my precious money to send James and his mother to Leominster market, to buy what we needed to repair the hall and to lay in supplies of food. I had worried that Lord Edward might take me to war too soon and now I saw that *whenever* it was, it would be too soon. I had much to do.

I took the opportunity, as we rode to the wood along the greenways, to examine the land I now owned. The farmers did not own the land, I did, and they paid me rent in the form of crops and animals. That Matthew of Yarpole had mismanaged the land was now obvious, for I saw fallow fields that should have contained either crops or animals. The combination of a poor landowner and bandits had almost killed Yarpole. I wondered now if Lord Edward had known this, or just thought I would be grateful for anything. I would make the best of it, for that was my way.

We halted well short of the wood and dismounted. Tom was not happy to be the horse holder, but I had trained my men to obey. John of Nottingham took his half (of the dozen or so men we had with us) around the wood, as my men and I strung our bows. We would be using hunting arrows rather than bodkins or war arrows. Our aim was to incapacitate, not to kill.

When we were ready, I nocked an arrow and carried my bow in my right hand. We had not bothered with our hats, for we did not need to keep bowstrings dry and we had more freedom this way. I followed the path leading into the wood and my men spread out on either side. We were archers and thus the most silent warriors in England. I was the lucky one, for I had the path. Those under the trees had to watch for twigs and branches, which might crack underfoot. We could do nothing about our smell, as my plan involved men coming from two directions.

Even as we walked, I saw signs of the bandits; there were footprints and broken branches that showed where men had passed through the wood. The wind was coming into our faces and I smelled the woodsmoke. I did not need to tell the others that it meant we were nearing the bandit camp. The direction of the wind meant that John of Nottingham and his men might well alert the bandits.

When I heard voices, I knew that we were closing with the bandits. My men were watching me as well as their feet, and I held up my hand to warn them we were close. I held my bow in two hands and watched for movement ahead, which would tell me that we had reached the camp.

The movement was slight, but the brown cloaked figure who moved told me two things; firstly, where their camp was and secondly, that they had their backs to me – for I saw no flesh. I guessed that they were preparing an ambush for John of Nottingham.

My men and I moved as one, and I saw the camp take shape. That some of the bandits were old soldiers was clear, from the hovels they had built and the organisation of the camp. As we moved closer, there looked to be no more than twelve of them, although there might have been more ahead of me and hidden.

I heard their voices as they spoke.

"Wait for my command and then loose your arrows! If there are too many of them then we flee." I kept the words low, but my men knew me anyway. They needed no shouted commands.

I now saw their weapons. They had bows, but not all were war bows. Some were shorter hunting bows and the arrows I could see were mere hunting arrows. I glanced to my left and right to ensure that we were all in a line, and then, I used a large poplar to shield half of my body and drew back.

The bow creaked and one bandit began to turn. I shouted, "Drop your weapons and you will live. I am Lord Edward's archer and I now own this land!"

One of them, possibly the leader – for he had a good sword, turned and released his arrow in my direction. Even as it headed for me, I had sent mine to smack into his chest and drive him backwards.

His arrow embedded itself in the poplar. Three other bandits made the same mistake and three more men died unnecessarily. Their surviving comrades, realising that they were surrounded, dropped their weapons.

"Raise your hands above your heads!" They obeyed, as John of Nottingham and the rest of my men appeared. I waited until all of the weapons were secured and then we walked in.

John said, "Two tried to run through us. I am sorry, Captain, we had no choice but to kill them."

I nodded. "It was their decision. When a man chooses to live outside the law then he has to deal with the consequences." I slung my bow over my shoulder and said, "You have two options; leave here, or stay – and I will hang you." I turned to David the Welshman. "Burn their bows."

One of the bandits shouted, "But we need them!"

"You should have thought of that before you took to banditry, or you should have kept a better watch! I give you your lives and that is all that you can expect." My voice was harsh because I was well within my rights to hang them all.

One of them, an older man, asked, "Where do we go, Captain?"

I shrugged. "Well away from here, but if you want employment then go to Kenilworth. Lord Edward needs archers and he is desperate enough to take you on."

The older man knew he had been insulted. "I am a good archer."

"And how long have you been here in this wood?"

"Almost three years."

"Then I am right, for you would have had the opportunity to be hired as an archer. Baron Mortimer has need of archers. Do not feel sorry for yourself. Do something about your station in life. Believe me, my friend, I know. John, escort them to the Ludlow road and make sure that they leave the area."

"Aye, Captain Gerald."

As we headed back to our new home, none of us felt good about what we had done, but we had people to protect. When the prince gave me the manor, he changed my life. I could no longer think just of myself. I was not married to a woman, but I was married to a village.

After I returned home, I thought no more about the bandits I had evicted – but I told David to assign two men to check the woods each day. From that moment, I became a landowner and until I left, I saw to the village and my hall. James and his mother proved a godsend and although my head was spinning when I retired each night, I felt as though I had put a long day in. It was harder than pulling a bow on a battlefield.

In the end, Lord Edward gave me and my men just three weeks without war.

Richard, Sir John's squire, rode into the courtyard of the hall and, handing me the royal warrant, said, "Captain Gerald, Lord Edward has need of you. He asks that you meet him at Oxford on the morrow."

I liked Richard and hoped that he proved to be as good a knight as his master. "Kenilworth has fallen?"

"No, Captain, Simon de Montfort's son, Simon, has fled to East Anglia and is raising men to fight another war."

I nodded. "Will you alight and sup some ale? We have a good ale-wife here."

"No, Captain Gerald, for we go to the muster early."

I think my men were as pleased as I that we were going to war but, surprisingly, Sarah was not. "But Captain, you have made such a difference to the village already. What if you should die?"

John of Nottingham laughed. "Gammer, the man who can slay Captain Gerald has yet to be born – and besides, we follow Lord Edward and he is as lucky a leader as a man could wish for. We will all return home and we shall have riches so that the Captain can make his home the finest in the county!"

I did not like to hear my men tempt the fates like that, but Sarah seemed mollified and James assured me that all would be well when I returned. Of course, we had no idea when that would be.

As we headed south, I led men who rode palfreys and had the best of weapons. We each had a metal cap, rather than a helmet. It did not give as much protection to the head as a helmet, but it was better than a leather cap. We each wore the same hose and livery; men would know that this was the company of Gerald War Bow. As well as working on our new home, we had also fletched a thousand arrows, for we each knew the value of a well-made arrow, and while King Edward had good fletchers, we took greater care than they would. It meant our arrows were all the same and we knew, in battle, whom we had slain. To us that was important. The arrows were carried on our spare horses, with our cooking tools and war gear.

The royal warrant afforded us accommodation in royal castles, and there were some knights who offered us shelter for our horses, giving us food. We did not have to eat into our dwindling supply of coins.

We reached Oxford in three days and I found a place by the recently-knighted Sir William and his men. It was always good to be close to men alongside whom you had fought.

"Well met, Gerald."

"And you, Sir William."

He shook his head. "I still cannot get used to the title and, between you and me, the title is expensively bought. I have to employ and arm a squire and a page. I have to provide men at my own expense for the king. There is little profit in knighthood. I hope this campaign is financially rewarding, else I fear I will have to hire my sword out in Aquitaine again!"

"Aye, I know what you mean. And where is Lord Edward?"

"Here in Oxford. We head to Alton in Hampshire, where there are, he has heard, rebels. You are needed, for the rebels have taken to the woods and will have to be winkled out before we head for Lincolnshire and de Montfort's sons."

"I hope that Lord Edward has not misplaced his confidence. Aye, we know our way around the woods, but the very nature of trees is that they limit the range of our arrows."

"I think he wants you as hunting dogs. You and your men will pin them down and Lord Edward will bring us in to finish them."

"There does not sound to be much coin to be gained from men who hide in the forests. Has not the king given the land of the rebels away?"

"He has, but there are still the rebels in Kenilworth. There is a rumour around the camp that the papal envoy, Ottobuono Fieschi, is speaking with them to end the opposition to the king." Although the sons of de Montfort had fled, there was still loyalty to them in Kenilworth and it would take an army to remove the remaining rebels. The papal envoy might save lives.

"And de Montfort's sons?"

"Are both in the east; they hide in the Fens close to Lincoln. We will not have a quiet autumn, Gerald, but we are men of war and what else would we be doing?"

"I would have thought, Sir William, that your new status would have meant you could marry!"

"As I said, Gerald, at the moment, my title is a financial burden. However, there is hope – for I have heard a rumour that when the rebellion is truly over, Lord Edward will take ship and take the cross. Many men flocked to de Montfort, for he had been on a crusade. The Holy Land is a place where a man can make a fortune."

"Aye, Sir William and, equally, lose his life!"

I knew the situation in Alton was urgent when Lord Edward came to our camp as dawn broke the next chilly, damp morning. My men already had a fire going and a pot of water on the boil. They had scavenged and found enough food to warm our bellies. Lord Edward came with just three men as guards. He was afraid of no one.

He rarely wasted words and he came directly to the point. "War Bow, you and your men are ready?"

"We are, Lord Edward, when we know what we are to do."

He frowned. "Still as impertinent as ever. You do that which I command!" Duly chastised, I nodded. "There are some hundred or so rebel knights and their men in the forests and woods around Alton. They are led by a knight called Adam de Gurdon. He is an irritation rather than a threat. My cuz, Henry Almain, is in the north dealing with the rebels there and my father and the Pope's envoy, Ottobuono Fieschi, are at Kenilworth. We will be scouring out the last of the rebels. After Alton is subdued, we head to the Cinque Ports and after that, we deal with the last irritation, de Montfort's sons." He smiled. "So you see, you will be busy. Have you enough men? For you will be my only archers."

I shrugged. "We could always use more men, Lord Edward, but we need men who know one end of an arrow from the other."

He nodded. "Hmm. You had some trouble with bandits by your new home, I believe?"

It took a great deal to surprise me, but that did. How had Lord Edward come to know of my encounter? "Yes, Lord Edward, but I dealt with them."

"Did you now? Four of the bandits were apprehended in Worcester, where they were found begging for work. They would have been locked up, but they told a story of archers who had not hanged them for their crimes, and they sought employment. It was fortunate that I was in Worcester and heard their story from the sheriff. I recognised you from their description. I brought them here and they are in the cells of the castle."

I wondered why he had done that.

He smiled. "I have had an idea, for these men know the woods and we might use them to augment your men. They are expendable, but they may be useful. I have bows for them and I would have you take them with your men."

"But, Lord Edward, *my* men know the woods and we do not know these men. I like to choose the men I lead."

His face darkened. "Do not get above yourself, Gerald War Bow. You are my man and do what I want. I will send them to your camp."

"Yes, Lord Edward. Have they horses?"

"They are now your men, you find them!" He handed me four silver coins. "See what you can buy with these. As for any more, you had better hope the men we seek have full purses. We leave at noon, be ready."

He carried on, to speak with Sir William.

John said, "What did he want, Captain?"

"To give me the glad news that we have to take with us four of the bandits we evicted from the woods at Yarpole."

"They will upset the balance of our men."

"I know, and we also have to find them horses." I handed him the four coins and supplemented it with another four of my own. "I know that they will cost a fortune, but find four sumpters for them. If we are slowed, then Lord Edward will just blame us."

"Aye, Captain!"

He left, and I went to the fire to explain to the others. They had mixed views on the arrival of bandits. Some of them had dubious pasts, but they had been chosen by me for the company and not dumped upon us. Lord Edward had made my life more difficult.

We had enjoyed but a few hours of rest. One of Lord Edward's pages, Henry of Buckfast, brought them. I saw that each had a bow and an empty arrow bag. None had any other weapon. I recognised the leader as the older man from the camp. The four of them looked worried as Henry of Buckfast spoke.

"My Lord Edward charges you with the care of these men, Captain Gerald. They have been sentenced for their crimes and if they run then the sentence will be carried out by you. If they prove themselves worthy, then Lord Edward promises them a pardon."

I nodded, absent-mindedly. "Thank you, Master Henry. You have discharged your duty and can leave them with me." Once he had gone and with my men looking on, I addressed the four newcomers. "I am an honest man and I will speak plainly. This does not sit well with me. I am Lord Edward's archer and I obey my lord at all times, but I like to choose my own men. You heard Master Henry, you are my responsibility – and if any of you try to run, then you had better be able to run faster than one of my arrows."

I was now a man of substance and I had acted as an officer of the law. I could not allow men to break the law in one part of the land without comment. I needed to know if I could trust them.

The older man spoke. "Captain, none of us chose this life. We obeyed your command and left your land to seek employment. We chose Worcester, for we thought we might be used against the Welsh – but know that I swear we will not run. You gave us our lives and we are grateful. If you will give us a chance, we will redeem ourselves."

Jack of Lincoln said, quietly, "That was well spoke, Captain."

I nodded, but I knew that men could use words to get what they wanted, and I had known many men who used oaths like others used coins, buying their way into the confidence of others.

"What are your names?"

The older man spoke. "I am Richard of Culcheth, and this is my son, Robin." I now saw the similarity between the greybeard and the young man. "The other two are John and Alan; they are brothers. Their father, Walter, was an archer who died fighting the Welsh in the north."

I nodded. "There is food here. Have you your own bowls?" In answer, they took out their simple wooden bowls and spoons. I had no doubt that they would also have homemade beakers. Living in the forest meant you learned to use what was at hand. "I hope you can ride, for when we leave at noon you will be riding with us. If John of Nottingham can buy four horses, then all well and good – but it may be you have to ride double."

John had done well and while the four sumpters he bought were just a step away from the knacker's yard, they would be able to carry the four men. We were the archers and, as such, the scouts. Sir William's knighthood had merely given him a title. He still had to ride at the fore with his men and so the two of us led the small column of knights as we headed south through the grey, rain-filled skies. Although the rebellion was now confined to one or two isolated places, we rode prepared for war.

The four new men rode at the rear and each led the horses with the war gear. The rest of us had helmets and swords at the ready. Sir William and his men at arms were similarly ready for an ambush. I knew why Lord Edward had chosen a noontime start; he wished to make enough progress to be close enough to the woods by evening, so that the next day, we could begin our sweep into the forest.

Chapter 2

We reached Basingstoke after a ride of no more than a few hours. It would be our last camp before we attacked, and I was summoned, along with Captain William and his other leaders, to meet with Lord Edward. I was the only one not wearing spurs, but I was gratified that after Evesham I was now accorded respect.

"Tomorrow we ride the last five miles to the forests where the rebels are hiding. We will use Captain Gerald's archers to find them. The rest of us will dismount and follow on foot. We have enough men to surround the camp and make a complete circle. I want none of the rebels to escape."

I saw a huge flaw in his plan. We had enough men at arms and knights to form a huge line of beaters, but my handful of archers would be spread out too thinly and I risked losing some – I knew that the archers in this part of the world were good.

I was about to voice my fears when Lord Edward turned to me and said, "We have few archers and so each archer must perform the task that a dozen such men would normally do. The archer who finds the camp shall have one gold piece from me as a reward."

There was little point in complaining but the gold was not the incentive he thought it was. We would always make more profit from the battlefield than we would from pay. We were amongst the best archers in England. The men of Cheshire were our equals and the archers of the Weald a close second to us. We trained hard and were effective on a battlefield, where we collected our spoils. Our skill in battle was why Lord Edward employed us. I merely nodded.

The details of the attack were quite meticulous and if you took out the single flaw I had identified, then it was a sound plan. I headed back to my men, who would have to be in position hours before dawn broke – for Lord Edward intended to use the darkness to disguise the number of men we would use. I assigned each archer to a position in the wood, choosing the most difficult for myself.

I would ride Eleanor all the way around the forest and approach from the Alton Manor side. We would not, of course, be alone. There would be knights and men at arms who would give us a head start and then follow. That was another potential flaw, as men at arms and knights are, perforce, noisy creatures. Mail and leather both creak, rattle and groan. However, by the time the enemy was roused he would be encircled, and the slaughter could begin.

The choice of men to take was easy: Jack of Lincoln and Tom were the most experienced men I had, while Peter and Martin were both younger and keen to impress. As we rode to our positions, I reflected on the way Lord Edward waged war. He was unforgiving. The way that Simon de Montfort had been butchered had terrified the nobility of England, for that was not the way war was waged. Lord Edward had turned a new and frightening page in his manual of warfare.

Sir William and his familiar men at arms were behind me. My other men had knights and their retinue close to them. Each archer was supported by up to twenty men at arms and knights. I tied Eleanor to a tree and turned to speak, albeit quietly, with Sir William.

"I know your men will try to be quiet, but I fear that the nature of their weaponry will negate their attempt. Give me a good head start, eh?"

"Is that not more dangerous for you, Gerald?"

"I am happy with the risk, for I am happy in the woods. I grew up in Flintshire, roaming woods every day. I will return when I have found their camp. I will use the password 'war bow' so that your men do not slay me."

He laughed. "I think they know you by now, Gerald. God speed!"

I nocked an arrow and set off along the track. We had no signal to enter and needed none. We had taken the longest route and by now the forest was surrounded; my archers would be making their way in. As Alton lay on the road where Sir William waited, the rebels had no escape. They would have to fight when we found them.

I stopped after I had counted forty paces so that my eyes could adjust to the darkness and gloom; it meant that I could smell what lay ahead of me. If this rebel leader, Sir Adam, knew his business then, unlike the bandits of Worsley Wood, he would have sentries out. They would be woodsmen and I would not dare to take any chances. If I saw one, then he would have to die – for these rebels were little more than mailed bandits.

As my eyes adjusted, I began to move along the path – but as soon as my senses warned me, I would move from the path, for any sentry worth his salt would be watching it.

I had learned to measure time in my head. It was not as accurate as a church candle or an hourglass, but it was better than nothing. I think I had travelled for half an hour when I smelled something. I had heard noises before then, but they were in the distance and behind me, made by Sir William and his men. This was a different smell, a human smell. A man had made water close by and I stepped off the path and held my bow in two hands.

I had stood watches in the woods before and knew that you moved away from your sentry post to make water and to defecate. By leaving the path and keeping to the wood side of the smell of urine, I knew that I would be approaching the hidden sentry from his blind side, for he would away from his toilet.

I was silent, but the sentry was almost my equal. I saw him when he smelled me and, had I not had an arrow nocked and my bow ready to draw, I might have lost the duel. His bow and arrow were rising when, at a range of ten paces, my war arrow drove through his chest and pinned him to a tree.

He could not speak, and I watched him die. I took his bag of war arrows. An archer can never have too many arrows. I nocked another of my own.

As dawn began to break, I deduced the camp would be close and that I had broken their line of sentries, but I needed confirmation before I returned to Sir William. I did not rejoin the path but made my way from tree to tree. The glow in the distance showed me where their camp lay but I wanted to ascertain numbers.

I spied, close to the path, their second line of sentries and there were two of them. There were tents in the clearing, but in the main, men were in hovels. I even heard the neigh of a tethered horse. I could not identify the nature of the men, for most were in the hovels or under blankets, but I estimated there to be fewer than two hundred of them. We had far more, for Lord Edward did not intend to lose.

Turning, I headed quickly back to Sir William and his men. I found them close to the dead sentry. I did not speak but used my fingers and my hands to tell Sir William how many men we had to deal with and how far we had to travel. I knew that I was lucky. Sir William and I had fought together so many times that he was as familiar to me as John of Nottingham.

This time I moved just four paces ahead of Sir William and his squire, Roger. Our silence was not needed for much longer, but we still moved as quietly as possible. In the dark, I heard a cry from the far side of the camp and a voice shouted, "To arms! To arms!"

We ran, then I stopped close to the path and sent an arrow at one of the sentries. He had, conveniently, turned his back to me and my arrow knocked him to the ground. I had nocked, drawn and released my next arrow as his companion turned around, and my arrow smacked into his head. I let Sir William and his men at arms pass me, for I had done my job and I would now protect Sir William with my bow. He and his men knew their business, and they protected each other with their shields as they ran into surprised and rudely awakened men. The last line of sentries rushed to meet them and there was a clash of metal and wood. I aimed my bow but I had no clear target.

I recognised Adam de Gurdon, for he had managed to don his mail and was organising his defence. I had no bodkin arrow in my war bag and so I did not waste a war arrow. I might hurt him, but the odds were that the arrow would be wasted – and a good archer never wasted an arrow. His men were loyal as well as brave and I saw shields around him as they defended their leader. For the rest, it was a confusing scene as Lord Edward's men flooded into the camp and little battles took place all over.

As Sir William and his men drove in so I followed, all the time looking for a target. The target, when it came, appeared from an unexpected direction – behind us. I sensed, rather than saw, the movement as a warrior with helmet and leather vest raced from the trees with a war axe, intent on killing Sir William. The noise of his charge alerted the former captain and he started to turn – but it was a turn that would be too slow. I released the arrow, and, at twenty paces, the force was such that the arrow drove through his body and hurled him to the ground.

Sir William raised his sword in salute.

It was at that moment, when we stepped into the camp proper, that I saw Lord Edward. He had his squires and knights with him; I saw Sir John Malton. Sir John had been Lord Edward's squire when I first met him and was now a baron. He was used by Lord Edward, for he could rely upon him. Sir John had been awarded honours, too. In his case, it was a larger manor, that of Malton in Yorkshire. It was a rich manor, for there were many farms, but there was no castle and it was so far to the north that it was unlikely he would live there. He had another hall, closer to London and Lord Edward. The manor of Wittering was close to Northampton and the main road in and out of the capital. I liked Sir John, but I noticed that he had changed since he had been elevated. I suppose it happens when men are ennobled. They were making for Adam de Gurdon; Lord Edward intended to end this as quickly as he could.

The rebel also recognised Lord Edward and he eagerly raced forward to engage him. Not a word was spoken, but the rest of the men did not interfere with the two leaders. This was old-fashioned combat between two warriors who led their own men. I knew that Lord Edward would not thank anyone for interfering, but I took aim at Adam de Gurdon. If he slew Lord Edward, he would follow him within a heartbeat or two. And, strange though this might seem, as the sun suddenly flashed through the clouds, everyone else stopped fighting and every eye was on the two men who were now the centre of attention.

Lord Edward was the tallest man I knew, but Adam de Gurdon was not far behind. They were equally matched, and both men had good swords, mail and almost identical shields. This would be a battle settled by skill.

The two men traded blows that were intended merely to test the basic skill of their opponent. It was clear that they were both capable swordsmen. Lord Edward had been fighting since he was a boy and practised at the pel every day. But I noticed a subtle change after the first flurry of probing strikes. Lord Edward began to use his feet and his body. He had a slightly longer reach than his opponent and his longer legs meant he could cover more ground. He used them to strike with his sword, first at the rebel's shield and then Sir Adam's sword side. He had the rebel on the defensive and that meant that Lord Edward had the advantage – but Sir Adam knew how to defend.

I stopped drawing the bow, for the bout would take some time, but I left the arrow nocked. It soon emerged that Lord Edward was the better swordsman; the offensive attacks from Sir Adam became fewer and less effective as he fended off such a variety of blows that it was almost like watching Lord Edward training with Sir John Malton. The end, when it came, was inevitable and quick. Lord Edward feinted and, after smashing his sword hard into Sir Adam's shield, punched him in the face with his own. Sir Adam fell backwards.

This was the moment we all saw a change in Lord Edward. Gone was the ruthless and vengeful killer who had happily had Simon de Montfort butchered. I half expected Lord Edward to put his sword to the rebel's throat and sink it into him, but he did not. Instead, he shouted, "Your leader, Simon de Montfort, is dead. Yield and let us not waste any more English lives!" Most threw their weapons to the ground but one, an axeman standing but four paces from Lord Edward, raised his axe. Without moving, Lord Edward said, "War Bow!"

In one movement I had pulled back and released the arrow which smashed into the axeman's left hand and forced him to drop the axe, which fell to the ground. The broad head tore such a hole in his left hand that he would become one-handed. I had another arrow ready in case anyone else was foolish enough to risk raising a weapon to threaten Lord Edward. My demonstration had been more than enough, however.

Lord Edward smiled at me and then, after sheathing his sword, held out his hand. "Sir Adam, even though you are a rebel I can see that you are a worthy warrior. Will you not forego your misplaced allegiance to de Montfort? I have need of warriors such as yourself."

I saw the knight, who had taken off his helmet and was looking around, debating with himself. Lord Edward added, "You may have your manor returned if you will follow my banner, and these rebels here, if they also so swear, will be forgiven too."

Sir Adam nodded and grasped the outstretched hand of Lord Edward. "In that case, Lord Edward, I am your man – and if you would ask your archer to lower his bow then I will breathe easier."

Lord Edward said, "War Bow!"

I took the arrow and put it into the war bag. My first thought, as the men who had followed me began, under the command of Jack of Lincoln, to strip the dead they had slain of valuables, was for the others I could not see. I saw John of Nottingham and David the Welshman. They were empty handed.

"Are any of our men hurt?"

John nodded. "One of the new men, John, was slain. He came upon a sentry and was too slow to raise his bow. His brother Alan slew the sentry." He gestured towards the camp. "We came too late to garner any booty."

"We had enough from our side and there will be pay for this."

"You are certain, Captain?"

In truth, I was not certain, but my actions in killing the axeman must have gone some way to gaining my men a reward. "We managed to kill men on this side of the camp."

We spent the night in Alton, and we needed the rest. My men and I had to camp, of course, while the lords stayed in the manor. It was to be expected. We had won the battle, but the generosity of Lord Edward had cost us, for there would be neither ransom nor the weapons of the defeated. They were now Lord Edward's men.

The deer which John of Nottingham hunted, albeit illegally, was our reward. As we cooked it, Lord Edward came from the hall. He frowned at first when he saw the deer, and then laughed. "A rebel deer, War Bow?"

I smiled, for he was not angry. "It could have been, but you know deer, Lord Edward, they are cunning creatures and you never can tell whose colours they sport!"

He nodded. "You and your men did well today, and it bodes well for the future." He took a coin from his purse. "Here is the reward for finding the camp. Who earned it?"

I took it and said, "We all did. We shall share it equally."

"You are a strange one, War Bow. Many leaders would have kept it for themselves."

I smiled. "But I wager, my lord, that they are not archers."

"Tomorrow we ride to the Cinque Ports. I do not think we will need your skills there, but we may. In any event, when we have taken them by whatever means we can, I want you and your archers to ride to the Isle of Axholme. I believe that young de Montfort, Simon, and his brother, Guy, are to be found there. I need you and your men to ascertain the facts."

When he had gone, Jack of Lincoln said, "I know the area, Captain and it is treacherous. It is almost an island and to get to it you have to cross over nasty little waterways."

"Are there any towns there?"

"A few, but they are mean little damp places and at this time of the year, they will be damper than ever. Crowle, Belton, Epworth and Haxey lie on higher ground and Owston Ferry and West Butterwick lie close to the River Trent."

At least I had local knowledge to help me.

The weather got worse as we approached Dover. We heard that Sir Roger Laybourne, who commanded the king's men in the Kent area, had already stormed and taken Sandwich. Men on both sides had been lost and so Lord Edward was attempting to end the rebellion by the powerful ports in one swift and decisive action. Although Dover was the strongest of the ports it was also strategically important. The wife of Simon de Montfort, King Henry's sister, Eleanor, the Countess of Leicester, had taken refuge in the castle.

Henry II's fortress was one of the strongest in England. As we rode towards the imposing structure I wondered at the wisdom of this strategy. Lord Edward, had, however, changed. I am not sure if it was the elimination of his greatest enemy or just a new maturity. It seemed likely that King Henry, who had suffered many illnesses of late, might not have long left to rule. Was this Lord Edward preparing to become King Edward?

His strategy became harder to fathom when he merely cut off the port rather than preparing siege lines. I sat with John and Jack before a roaring fire and we spoke of the choices Prince Edward had before him.

"He could use ships and attack the sea side of the port."

"Nah, Jack, we don't have the ships and the Cinque Ports have a whole fleet. He would lose."

I nodded. "And he doesn't want to lose. Evesham didn't end the rebellion, it just cut off the head! I wonder if he is using words to win this battle for him. We won the battle, but Englishmen have died fighting Englishmen."

"Words, Captain?"

"Aye, John. Adam de Gurdon was persuaded to change sides. Perhaps he can do the same with the burghers of Dover."

Perhaps I was becoming cleverer or, more likely, I had been around Lord Edward so often that I was used to his mind and the way it worked. I was proved right, and he chose diplomacy – but it was tinged with a threat and that threat was my archers and me. He took us with him when we went to negotiate with the Constable of Dover Castle, who was also known as the Warden of the Cinque Ports. Before we left for the negotiations, he gave clear instructions to me and my archers. We listened and I made my men repeat them when he had gone.

Along with my archers, he also took five of his senior advisors and Adam de Gurdon. The latter was a clever move, for Sir Adam was popular and the fact that he had chosen to follow Lord Edward might well sway some of the important men in the ports. Lord Edward reined in well within the range of crossbows and it was a courageous act. He cupped his hands and said, "I would speak with the Constable, Sir Stephen de Pencester."

We waited, and I had the chance to admire the stonework and the defences of the mighty castle. This would not be an easy place to take. My archers and I each had an arrow nocked, but our bows lay across our horses' necks. We were all ready for the command whenever it came.

The knight arrived and he was younger than I had expected.

"Sir Stephen, you are Constable of Dover Castle and that appointment is a royal one. Why do you bar your gates to us?"

The simple nature of the request, delivered so calmly and reasonably, made the delegation at the gatehouse look at each other.

"Lord Edward, this is not a simple matter. I am also Warden of the Cinque Ports and it is all of the ports who oppose the will of the king."

"Then you are all traitors? You would defy me and risk hanging, drawing and quartering?" He turned to Adam de Gurdon. "Sir Adam, now do you see how wise you were to become our ally rather than our enemy? Sir Stephen here seems to lack that sense of survival which even a rabbit possesses when it sees a hawk."

Sir Adam, as he had been instructed, merely nodded.

"As you can see, Constable, we have not, as yet, dug our ditches nor prepared our rams, for I come here to speak with you. If I have to take action, then it will be one which will leave every home in your town bereft of men – for I will hang them all!"

"I am sorry, Lord Edward, but we will keep our gates barred and you and your men can do your worst. We survived attacks by the French, and we will survive attacks by you."

Lord Edward never moved his head and he spoke so quietly that his lips barely moved, but we were all waiting for his command.

"Now!"

As one, we raised our bows and sent our arrows towards the walls. We had aimed at the hoardings that protected those on the fighting platform. Our arrows thudded in as one, stitching a neat line directly above the heads of Sir Stephen and the other important men standing there. It looked spectacular and sounded terrifying, but there was no danger for the wooden hoard was just forty paces above our heads. The men on the fighting platform all ducked and then, when they realised that they had not been hurt, raised their heads fearfully over the parapet.

Lord Edward's voice was commanding. "Had I given a different order to my archers then each of you would now lie dead, so do not talk to me of defiance. Do you yield?"

There was a hurried conversation and then Sir Stephen said, "Lady Eleanor, the widow of Simon de Montfort, is within our walls. She would leave for France and there is a cog waiting to take her."

"I do not make war on women, especially not my aunt. She may leave – and then I will expect the gates open and for all of the Cinque Ports to swear loyalty!"

"It shall be done."

And so the jewels of the south coast fell into Lord Edward's lap, and it cost him just a sheath of arrows. He turned to me and tossed me a purse. "A reward for you and your men. You have saved many Englishmen's lives this day. Now, hie you to the Isle of Axholme. We shall follow within seven days."

"Aye, Lord Edward, and congratulations."

"This is just the beginning, Gerald War Bow. For now, we take back the hearts and minds of our warriors!"

Chapter 3

I disobeyed Lord Edward, for I had no intention of riding directly to Axholme. We rode instead for Canterbury, and there we stayed in a well-known inn, The Pard. Its sign displayed a symbol of England, a leopard. I headed there for I knew that it was popular with pilgrims and had many rooms. The civil war had dried up the number of pilgrims travelling to the shrine of St Thomas and I hoped for comfort and good service. It was likely that we would be in hovels for the rest of the month!

I was proved correct on all counts and the landlord could not do enough for us, especially as my fame at Evesham and Alton had preceded me. All had heard of Lord Edward's archer. When I examined the purse, I found that Lord Edward had given each of us one gold coin. It was not the largest gold coin, but to some men, Richard of Culcheth and his son, in particular, it was a fortune. It went some way to easing Alan's pain at the loss of his brother John. However, I also needed to ask, now that they had fought with us, if the three of them still wished to be part of my company. Thus, I sat with the three newcomers and waited until our much-needed food arrived and the others were bantering and joking before I spoke.

"I am sorry for your loss, Alan." He nodded and I tore a piece of white bread to dip into the stew. We were used to barley or oat bread and this was luxury. "The three of you did well both at Alton and Dover, but I know that Lord Edward almost forced you on to us and I realise that there may be bad feelings harboured amongst you, for we killed your friends. You now have money in your purses and if you choose to leave us then I will understand. As far as I am concerned, you have nought to answer for your banditry."

Richard of Culcheth was still their spokesman and he smiled. "Captain, you are young, but we can all see in you a leader. For myself and my son, we are happy to stay with you if you would have us. But there are two sides to this coin and these grey hairs tell me that your men are better than we are."

"You are raw clay, Richard, and I know that you are older and will find it harder to learn, but my company needs young and old, experience and youth." I turned to the silent Alan. "And you, Alan?"

"At this moment I do not know, Captain, and that is the truth of it. When our parents died, John and I had to rely on each other. I feel like I have lost a limb and I know not if I wish to tread this warrior path."

"But you have not. Your loss is too raw a wound for you to make a good decision. The offer to let you leave remains open but, I pray you, if you choose to go, then tell me. Do not just run."

He nodded and looked relieved. "I will do that, Captain, for I can see that you are an honourable man."

The others had been aware of our words and the banter had died a little. Jack of Lincoln said, as he nodded towards the food and ale, "There will be precious little like this when we are in the Fens of Lincolnshire, Captain. We have oiled cloaks, but the new men do not. They have a saying in Lincoln. If you see a single white cloud in the sky it is going to rain soon and if you cannot see a single cloud…"

The others chorused, "It is already raining!" It was an old joke and it seemed to make the atmosphere lighter, for even Alan smiled.

I nodded my agreement and gave some advice. "There is a market here where we can buy oil for the company. Richard, you three should invest a few pennies in good cloaks and, perhaps, buskins. I can promise you that while we might not always have gold coins from Lord Edward…"

John of Nottingham murmured, "This one is the first!"

Ignoring him, I carried on, "…we do profit from our arrows. Soon, you too will have helmets, swords and daggers. We can do nothing about your mounts, but when we reach Axholme we shall not need them and mayhap we can take better from the rebels."

"We have no bodkins, Captain." Richard of Culcheth was an archer. The other two were young and had much to learn.

"We may not need them at first. Our task is to find the rebels for Lord Edward. We have a supply of bodkins, but I am not certain that this will be a battle. I do not think they have a Dover or a Kenilworth in which they can hide." I patted my bodkin blade in my belt. "This may be a time for a knife or a sword. Let us see."

Two days later, bedraggled and soaked, we left the Great North Road and began to trudge along the muddied Lincolnshire tracks and roads. The land was already wet and filled with streams, becks and dykes as we headed east and often, our horses were wading through puddles which threatened to become pools and then lakes. I took comfort from this, as the knights who followed the de Montfort brothers were not used

37

to such conditions. Jack of Lincoln led us, as he was familiar with this land. The isle covered a large area, but he had an idea where the rebels might be. He also knew a farmer who might be persuaded to let us use his barn.

Jonathan of Stamford's farm was a mile from the village of Haxey. The old man lived alone, and his farm was run down. It turned out that Jack was his nephew. We learned this in the last mile, when Jack told us how old Jonathan had been fighting in Aquitaine for King Henry when a plague had swept through Lincolnshire and decimated the villages. In Jonathan's case, it had taken them all – the old soldier had returned to the ghosts of his family. The plagues and pestilence that swept through England were sudden and savage. They came, they killed and then they were gone. None could predict whence they would come, and most people thought it a punishment from God.

Jonathan was pleased to see his nephew and I knew why. The old man was dying. The presence of so many young warriors, archers at that, seemed to lift his spirits, but Jack confided in me that his uncle was a shadow of the man who had been a man at arms. We did not impose on Jonathan's food, for we had brought our own, and his mean home was too small to accommodate us all. And so we ate in the barn, with a bright and warming fire burning outside.

"Owston Ferry, that is where they will be."

"You know that for certain, Jonathan?"

His eyes were still able to twinkle and the ale we had brought had reddened his pale cheeks. He chuckled. "Nay, Captain but they passed by here a couple of months back and the ferry is just three miles or so east of here. You say they are still in the area?" I nodded. "Then that is where they will be, for the river makes it drier than most places around here and they can get to sea. The Humber is not far away."

The local knowledge was important. I turned to my men. "Then we do not need to use our horses. If the ferry is just a few miles away, then we can use our legs and the cover of this land to spy them out. Tomorrow, I will go with Jack and scout out the ferry. If we do not find them, then John of Nottingham and David the Welshman can try their luck the day after. Tom and Peter, tomorrow I want you to ride to the Doncaster road and wait there for Lord Edward. I will have you relieved in a day or so. Bring him here." It was not a long ride, but I wanted Lord Edward to be safe.

They all nodded. I had a plan and I was always happier when I had created the plan. Lord Edward would not have been so thoughtful about my men. My new men could become stronger with more rest and leaving them with the others could only fortify our company.

When Jack and I left to scout, I did not string my bow but carried it over my back in its case. Nor did we wear helmets, for we wanted to be able to hide or to pretend to be what we were not. The rebels had worn white crosses at Evesham, and I did not know if they would still identify themselves. We had removed our red crosses but the stitching remained; we might be able to persuade them that we had removed white crosses to pass through the royalist lands. We had no idea of numbers and Jonathan had only seen forty or so knights heading east. If that was all de Montfort had, then Lord Edward would have an easy victory. If there were more, it might be a bloody battle.

Jack's knowledge, augmented by his uncle's, proved crucial. We took little-used lanes and greenways, which twisted and turned towards the river and the ferry. The absence of hoofprints told me that knights had not used them.

Our hidden route meant that we heard the enemy before we saw them. A large number of horses and their attendant men are never silent.

It meant that we took cover before we could be seen. Knowing that the enemy was close, we hid our bows and arrow bags under a hedge and then, with our cloaks wrapped around us and the hoods covering our heads, we headed along the lane towards the camp. It was raining once more. This December had not yet seen snow, but it had seen rain of Biblical proportions.

The problem we had, was that the land was low-lying and it was hard to find a vantage point from which we could view it all. We followed the lane that headed down towards the river. Rebels or otherwise, people would still use the ferry, and so I took the bold decision to simply march towards the river and attempt to cross it. We had coins in our purses and even if we had to use the ferry, it would allow us the opportunity to spy out the enemy. I guessed that the de Montfort brothers would feel safe with Lord Edward, King Henry and Henry Almain all busy in other parts of the country. Two strange men passing through should not be cause for too much attention.

The rain helped us, for most men had their hoods up, and we shuffled down the lane to the ferry. From beneath our hoods, we spied the hovels the rebels had made – for there were few houses to accommodate the remnants of the rebel army. Simon de Montfort, Guy, and his knights would have commandeered buildings, but the men who followed them, probably in the hope of some pay, were in small camps that lined the road. Their numbers would be in the many hundreds – rather than thousands – but these were the ones who would keep fighting, for they had nothing left to lose. Realising that we could get more information by talking than watching, we took shelter beneath a tree as a particularly hard shower cascaded water and made a small river that ran down the lane to the river. The camp was at the top of the slope and afforded a good view of the river and the houses.

There were four men beneath a cloak, playing with dice. Jack had a real skill when it came to gambling. I suspected him of cheating, but I was not a gambler and had not suffered at his hands. I nodded towards the game and Jack took out his purse and said, "Room for a little 'un?"

One of them laughed and said, for Jack had an archer's chest and was clearly all muscle, "A big 'un more like."

Another said, "Aye friend, so long as you have money. Pay has been in short supply of late."

Jack nodded as he sat and took out a half dozen pennies. The eyes of the men widened as it was more than the pot they had. They were playing for farthings and halfpennies. I wondered if it was a mistake, but Jack had a wise head on his shoulders and had the answer ready when he was questioned. His answer to the interrogation he received surprised me, but it worked.

"You have been paid well or you are a cutpurse; which is it?"

"I am no cutpurse, friend, but as you do not know me, I will excuse the insult and I will not draw my bodkin. We have been paid well for, unlike you, we chose the winning side."

I held my breath.

One of the men shook his head and said, "I might have known you fought for the royalists. Why are you here?"

I answered, "We seek the ferry. With the rebellion over we thought to take a ship to France, where they have need of men who can use swords."

They looked at our weapons. "Piss poor weapons to be swords for hire!"

"My friend told you, we were paid well, and we can always buy better swords. These will do for protection. You should come with us. You look handy!"

"Aye, that we are but we have no coin for the ship across the German

41

sea." He grinned. "Still, we might relieve your friend of his coins, eh? Would you not care to join the game?"

I shook my head. "Gammer Murton did not raise me to throw away my money. Jack here is a gambler, I am not."

I watched them play for a while and Jack made sure he lost a little and that allowed me to ask questions, for they became happier. "So why do you all wait here? I thought Kenilworth was where the rebels were holed up."

"Aye, and at Chesterfield, but our master, the son of the Earl of Leicester, cannot make up his mind about what he should do."

Both places lay to the west of our position.

Another said, "Aye, he is a shadow of his father! We wait for payment and then we take off these crosses and seek another master. Whom did you serve?"

"Sir John of Avebury."

Sir John had been killed at Evesham and it explained why we had left the royal army.

"Was he a good man?"

"Obviously not good enough, for he was killed." I looked around. "De Montfort has enough knights here to fight?"

Shaking his head, the leader of the dice players said, "There are not above twenty here. The bulk of the men are like us. We fight for pay and until we have it, then we remain."

We had learned enough, and I sought a way out. Jack had begun to make back his money – and more – when I saw three mailed men at arms striding up the lane. One of them stopped to talk to men in a small camp and the two others came closer. I vaguely recognised one but, worse than that, he recognised me – despite my hood and the rain.

"I know you! You are Gerald War Bow and you slew my friend, Henry Sharp Sword!"

The men with whom we had been playing dice knew we were royalists and they did not reach for weapons. I think that they were surprised and stunned. They delayed. That saved our lives, and Jack's story had been a wise decision. I grabbed the unburned end of a burning brand and hurled it at Henry Sharp Sword's friend; I had a good eye and it hit him, making him and his companion reel. Jack and I took to our heels and ran. I did not look back and I guessed that we had perhaps a twenty-pace lead. We had no mail and they did; if they had mounted horses, then we would have been caught, but their mounts were at the bottom of the slope. I had to hope that there were just three of them following us, for then we had a chance, albeit a slim one. We needed to get back to Lord Edward, for he could snuff out the threat that was Simon de Montfort by Christmas.

Apart from our lack of mail, another advantage we had was that we had travelled this road more recently than the men who were chasing us. We had crossed ground that was flooded and impassable, as well as other areas which were so muddy that a mailed man would sink. We had, perhaps, four hundred paces to reach the hedgerow where we had secreted our bows and arrow bags. We left the road to hop, like deer, from one dry patch to another. I realised I was faster than Jack and I said, without turning, "I will get to the bows!"

I lengthened my stride and began to leave Jack behind. As I neared the hedge, I looked around and saw that the three men were still running but they were spread out. The nearest was the friend of Henry Sharp Sword and he was closing with Jack and a mere twenty paces behind; Jack was showing his age. All the years of training came to the fore as I ducked behind the hedge, took out the bow sheath and extracted my bow. Although I made it look easy, as strong as the men at arms were who chased us, they would have struggled. I took out a string from under my hat and strung the bow almost without thinking. I did not choose an arrow, I grabbed the first one I found and, nocking it, stepped out from behind the hedge. I aimed at the man at arms whose drawn sword was now just ten paces from Jack.

"Stop and back off or you die!"

He did not stop, but he slowed and snarled, "That is not a bodkin arrow! I will have vengeance for my friend!"

As Jack ran behind me to grab his bow, I released. The man at arms was a mere ten feet from me, and my arrow smashed into his nose and erupted from the back of his skull. The second man at arms was so close that he was spattered with the brains of Henry Sharp Sword's friend.

I had no time to draw another arrow and so I swung my bow across him. The sharp tip hit his face, then ripped across it, and he stumbled – giving me the chance to pull my sword and bodkin from their sheaths. The third man at arms was now closing and unless Jack managed to nock an arrow, I was in trouble. The second man at arms had a bushy black beard and looked to be taller than I was. He also had a long sword – and a longer dagger. My bow had cut his face, and he was bleeding. He was also angry.

"I will have your bollocks for that, and I will claim the reward from the earl for killing you!"

I heard the words but ignored them as I concentrated upon finding a way to defeat a man at arms. I had done so with a sergeant at arms when I had first served Lord Edward, many years ago in Wales, but I knew that I had been lucky. This time, I might not be. The third man's longer sword swept towards me and I danced out of the way. It was a mistake, as I slipped in the mud. He saw his chance and tried to bring over his sword to lay me open. I rolled in the mud and saw Jack emerge with a nocked bodkin arrow. I just had black beard to worry about. I got to my feet as he tried a clumsy swing at my back. It was clumsy because he lost his footing too, and I was able to get a swing in. My sword connected with the back of his left hand and tore it open. He shouted, not in pain so much as anger that an archer had hurt him. He swung at my head and it took all of my strength and speed to bring up my own sword and block it. If this became a test of swordsmanship, then I would lose – and so I rammed my bodkin into his right ear and drove it into his brain.

At that moment, I heard the whoosh of an arrow and Jack's bodkin slammed into the third warrior's chest.

I looked beyond the body. It seemed the three had been the only ones to follow us, and that made sense. They came to avenge their friend. As the dice players had indicated, the men with de Montfort just wanted money and his knights wanted their land back. No one else had followed what they believed to be a gambling feud.

"Are you hurt, Jack?"

He shook his head. "Just embarrassed that they nearly caught us because of me! I should walk more and ride less."

"It is done now. As much as I would like this mail, for it would fetch a great deal of silver, we dare not stay – and we have news to report. Take their weapons for the new men and see if they have coins in their purses."

They were men at arms so had more coins, but not many more, than the dice players. But their swords and daggers were good ones. We hurried back to the barn, where I sent Martin and William of Matlac to relieve Tom and Peter and to bring Lord Edward to Haxey. I shared out the weapons with the new men and the coins with all of my company. That was what we did. We shared.

Lord Edward arrived at noon the next day. He had with him plenty

45

of knights but few others. I told him what we had learned. Over the years, I had grown less fearful of reporting to the fierce Lord Edward, and he had also come to trust me. I told him the facts and then my assessment. "Lord Edward, this is a beaten army. There are three ways for him to escape: across the river on the ferry, but I have spied it and it can hold just four knights and their horses. They could go upriver towards the Humber or downstream towards Gainsborough."

I was concise and gave just the facts. Those were qualities Lord Edward admired.

"Take your men and block the route north." He turned in his saddle. "Sir John, take ten knights and ride south to stop the enemy fleeing to Gainsborough. War Bow here tells me that they are less than three miles from here. I would capture them and avoid needless casualties, as we did at Dover. This civil war has cost us enough English lives already."

My men and I were in the saddle almost immediately, and because I knew the land, we were heading north before Sir John Malton had given his orders. I stopped just a mile upstream from the ferry and positioned my men so that Peter and Tom held the horses while the rest of us strung our bows, nocked an arrow and waited.

We heard the horns sound the alarm and then saw, to the south of us, men rushing to the ferry. The ferry was small, and I watched as too many men tried to board it. I did not recognise the de Montfort livery, and when the ferry capsized, enough men were on hand to rescue the sodden knights.

A handful of knights who had already mounted their horses turned them to ride north along the river. "Ready lads, remember we are just to stop them." I did not fully draw my bow but readied it as the eight knights, oblivious to our presence, hurtled north along the river path. It was only wide enough to allow one knight at a time to ride along it, and that suited us, for it meant we only had to stop the first knight and the rest would be forced to halt.

I spoke without turning. "Jack of Lincoln and John of Nottingham, be prepared to stop the horse if the knight does not heed my command to halt."

"Aye, Captain!"

I recognised the younger Simon de Montfort, and his brother Guy, with the knights. The others were unknown to me. The leading knight had a red and white quartered shield with a hunting hawk in the right quadrant. I vaguely remembered it from Evesham. I waited until they were just thirty paces from us before I shouted, "Halt, in the name of Lord Edward!"

The eager knight at the fore drew his sword and rode at me. I loosed an arrow at his right leg as two arrows struck his horse. At that range, and with the power in my two archers' arms, the animal died immediately. As its knees buckled so the knight, with an arrow sticking from his knee, flew from the saddle. His sword fell into the river and he crashed into a willow, where he lay still.

"Peter, Tom, see to the knight." As they hurried to obey me, I aimed my bow at the eldest son of the rebel leader. "Sir Simon, surrender, for none of you wish an ignominious end from a bodkin arrow, do you?"

Snarling, the son of the man who had been butchered at Evesham, Simon de Montfort, said, "We will surrender – but not to a peasant!" Then he turned his horse and headed back to the ferry.

I did not mind, for we had the horse furniture and weapons from the fallen knight.

"John of Nottingham, take half of the men and follow them; Lord Edward will want to be there when we take him. Jack, see what can be taken from the dead horse. How is the knight?"

"He lives, and we have stopped the bleeding."

"Then sling him on the back of a horse and we will be rid of him soon enough."

It was the end of de Montfort's war. I heard Lord Edward's horn sound the recall and we mounted and headed downstream. By the time we reached the stream, Lord Edward was there and examining the prisoners to see if he had his prey.

Sir John was organising the knights so that Lord Edward could examine each and every face. The young squire had grown since the first time I had seen him in Aquitaine. Lord Edward's face lit up as he saw John of Nottingham leading the leaders of the rebels. He gave me a wave of his hand and then he and his senior knights led off the men we had captured.

Sir John was mounted on his horse and he shouted, "All of you have surrendered to Lord Edward and he has spared your lives. Your lands are now forfeit as punishment. Your leader, Simon de Montfort, when we take him, will be tried for treason in Northampton. Depart – and thank Lord Edward for his kindness."

I saw the leader of the dice players. He was standing with others who had followed de Montfort in hope of pay. "And what of us, my lord?"

For once, Sir John looked perplexed and I nudged Eleanor next to him. "My lord, these men seek pay. They care not about the rebellion; that is the province of knights and the nobility. It is winter and these men do not know whence they will get their next meal."

Realisation set in. "I say to you that we will not restore pay to rebels, but if you wish to follow our banners then you will be fed and we will endeavour to pay you. We go west to the county of Derbyshire, to fight the last of the rebels. That is your choice; fight against your former comrades or depart and fend for yourselves."

To be fair, half chose the latter, but Sir John and the knights he led had their numbers swollen by sixty men who swapped the red cross for a white one. When you were hungry and poor, pay and food were more important than the colours you wore.

The knight we had hit was Sir Walter of Mansfield, and as the healers worked on his leg, he scowled at me. I had made another enemy – and one who was a powerful knight in this part of the world. It did not worry me, for it was a long list.

Chapter 4

We did not leave Lincolnshire directly, for the weather had made the roads impassable, and so we spent a month in Lincoln where we used the coins we had made to buy better horses for our three new men. Lord Edward had also provided back pay, and whilst I did not need it, many of my men did – and they spent it wisely. Lincoln made good cloth, and I invested in some better-made clothes. The cloth was superior to that I normally wore, though still hard-wearing. I knew that, with my elevation in status, I would have to entertain and have clothes other than the ones I used for war. We also bought some leather, to make better bags for our war gear. When we finally left Lincoln, we all looked better for the enforced rest. God smiled on us and gave us better weather as we had headed south and west.

Henry Almain commanded the men who were scouring the rebels from Derbyshire. This was like war had been against Adam de Gurdon, and it did not suit knights, whose fine horses could be harmed by the rough land. A courser or warhorse could be worth ten or twenty marks and riding through forests could easily break a leg. Robert de Ferrers, the Earl of Derby, and his men used the forests and woods of the Derbyshire hills to resist all the efforts of Lord Edward's cousin to capture them. I often wondered if that was why Lord Edward did not lead us – for there was little glory to be had, and he had already enjoyed much fame from his single combat against Sir Adam. Robert de Ferrers was no fool and would avoid all such conflicts. This was his land, and he and his men knew it better than any. I learned this as we rode south and west, when Sir John and I were given a clearer picture of what we might find. Sir John Malton was a good leader who listened and, more importantly, understood that those who were not noble born could still contribute. He was growing into the lieutenant Lord Edward would use as a reliable adviser.

"We need you, Gerald, and your men. We need to find their lairs and to eliminate their refuges. There are three knights who lead the rebels and if we can neutralise them, the rest of their resistance will crumble. It happened with young Simon and it will happen here."

I was interested in the identity of the other knights, for I had known some at Evesham. "And who else leads this band of rebels?"

"The leaders are Baldwin Wake, Lord of Chesterfield and John d'Ayville. It is John d'Ayville who is the most dangerous of the three. I met him a number of times and he has surrounded himself with good men at arms as well as using the outlaws and bandits of the northern forests."

"My lord, if they are in any sort of number, then my handful of men will be outnumbered."

"I am mindful of that, and so I have asked Sir William to bring his men at arms. You worked well together when you were both captains and I have no doubt that you can revive that association. You and your men will be the beaters, and you will drive the rebels into the waiting swords and spears of Sir William. First, however, we need to find them!"

Our three new men had shown themselves to be good campaigners, and so they no longer rode at the rear with the baggage. Our enforced stay in Lincoln had allowed us to make Peter a better archer and to build up the strength of Robin, Richard's son, so that our company was more skilled, and I no longer feared for weaknesses. We rode at the fore with Sir William and his men behind us. Sir John Malton, his squire and his pages, as well as the captain of his guard, rode with Sir William and me. I was the only one, apart from the pages, who did not wear mail. I did, however, wear my helmet – although the wind was still chilly enough for me to have the hood of my cloak up to give me additional protection. John of Nottingham and Jack of Lincoln rode behind me and they were a comfort, for I knew that my back was safe.

We had spent a night at Ollerton and as we headed west, we spied Bolsover Castle in the distance. A favourite of the king's father, John, it had been the centre of power when the barons had tried to wrest power from him. I wondered if Sir John thought to attack it.

It was as though he was reading my mind. Pointing to it he said, "Henry Almain has men watching the gates of that castle, as well as guarding the road, but it is not a siege. There are too few men within it to be a threat to us – and yet those few are too many for us to take it without heavy losses. Lord Edward and his cousin both remember the good men we lost at Evesham, and we are besieging Kenilworth as it is. Kenilworth is the most powerful castle in this part of the world. When that falls, then the rebellion is over. Lord Henry Almain and the bulk of our forces are watching the road to Sheffield and Lord Edward hopes that de Ferrers' eyes will be fixed on him. It will allow us the freedom to attack those men who are around Chesterfield. Once we have begun to start the enemy, then Lord Henry will bring his men and we will trap the Earl of Derby and his rebels like nuts in a nutcracker."

I could see how the strategy would work. The rebels were using strong castles as bases and waiting for Lord Edward to try to take them. Lord Edward was using himself as bait. Just as Simon de Montfort had been the target of killers at Evesham, so Lord Edward might become the target of the rebels. By drawing them out he hoped to defeat them and end this war.

It was a good plan, but it only worked if my archers could make a larger number of men than we had flee from us – and that would be some trick. If we had not been working with Sir William and his men, then I would have feared that we would fail. Sir John Malton and his men would drop back so that we would become two bands of men. We would have a gap of just one hundred paces between the rear of our band and Sir John, but it might fool any careless sentries into thinking that we had fewer men than we actually had.

"So, Captain Gerald, do you have a man who knows these woods?" Sir William was a practical man who knew how to use men to the best of their ability. If I had a good archer, then he could use his skills. "John of Nottingham, although he is not as familiar as we might like. What we do know is that the rebels have camps in the woods as well as in the villages to the west of Chesterfield. The bulk of their knights are within Chesterfield itself. My plan, Sir William, is to start in the west and destroy their smaller camps. It will take three or four attacks before they start to panic."

Sir William nodded. "You find the camps, eliminate the sentries and my men attack them? Much as we did at Alton?"

"Aye, and drive them into the waiting arms of Sir John."

Sir John beamed. "You give me the easier task. I wait to hit them as they flee to their knights, and if their knights are foolish enough to venture from behind Chesterfield's walls to come to their aid, then Lord Henry will fall upon them! With luck, there will just be Kenilworth left to oppose us. I will drop back with my men when we find their scouts."

I did not approve of such optimism. It rarely occurred amongst those who had been born poor, but the nobles of the land seemed to think all would come their way by right – and they were normally correct.

The optimism was misplaced, for the rebels here were not hiding as they were in Lincolnshire; here they were the men of Derbyshire and it was their land, which they defended. In this part of the north, as we discovered, although they knew that they had lost the Battle of Evesham, they did not believe that they had lost the battle of England. They would fight on, for they were stubborn men. It was in the late afternoon, when we were seeking shelter for the night, that we encountered a small group of knights and their followers who had blocked the road. They were either very brave or they had underestimated our numbers.

It was getting on to dusk and I had been listening to Sir John and Sir William discuss signals when I smelled woodsmoke. From the local men, the royalists who had joined us to rid this land of rebels, we knew that there was a crossroads ahead and when I smelled smoke, I unslung my bow. John and Jack behind me reacted as quickly, so that when the arrow slammed into the shoulder of Robert, Sir John's page, I was digging my heels into Eleanor so that I could find space, dismount and use my bow. I shouted, "Archers, dismount!"

Sir William called out, "Line of shields! Healer!" Sir William was quick thinking and while he would react to the attack, he would have the wounded page tended to.

I then concentrated on finding the enemy. A darkening gloom filled the road; I heard the sounds of metal from ahead and of arrows sent from the trees. I dismounted and just left Eleanor where she stood. I had trained my horse well and she would simply graze until I returned for her. Nocking an arrow, I walked along the tree line. My dark clothes helped me in my position east of the camp, which was now darker than the west. Behind me, I sensed rather than saw John and Jack as they marshalled my men into a skirmish line. The noise and the shouts from ahead and behind were a little distracting, but I used the same method as when I had an arrow to send at a target: I cleared my head of all else.

The rebels had a fire at the crossroads. Upon our approach, they had doused it and clouds of smoke rose. But, from the dying glow, I saw a sergeant at arms, just one hundred paces away. He was giving orders. I drew and sent the war arrow to slam into him. As he dropped, the men he had been ordering faced us with their shields.

I chose another arrow and turned to John of Nottingham. "Take half of the men and scour this side of the road. We shall meet you on the other side of the crossroads." He nodded and signalled to the men he would take. "Jack, we will use our bows to clear the woods opposite." By hitting the sergeant, I had fixed the knights and men at arms, who would let their own archers deal with our mounted men. The men at arms would simply hold their position and wait for orders. They had lost a leader and initiative.

I looked to the woods, which were opposite us. The archers were there but, like us, they were hidden by their dark clothes and the trees. I saw a movement and drew my bow. If the rebel bowmen were to hit our horsemen, then they had to step from the trees to do so. As soon as one did, he was exposed – the first to do so was hit by both my arrow and that of Jack of Lincoln.

I had just stepped back to nock another arrow, when an arrow cracked into the tree I used for shelter. I saw Martin, release an arrow and I heard a body fall. I knew that while the rebel bowmen knew these woods better than we did, we were the better archers with better equipment. I made the decision. "We cross the road in pairs! One of you watch the road for danger while the other runs."

I heard them acknowledge me. We used this technique often and had our pairs already. Jack would cover me.

"Draw, Jack!" As I heard his yew bow creak, with an arrow nocked I ran across the road. Sir William's men had dismounted and were preparing a wall of shields to advance down the road, but they needed safe passage first. I saw the rebel step from the tree and pull back. If I had not trusted Jack completely, I might have hesitated, but I kept running and as the archer tracked me, Jack's arrow went into his shoulder and knocked him from his feet.

I saw that my other archers also reached the safety of the trees and our sudden rush had taken them by surprise. I raised my bow and saw a surprised rebel just ten feet from me. "Drop your bow!"

He must have thought that he was quicker, for he began to turn, but it was too late. My arrow hit him in his forehead, and he fell.

Jack ran next to me and we headed into the woods. It was dark when I called a halt to the pursuit. We had cleared the threat of their archers, but the rebel bowmen knew the woods and would be long gone. We headed back to the crossroads and reached them as Sir William and Sir John were searching the bodies. We had killed more than half of the men we had encountered, and we had another eight as prisoners.

I led Eleanor into the improvised night camp and from Sir John's voice, I knew he was angry. Young Robert, who had been hit, was his nephew and he was in danger of losing his temper with the men he questioned.

"Where is Robert de Ferrers?"

The sergeant at arms he questioned was the one I had hit, and I saw the bloody dressing on his shoulder. "We heard he was in Brampton, lord, but I do not know for certain. We were told to stop the royalists using this road."

I saw Sir John bunch his fists as he towered over the wounded man. I think he was going to strike him. If he did so, then he would regret it.

To distract Sir John, who was clearly not thinking straight, I led my horse towards the fire and said, "Sir John, we have chased the rebel archers into the woods, should we make this our camp?"

"What?"

"There is little point in moving on, for your page will need to rest and we now know where the rebels are." I pointed into the woods, which lay north of the road. "Our plan can still work, and this will be as good a place as any to begin putting it into action. Brampton lies to the north of us and if de Ferrers is there, we can drive the enemy to him. They know we are here now. Let us make the best of it."

I had made Sir John forget his nephew's wound and think of the task before him. "You are right, Gerald, and I can take my men around the woods to Brampton. If de Ferrers is there, then I can end this quickly."

Sir William nodded. "Aye, Sir John, and we can send a rider to Lord Henry and tell him what we have learned."

We had only killed the rebel archers, but their bodies yielded booty we could use; there were bowstrings and arrows. Whilst the arrows did not have good heads, they were well made and fletched. We also recovered a couple of short swords and daggers. A man could never have too many daggers.

I went over, after we had eaten, to see how Robert the page fared.

The arrowhead was poorly made and had broken when it had hit him. It meant that while the head had not been driven deep into him, the doctor had to dig out the metal and I saw, as I approached, that the page had passed out from the pain. That was probably a mercy. I picked up the discarded head.

Sir John was sitting, looking at his nephew, and I saw that his face was wracked with guilt. "How is he, Sir John?"

"He will recover, but that does not make me feel any better, for I should have had him with the baggage. You do that when you have inexperienced men, but he wanted to ride with us, and I allowed it."

I nodded. "We always see clearly when we look back, Sir John. He will live and he will learn from this. If he cannot yet have mail, then give him a hide vest with padding beneath. Stud the hide with metal." I held the broken and bloody arrowhead in the palm of my hand. "If this had been one of our arrows, it would have driven deep into his shoulder and would have torn muscle and chipped bone. Then, he might have been crippled for life. Robert has been lucky, as have we. The ambush could have been worse, and we could have lost men. We are whole and can complete our mission. If they had been better led, then it would have been a real ambush and they would have emptied saddles."

I knew that Sir John was annoyed at having men at arms and knights escape us, but I saw this as something we could be pleased about. We had killed archers and I knew how dangerous an archer could be in woods.

Sir John took the head. "Thank you, Gerald, you have comforted me and reminded me that I lead a company of men and not just my nephew."

The next morning, Sir John and his prisoners continued down the road to sweep around to Brampton, where he would join up with Henry Almain. The wood lay between us and Brampton. Leaving horse holders, I led my men into the woods in a long line of skirmishers. Sir William and his men walked ten paces behind us. At first, we followed our own trail from the night before, and then the trail of the fleeing archers. That they would feel safe in their own woods was obvious, but they would also feel concern that Lord Edward's men were close. We each walked with an arrow and our bows in our right hands. If we sensed an enemy, then we would have an arrow nocked and our bows drawn in an instant.

The day, which had begun damp and gloomy, soon brightened as the sun and the wind made the clouds scud away, and the path we followed became brighter. My archers all had clear instructions and it was Richard of Culcheth who loosed the first arrow. I heard the cry as his arrow slammed into a sentry and I heard cries from ahead as the archers, who had made an improvised camp, realised that we had pursued them.

My arrow was nocked and my bow levelled as I ran along the trail I was following. I saw the camp, which was like a disturbed ants' nest as the rebels ran for bows. I stopped and loosed an arrow at a running rebel who was struck in mid-stride. No matter how good they were as bowmen, they were at a disadvantage, for we had arrows ready and they were looking for their bows which would have to be strung. We stood and drew our bows as Sir William and his men ran into the camp. It was all over in less time than it took to tell the tale. We led the ten prisoners who had surrendered as we carried on to Brampton.

We heard the battle before we saw it, although the term 'battle' is a little grand for the skirmish we encountered. Lord Henry and Sir

John, more by luck, I think, had managed to trap the Earl of Derby and his rebels in the village of Brampton. Perhaps the men who had escaped us had ridden there and warned him, though if he had more sense he would have left for the woods where there was more chance of escaping. Brampton was a trap, for there was neither wall nor keep. It would have been a complete victory for Lord Henry, except that one brave rebel knight, Sir John d'Ayvile, managed to lead five knights and, with levelled lances, cleared the knights sent to capture them. Then, Sir Gilbert Hansard, who was one of the local rebel leaders and an important man, was unhorsed, and a small number of rebel knights managed to escape in the confusion. Had we been there, then it might have been a victory in full. A mailed knight was still vulnerable to a good archer with a bodkin headed arrow. However, we had the prize; we had the Earl of Derby and, for us, our work was done.

Lord Henry Almain had the earl sent to London and with Bolsover and Peveril Castles now in our hands, declared that he would lead the knights to the siege of Kenilworth. It was clear to everyone that with de Ferrers and the young de Montfort our prisoners, Kenilworth would soon fall. We were all rewarded and Lord Henry Almain himself gave purses filled with coins to Sir William and me.

He knew my value, but also knew that I would not be needed at Kenilworth. I was dismissed and I was grateful. "For now, Gerald War Bow, your war is over, and you may return to Yarpole. Make the most of the peace you have won, for I know my cuz and he will need your war bow before too long. We have won the war – now it is up to the king to win the peace!"

Travelling the roads of England took time. None of us wished to hurt our horses and the campaign had taken us from Worcester to Southampton, the Fens and then Chesterfield. We had seen the seasons change. Of course, waiting for pay always took time. I had learned that lords were quick to promise pay but they did not pay on time.

It was early summer as we headed back to the village that we had seen for but a month – and that had been more than half a year ago. In that half-year, we had changed; now we were well mounted and had more experience. We had learned to fight in woods against archers who were almost as skilled as we were, and we had defeated them. We had devised ways of fighting which were unique to my company. I was relieved to see, as we rode towards our land, that the fields were filled with both growing crops and young animals. Sarah and her son had done that which they had promised. John and Jack flanked me, and John said, "Can we get used to peace, Captain?"

I laughed. "I know not for I have followed the way of war since I was a youth. Perhaps I shall give it a try."

"You are a man of wealth now, Captain. Take a bride and father children."

I turned to John of Nottingham. "You think I am ready?"

He laughed. "No man is ever ready for marriage, but you have land and it is expected of you."

I nodded. "Let me learn to be a landowner first."

In truth, it was easier than I had thought. James knew his business and both he and his mother were keen for me to be a success. I think I helped by not pretending that I knew what I was doing, and Sarah became the mother I had barely known. She was not afraid to comment on the way I dressed, and it soon became clear that I had to match the high standards she expected from what she termed, 'the lord of the manor'. Of course, that title was not mine. In essence, I was the tenant and it was Baron Mortimer who was the lord of the manor.

I found that James was a good reeve and steward. The land was more productive, and I was learning all the time. Farming had been something other people did and I had enjoyed the fruits of their labour. Now, I could see that there was a plan to it.

Sarah was also not afraid to criticise other things, apart from my dress. She thought I ought to be wed! I know not when she thought I had the time to look for a wife. Each day saw me busy on the manor, either with James or with the farmers and those who made a living from the manor. The days flew by.

It was in the late autumn and the crops had been harvested when we were visited by Lady Maud and Baron Mortimer. I had not seen Lady Maud since I had delivered the head of Simon de Montfort, but the baron was my liege lord and this visit was to be expected. The timing of the visit threw Sarah into a frenzy of activity, for she thought my home too bare and mean for such a great lord and lady.

Lady Maud, for her part, did not appear to care. I liked her, despite her macabre trophy, and I know that she had affection for me. She greeted me not like a lowly archer, but a son.

"You have done well, Gerald War Bow, and you have helped make England safe." She allowed me to kiss the back of her hand.

"Is the rebellion over, my lord?"

"Aye, we have had the Dictum of Kenilworth. King Henry, advised, I think, by his son, Lord Edward, has offered to let the rebels keep their lands."

Lady Maud snorted. "I would have hanged the lot of them!"

Baron Mortimer sighed. "And the siege would have continued,

my dear. The rebels have to pay a fine, which is the equivalent of five years' rent on their properties, so it will give Lord Edward the funds he needs."

His wife shook her head. "Aye, but young de Montfort is at large!"

This came as news to me, for the last I had heard he was being watched and guarded. "I thought he was in Northampton, your ladyship?"

"He was, but Lord Edward is changed. He did not keep as close a watch as he should, and de Montfort fled to France!"

Baron Mortimer was less bellicose than his wife and wanted an easy life. "Good riddance, I say. He is not the threat that his father was and de Ferrers has been completely disinherited. We have peace."

I nodded and then asked, "You said Lord Edward had the funds he needed, for what did you mean, my lord?"

"Ottobuono Fieschi is now Pope Adrian and Lord Edward has decided to join King Louis of France and take the cross. He will go on crusade."

Lady Maud smiled. "Enjoy Yarpole while you can, Captain Gerald, for I am certain that Lord Edward will wish your archers to accompany him."

My heart sank, for my men and I were enjoying life at Yarpole and I did not relish the prospect of a journey halfway around the world to fight heathens in the Holy Land – despite the promise of heaven at the end of it. "Will this be soon, Baron?"

He shook his head. "These things take time and besides, it is winter. The earliest that Lord Edward could leave would be the summer, but it may well be the summer after that. His father is unwell again and Lord Edward knows that the rebellion, whilst over, is still a pile of glowing embers which could be reignited. He will wish it to be ash before he ventures from these shores. You have at least a year. Enjoy your time!"

Lady Maud smiled. "Aye, take a wife!"

Everyone, it seemed, was keen for me to wed. Everyone, that is, except for me!

PART 2

The Crusade

Map of The Holy Land at the time of Lord Edward's Crusade

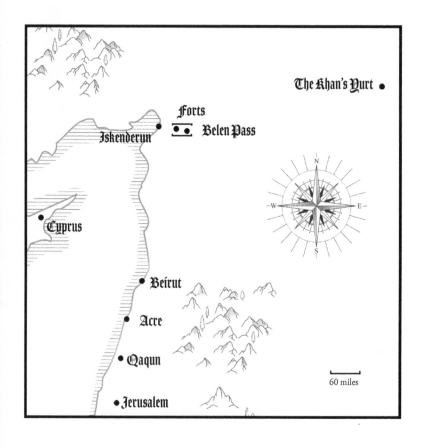

The Khan's Yurt •

Forts
Belen Pass

• Iskenderun

• Cyprus

• Beirut

• Acre

• Qaqun

• Jerusalem

N
W   E
S

60 miles

Chapter 5

Lord Edward granted me a year – and it was a year in which Lady Maud and Sarah tried to ensure that I was wed. I was invited to Ludlow castle, which was just a few miles away, almost on a weekly basis. There, young ladies would be presented to me almost as though I was a buyer at a cattle market. Sarah did the same with farmers' daughters. To speak the truth, I was not attracted to any of them and none seemed like the woman who would be the mother to my children. I enjoyed the dining at the castle, and I enjoyed the conversations with other warriors, but more than that I had grown to enjoy what amounted to the life of a gentleman. Lord Edward had not given me that title but, somehow, I felt that I had earned it.

That year showed me my land and my people as they changed with the seasons. I did not think I would ever become a true lord of the manor, for I still enjoyed my trade too much, and my archers and I continued to train and to practise daily. They were paid from the income of the land and that meant my fortune did not grow. I did not mind, for I knew that when we went on the crusade there would be a great deal more money.

The command to crusade was confirmed when I was summoned to Worcester to meet with Lord Edward. He was visiting the castles that bordered Wales, for whilst the Welsh were quiet, Lord Edward knew that it would not last. I went with Tom and Peter. John of Nottingham and Jack of Lincoln had shown an interest in a couple of local widows and I suspected that, in the future, they might marry. Tom and Peter were two of my younger warriors and I wanted them to have the same experience I had had when I was much upon their years; I wanted them to meet the men who would lead us into battle.

Although I had been summoned by Lord Edward, I was not accorded quarters in the castle and we had to use some of my money to pay for rooms in an inn close by. It would only be for one night, but I begrudged the expense. Nor was I admitted promptly. I had to cool my heels in an antechamber, while my two men visited Worcester market.

It was on this visit that I saw more of Lady Eleanor, Lord Edward's wife. He had married more than ten years earlier, but she had not accompanied him to war. With her children no longer babies, she began to accompany her husband. One day, she would rule with her husband and she needed to know the land and its people. She sat on the throne next to him and I think this was an attempt by Lord Edward to show his subjects the future Queen of England. The court at Worcester was like the court in London. There were nobles who hovered around, without an invitation, hoping to catch Lord Edward's eye or petition the future king. It was noisy on the periphery but at the centre, rather like a wild storm, there was peace and tranquillity. I dropped to my knee.

"This, my love, is my secret weapon; this is Gerald War Bow, and he has saved me on more than occasion."

Lady Eleanor took my hand and raised me so that she could kiss my cheek. "This, Captain Gerald, is for saving my husband from captivity. England owes you a great debt." She took a garnet from her finger.

"And this is part payment for that debt. I hope you will continue to serve Lord Edward."

"Of course, Lady Eleanor."

I saw a slight frown on Lord Edward's face. Such a show of affection was not in his nature. He then changed the scowl to a smile. "And he shall do so when we go on crusade. You have been warned?"

"Yes, Lord Edward, I just await the summons to the port of embarkation."

"It will not be until next year at the earliest, for we wish to join King Louis, who has yet to sail for the Holy Land. I require you and your best ten archers. You will be paid for the time you serve. I intend to tax the laity to provide the funds, so do not worry about payment. It will be there. We will be sailing from Dover and you should make yourself available from midsummer's day."

His smile at the next man in line told me that the interview was over. I bowed and said, "Thank you, Lord Edward. Thank you, Lady Eleanor."

She smiled and it was like a summer dawn. "And as we shall be travelling on the same ship, Captain Gerald, then I look forward to getting to know you better!"

I headed for the inn, The Roebuck Deer. It was too late to go home and I hoped to find out more about the force that would be going. Fate intervened once more when I encountered, for the second time, Captain Hamo l'Estrange, the sergeant at arms I had met after Evesham. He was a sword for hire, and he had travelled and served in France as well as in the Holy Land. He was a bluff fellow, but a good warrior and someone who would stand by a fallen comrade. I had liked him as soon as I met him, and it seemed fortuitous that I met him in the Roebuck Deer on the day that I discovered when we would be sailing.

I bought a jug of ale and he joined my men and me. "Tell me, Captain Hamo, what is it like on a crusade?"

He nodded. "I took the cross once, when I was younger, and went on the baron's Crusade with the Earl of Leicester, but I left because I did not like the way some of the Franks there sought power and because the rest of the English came home. You ask what it is like. It is like being in a pit of vipers, any of which will bite you when your back is turned. The enemy – the Turks, Mamluks and Turcoman – are deadly warriors. I was glad to leave the land, but I stayed with Richard of Cornwall briefly and made some coin. When the king's brother returned home I was able to come with him and find a woman. I fathered two children, but the life bored me and so I joined Lord Edward."

I have to say that I did not approve of his attitude. If you were a father, then you had a responsibility. Other than that flaw, I liked him. "Where are your wife and children now?"

He laughed. "I did not marry her, for she already had a husband. He was in the land of Estonia fighting the heathens there. At least the children I fathered have some decent blood in them!"

Hamo was unique.

He also seemed to have sources of information that I did not. "King Louis has paid Lord Edward more than seventy thousand livres to encourage him to go on crusade."

That was an extraordinary amount. I shook my head. "I know nothing of such things but why would the King of France do that?"

"A crusade needs more than one nation to take part, for if a single country went there, the lords of Outremer might think that the king sought an empire. I think King Louis would like men like you, archer. Have you been asked?"

I nodded. "But I am only required to take ten archers."

"Then that is interesting. I would have thought he would have chosen all of your company; I heard how well you did after Evesham and I know that Lord Edward thinks well of you. You never know, he may be taking cheaper archers who do not cost as much as the best. I have yet to be invited, so if you can speak on my behalf then I will be in your debt. Peace suits many people, but not me."

"I am not sure I have much influence."

He laughed. "Everyone knows that you are Lord Edward's archer and that he values not only your skill with a bow but also your judgement."

"Thank you for your kind words. I will do what you ask. We are due at Dover next midsummer's day. The King is still raising money."

"Then I will take a lesser paid job to feed me over the winter, and I shall join you. I have confidence that Lord Edward will listen to you."

We spoke of other matters and he told me that Simon de Montfort's two sons, Simon and Guy, were now living in France. He shook his head. "They should have been executed. Lord Edward will regret that decision, but he did change after Evesham."

Hamo l'Estrange merely confirmed what many men had said to me – that they saw a slightly less ruthless leader after we had defeated his enemies.

As I rode home, the next day, I was silent – for I had not seen myself as a confidante of a prince, but I supposed he was right. Lord Edward always seemed to listen to me. It would not harm my cause if I spoke up for Captain Hamo l'Estrange, as he was a good soldier – even if I did not approve of his morals.

Tom asked as we neared Yarpole, "I suppose that you will be taking warriors like Jack and John with you, Captain, as they are the best?"

I smiled. "There are many months before we have to leave and both you and Peter are improving. I will make my decision next Easter."

71

That seemed to brighten them both, and I knew that I would not need to tell the others. Once we reached my hall, word would spread.

Over the winter I spoke at length with my entire company of archers, as I wanted to find out who really wished to take the cross. I was keen, for it was said that a crusade guaranteed your passage into heaven. I had killed many men – and not all of them in battle. I needed all of the help I could get. I discovered that neither John nor Jack were keen to leave England. Oh, they said all the right things – but when you have faced death with men, then you know the look in their eyes that tells you that they are speaking what is in their heart. Both had had enough of war and killing. Both had grey-flecked beards, and both were courting widows. That was enough for me, as I had more than enough men to choose from. When I told them that they need not come then they threw themselves into training the younger archers so that I would have the best to choose from.

Mark the bowyer was another who indicated he would rather stay in England. In his case, it was because he had courted and married a farmer's daughter. I had him use his skills to make two spare bows for each of the men I would take. His skill as a maker of bows was the equal of his skills as an archer and I would miss him for he was solid and dependable. I understood his reasons.

By the time Mark had wed, I had an idea of the twelve men from whom I would choose the ten. Hamo had told me of the climate in the Holy Land and I feared that our bows might not endure as long as in England. It was better to be prepared and, by the same token, I had Walter the blacksmith make a good supply of both bodkin and war arrows. They were easier to transport than sheaths of arrows. I was not certain how much room there would be on the transports. From what Hamo l'Estrange had told me, it seemed likely that we would sail to France and then march through the land before embarking for the Holy Land from Aigues-Mortes.

One man I did not expect to take was Will Yew Tree. Other than Jack of Lincoln, he was the best of my archers and a fierce warrior. He had left my service, after Evesham, to marry a widow and run an alehouse. That it had not worked out was not Will's fault. He had earned money as an archer and invested it in the inn at Easingwold, but the widow he married had fallen ill with a pestilence that left her bedridden and struggling to breathe. Tending to a sick woman and running an alehouse in a village where many people were dying took its toll, and when she died, he lost heart. He was almost penniless and so he returned to me. I was more than happy to have him re-join my service, but I felt sad – for he had had a dream and it had been shattered. Our world was a hard one. For men it meant war and for families it spelt disease.

By the time Easter came, I had selected my men and the two I did not choose were disappointed. I then rode to visit with Lady Maud and her husband, the baron. I wondered why the baron was not participating in the crusade but as I sat with them speaking of what I might encounter, the reason became apparent: the baron was not a well man. He looked thin and coughed a great deal.

Lady Maud looked more than concerned and, as I left, she said, "Gerald, if you are able, I would have you say a prayer for the baron when you reach the Holy Land. I know that the barbarians have Jerusalem but…"

The strongest woman I had ever known looked suddenly vulnerable and I wanted to put my arm around her to comfort her, but this was Lady Maud. "Of course, for both you and the baron have been more than kind."

She threw her arms around me and wept as she hugged me. "And you are a noble man, even if the king cannot see it! Thank you, and be assured we will watch over Yarpole and your people while you serve Lord Edward and God!"

I was touched, for Lady Maud could be a fierce and unforgiving enemy – as Simon de Montfort had discovered – but her soft side was just as powerful.

Our departure from Yarpole, in contrast, was more subdued. Jack and John were the two who showed the most remorse for they both felt guilty about not accompanying me, but I knew that they would be happier at home – and so we headed south and east towards Dover. I intended to avoid the cesspit that was London. We would be better off in so many ways if we crossed the Thames further west. London was crowded and expensive, in addition to which there were more bandits there than in all the forests of England. They were just harder to spot.

We were able to take our time and we did not push the horses. They would have a long journey through France, as well as a difficult sea voyage. We made certain that the horses grazed good early-summer grass each day and I had bought oats and grain already. I would not pay the inflated prices closer to Dover. We had four sumpters with war gear and grain. They were the horses we bought for our new men, but we had been able to treat them well and build them up. They were not fast, but they were strong.

We reached Dover at the end of the second week of June. We were early for the muster and, when we reached the port, I discovered that we were amongst the first. I headed north with my men to the small port of Deal, which was not far away, and I negotiated with a local farmer to camp in his field. We hunted for shellfish and fed ourselves while we awaited the arrival of the army. Each day, I would walk into

Dover to check on the progress of the muster. On Midsummer's Eve, Hamo l'Estrange arrived and I invited him to stay with us at Deal. He agreed and when I saw the state of his clothes and boots, I realised why. He had had a lean year.

"I confess, Gerald, that if it was not for this crusade, I know not what I might have done. The borders are quiet and without war, what does a sword for hire do? I am glad that I met you in the inn in Worcester, especially as you have the ear of Lord Edward."

"I cannot promise that I can get you a berth on the ship."

"So long as you try, I shall be grateful."

And so it was, the two of us walked into Dover each day. My new friend was an expense, for he had no coins to speak of and I paid for twice the food and ale, but I had been poor once and an act of charity like this would stand me in good stead when I went to heaven.

It was the first week in July when Sir John Malton arrived. He had been put in charge of commissioning the ships he would need. I think he was relieved to see us, for it gave him two helpers. Richard, his squire, was not enough. Many ships had been commissioned already and Sir John had to find many more. There would be more than two hundred knights sailing to France, along with a thousand men. As every man would need a horse and the knights two, not to mention the baggage train, the horses alone would take twice as many ships as the men.

One evening, as we ate in an inn and before Hamo and I headed back up the road to Deal, Hamo l'Estrange showed his experience. He had been a warrior since boyhood and forgotten more than I would ever know about campaigns. "Sir John, have you not thought of sending men across the Channel now? It would mean you would need to hire fewer ships and you have boats that are idle. If we were sailing directly from here to the Holy Land, then I could understand the delay for you would all need to arrive at once. But as it stands, you should send over men and horses as they come, and you will need fewer ships. It will cut the cost."

Sir John was a clever knight; he had already realised that the Dover captains did not want their ships idle and was struggling to hire them for future use. Inspired by the words of Hamo l'Estrange, he took the momentous decision, and so my company were the first to cross. It coincided with the arrival of the first knights, including Sir William, and so we would have company. Calais was not France, and we would have accommodation there.

I had been abroad before, as had Hamo l'Estrange, but for my men, this was a new experience and the short sea voyage exposed those who had weak stomachs. I found it a short and gentle journey but for some of my men, it proved to be anything but.

I saw the wisdom in Hamo l'Estrange's suggestion. Being the first to arrive, we were accorded the best accommodation. Sir William was housed in the castle while we were given a warehouse, which adjoined the harbour. It suited us, for it was roomy and close by to some inns.

Sir William brought news of the knights who would travel to the Holy Land. Surprisingly, Henry Almain was not going with his cousin, although he had taken the cross. He was in France, but he was not following Lord Edward's banner and had business of his own. Sir William said that the son of Richard of Cornwall would join us, further south. Lord Edward's younger brother, Edmund, would eventually be with us too. As for the rest of the knights, they were unknown to me. Some had fought at Evesham, but with the king and not with Lord Edward.

Forewarned, the constable prepared chambers for Lord Edward and his wife, for we had been warned by Sir John that Lady Eleanor would accompany her husband. For a week we had the town almost to ourselves, while the army trickled across the Channel. Hamo l'Estrange and I had become firm friends and I liked his bluff way, for he had many tales to tell. We took to wandering Calais as both of us had enquiring minds.

One evening, as we headed back to the castle, I said quietly, "We are being followed!"

He was a wise old bird and did not turn, nor did he bombard me with unnecessary questions. "How long have you been aware of them?"

"When we reached the town gate and turned, a fellow looked away too soon and when I stopped to take a stone from my buskin, I saw him beneath my arm."

"Describe him to me."

"He is thin and has long lank hair, which covers part of his face. He wears breeches and a tunic of indeterminate colour, but I am guessing that he served a lord at one time."

Hamo l'Estrange nodded. "Let us see which one of us he follows. At the next square, I will stop and enjoy a beaker of ale. You carry on."

"You will be safe?"

Laughing, he patted his dagger. "Bess here is all that I need. If your lean and hungry fellow tries aught, he will learn that she has a savage bite!" His smile was that of a hunter, a wolf.

When we reached the square, he clasped my arm. "Fare ye well, archer!"

I headed back to the castle and was aware of the presence of my stalker. It was me he was following, but I did not recognise him. Perhaps he sought my purse – although now that knights had begun to arrive in Calais, there were better opportunities than an archer. I turned when I entered the gate, but there was no one behind me.

Hamo l'Estrange arrived after dark. He sat with me at the table in the warrior hall of the castle. "He followed you and I followed him.

He was good, but not good enough. After you entered the castle, I followed him to an imposing house. It was the house of a merchant; your follower entered by the servants' entrance. While I waited, I spoke with the neighbours and they told me the merchant is a rich man with lands in Poitou. I waited for an hour or so and was about to come back when I spied a knight emerging. He had a limp, his right leg had been hurt, and he had quartered red and white livery with a hawk in one quadrant." He smiled. "You have an honest face – you know this man!"

I nodded and told him the tale of my striking Sir Walter of Mansfield.

"Then it might well be that the de Montfort brothers are here, too." He smiled. "This may be profitable, for since they escaped Lord Edward, he might well reward those who find them."

"Let us go and speak with Sir William and the constable."

We spoke to them both together and the constable's reaction surprised me. "That merchant is Aubrey de St Gilles, known to be a supporter of the deceased Earl of Leicester. Sir William, on the morrow, go with Captain Gerald and seek this knight with the quartered livery. From what you have told me, he is known to be a supporter of the rebels. I would like him brought in for questioning."

Hamo l'Estrange shook his head. "Surely it would be better to strike now, before the enemy can flee."

"It is the opposite. I do not want any to escape. With Sir William's men and Captain Gerald's archers, we can surround the house and ensure that none escape. At night, we will not know if any has fled."

And so we listened to the constable and, in hindsight, it was a mistake, but at the time I saw the constable's logic.

Our second mistake was in walking and not riding to the house. Sir William and I roused our men before dawn, and we had the house surrounded as the sun rose in the east. We were too late. The merchant had guilt written all over his face and a smug look that suggested we could do nothing about it.

I acted first. "Will Yew Tree, have the horses for our men brought here."

"And mine!"

"And that of Captain Hamo l'Estrange." Hamo would not miss the chance for action.

Sir William turned to his sergeant at arms. "Have this man arrested and taken to the constable. He will have men there who can loosen his tongue." He was marched away, protesting.

Hamo l'Estrange was a clever and resourceful man. He disappeared and came back just as our horses arrived. "I spoke with the stable boy. Some lords never pay their men enough, and he was happy to tell me that Guy and Simon de Montfort, along with four of their knights, left before dawn. A further coin told us that they were heading north, for Flanders."

When we had mounted our horses and set off, Hamo l'Estrange said, "If we can catch them in Flanders or Hainaut, then we have a chance, for the Count, Guy of Dampierre, is no friend of France nor of rebels."

"And if they cross Flanders?"

"Then they are lost to us."

My archers and I, along with Hamo l'Estrange, were able to ride faster than Sir William and we hurtled along the road. I guessed that my lighter men would be faster than the knights we pursued. Even so, we saw no sign of them for some time. When we stopped in the villages, we learned the direction the men were taking, for they were riding fast and drawing attention to themselves. They were heading due east, through Ypres towards Brabant. There, they would be lost to us for the lords of Brabant were no friends of the English. It was as we passed through

Ypres that I spied hope, for I saw riders in the distance. Flanders is a flat land and many roads are straight. The sighting encouraged us and I had Tom, who was the last man in our line, signal to Sir William that our prey was close.

As we gradually reined them in, Hamo l'Estrange said, "Can your lads use their bows from the back of a horse?"

I shook my head. "It would be a waste of an arrow, unless we were stopped."

"Then it will have to be swords." He lowered his voice. "Can they use swords?"

Equally quietly I said, "Not as well as I would like."

He nodded. "Then, when we catch them, you and I will test their sword skills while your archers try to hurt them. I am guessing that Lord Edward will want prisoners."

I said sourly, "He might, but I would just as soon put an arrow in them and end this rebellion once and for all!"

I saw that there appeared to be two groups ahead of us. Four knights and their squires were struggling to keep up with the de Montforts. I recognised their livery. Three other knights, along with their squires, appeared to be better mounted and were pulling away. I glanced over my shoulder and saw that Sir William and his men were now just a hundred paces behind us. The labouring horses ahead were visibly slowing and we were catching them.

Suddenly, the four knights and their squires slowed and began to turn. I realised later that the line we were taking meant that Sir William and his men were hidden from them, and seeing the lack of mail, the eight men turned to rid themselves of the annoyance that was one man at arms and some archers. If the knight I had wounded at Axholme was with them, then he would wish vengeance upon me.

"Will, be ready to stop, nock an arrow and try to hurt them. If you can avoid it, then do not kill them. We need prisoners."

"Aye, Captain, and you?"

"I think it is me they want. Captain Hamo l'Estrange and I will act as bait."

Unconsciously, we slowed our horses for both Hamo l'Estrange and I were weighing up the opposition. The eight of them had, obligingly, spread out. I confess that I was uncomfortable fighting from the back of a horse. I had done it before, but I preferred the good earth beneath my feet. I heard the sound of hooves thundering behind us on the road and knew that Captain William was on his way.

Will Yew Tree shouted, "Dismount!"

The four knights were the more dangerous, including the wounded one, for they were mailed and I was not. I would have to use guile. When they were just forty paces from us, the first arrows hit them. Some struck shields, but at least two knights had their mail punctured by arrows. It made the two who were struck, and their squires, turn and flee.

I let Hamo l'Estrange go for the other knight as I rode at the man I had lamed, Sir Walter of Mansfield. He had a shield and a long sword and his wound would not impair him whilst on horseback. I saw him pull back his arm as he rode at my sword side. Eleanor was a quick-witted horse and when I jerked my arm to the right, the swing of the rebel's sword struck fresh air. I clumsily swung my sword at his shield and although poorly executed, the strength of my arm made him reel. I saw a squire plucked from his saddle by an arrow as Sir William and his men galloped up the road after the two wounded knights and their squires. The three squires who were still close to us all shouted, almost as one, "We yield!" when their companion was killed.

81

I was now behind Sir Walter of Mansfield, but he had good skills and he wheeled his horse so that he faced me sword to sword. If we fought a duel on horseback, then I would lose. I raised my sword and stood in my stirrups. Instead of swinging my sword, I leapt at him. My move took him by surprise, but he managed to bring his shield up. His body took the brunt of the fall while it was the knight's shield which afforded me protection. I leapt to my feet and he struggled to his.

"Yield!"

"To an archer? Never! Lay on!"

I whipped out my dagger and stood balanced as he tried to come at me. His weakened knee would not support him, and the blow he struck was easily fended by my dagger. I did not have his skill, but I had strength and when I swung at his shield, I hurt him – but there was more. He had an open-face helmet and I saw, even before my blow struck, he winced and his back arched. The fall from the horse had broken something. I heard a noise behind me as Captain Hamo l'Estrange killed the other knight. We had one chance of a prisoner, and that was the knight with whom I was fighting.

"Yield! Your companion is dead and you are hurt."

He did not even bother answering but tried to come at me again. I blocked his stroke with my dagger and repeated my swing to his shield. This time, he could not keep his feet. His weakened knee gave way and he fell. As chance would have it, when he landed, he fell on the helmet and head of the man who had just been killed by Hamo l'Estrange. His scream was that of a pig when it is being castrated, and his sword and shield fell from his hands. I could not see a wound and I approached cautiously.

"I cannot feel my legs!"

Captain Hamo l'Estrange shook his head. "His back is broken. I have seen the same in a tournament." He looked down. "Sir knight, you are sorely hurt, and I fear that your wound is fatal. Would you have me end the pain?"

In answer, he said, "Curse you, Gerald War Bow! Lord Edward would be dead but for you! Curse you!" He tried to use his arms to push himself to his feet but it was too much and, as he sighed, I saw the light go from his eyes.

Captain Hamo l'Estrange said, "That is a mercy. He has finished the work the fall started." He reached up and pulled one of the squires from his saddle. The youth, of no more than nineteen summers, looked shocked. "What did he mean about Gerald War Bow's saving Lord Edward?"

In answer, the terrified squire said, "Sir Walter here, who was my lord, did not tell me but when he spied you in Calais, he had Henry follow you, for he said where you were there would be Lord Edward. That is all that I know."

I shook my head. "You know more, for Sir Guy and Sir Simon de Montfort were with you, were they not?"

He nodded.

"What did you hear?"

"That they sought vengeance on the killers of their father. I swear that is all that I know."

Just then, Sir William rode up with the two knights who had fleed. They too were dead and draped over their horses. He nodded and said, "We will take these back to Lord Edward. He is due in tomorrow. They can enjoy his justice."

We had done well out of the encounter. Captain Hamo l'Estrange had a good horse and we had two further horses as well as Sir Walter's mail, sword and weapons.

We did not reach Calais until dark. More knights had arrived and I was invited to dine with them, where Sir William and I were quizzed about the encounter. All of them were worried by the fact there were knights who would happily kill outside the rules of combat. I was not as worried, for it was our way to do whatever we had to in order to sleep safely at night.

Had the constable heeded my advice, then the tragedy which ensued might have been prevented.

Chapter 6

When Lord Edward arrived with the bulk of the army, the constable apprised him of the threat and the previous, ruthless version of Lord Edward emerged. He had the squires held for ransom against their estates and after confiscating the merchant's home, he fined him a sum equal to the contribution of the King of France. He sent for me, along with Captain William, later in the day. Lady Eleanor was there.

"It seems that I am in your debt once more. What do you make of it, War Bow? You seem to have an affinity with cutthroats."

Lady Eleanor looked skyward at the insult, but I did not mind. I was under no illusion and knew what Lord Edward thought of me.

"I think they were here to kill you, Lord Edward. This would be the perfect place. It is crowded with armed men and many are unknown to each other. I believe that Sir John's decision to cross to Calais early upset their plans. As soon as you arrived, there would have been men seeking your attention. All it takes is one knife in the right place. It is not as if you are an anointed king yet."

"You are right, and this makes perfect sense. Perhaps those advisers who told me to execute the young Montforts were right. I shall not make the same mistake again!" He nodded. "Then you and your archers will guard me, War Bow. When my cousin, Henry Almain, reaches us, then, Captain William, you will guard him. War Bow, you shall be our chamberlain and sleep inside our door each night."

Lady Eleanor shook her head. "My husband, that is unreasonable!"

I smiled. "Do not worry, my lady, I serve Lord Edward and the rewards are worth it."

Lord Edward laughed and threw me a purse. "Aye, and I know that I can trust you. Set a murderer to catch a murderer, eh?" Lord Edward knew all of my secrets. "We leave tomorrow for Aigues-Mortes. King Louis and his sons could not wait for our arrival, it seems, and they have left for Tunis already. He will win the war before we reach the Holy Land unless we hurry!"

I was about to leave, then he said, "And this Captain Hamo l'Estrange, what of him? I did not hire him." His aggressive tone told me that he was less than happy.

"He is a sword for hire and came here on the off-chance that he would be hired."

Captain William said, "If he had not been so resourceful, we might not have known of this plot, Lord Edward, and he is a useful fellow. He is not a knight, but sometimes, Lord Edward, you need men who have fewer scruples than a knight."

He laughed. "Aye, take him on. It seems I am to be surrounded by bandits!"

Lady Eleanor shook her head. "Do not listen to him, Gerald War Bow, for I see nobility within you and I for one will sleep more safely knowing that it is you who watches our door."

Captain Hamo l'Estrange was delighted, although a little concerned that no price had been agreed for his services. For my men and me, it meant that we rode at the fore and not in the rear amongst the baggage and the dust. While I always had a roof over my head when we slept, at the very worst my men had the stables. We stayed in the castles of knights and lords who were keen to gain favour with King Louis of France and the future King of England. Most nights saw me sleeping in the antechamber of Lord Edward's room and there was normally a comfortable fur for me. I did not mind. The best part of my position was that I was privy to all that went on around Lord Edward. I think he might have benefitted more from the proven killer that was Captain Hamo l'Estrange, but he did not know him. I was completely trustworthy.

News was constantly arriving in the Holy Land as more and more men arrived. Each one added to not only our numbers but our knowledge of the world outside. I was there when the terrible news came that Henry Almain had been murdered by Simon de Montfort's two sons in Italy. I have never seen Lord Edward rage so much. He and his cousin had been as close as brothers. I witnessed the charm of his wife, who was the only one able to calm him. That she loved him deeply was obvious.

She gave him a sleeping draught and then came to speak with me. "He and Henry shared a vision for England, Gerald. I believe that the two of them could have righted the wrongs of their grandfather, King John."

"Lord Edward is a good man and he will make England stronger."

"He is strong, but he is now alone. Perhaps his brother, Edmund, will grow to become Henry Almain."

"Perhaps, but when you fight alongside someone, as Lord Edward did with his cousin, then you develop a trust which – although invisible – is as strong as steel."

She smiled at me, for she was a very perceptive woman. "And you have that bond, too."

"But I am an archer and will never stand next to Lord Edward. I can guard him, and I can fight for him, but I can never be a Henry Almain."

"You are something different but no less necessary." She held her hand for me to kiss its back. "Goodnight, Gerald. I shall join my husband." She looked at the fur on the floor. "I do not know how you can endure such discomfort."

I shrugged. "Until I was given Yarpole, I slept most nights on the hard floor. This is fine!"

She closed her door and I spent a few moments before sleep reviewing all of her words and recalling the soft skin on the back of her hand. After I said a prayer for the dead Henry Almain, I slept well. I had followed Lord Henry's banner and was there when he destroyed the Derbyshire rebels. I knew his worth. If I had the chance again, then Simon and his brother Guy would not have had the opportunity to surrender.

When we reached Aigues-Mortes, I was one of the first to see the ships waiting to carry us across the sea to Tunis. These were ordinary sailing ships and galleys. But the sheer numbers made it a formidable fleet. It was here that we would be parted from Captain Hamo and Sir William, for they would not be travelling on the same ship as Lord Edward. Lord Edward planned on sailing first to Sardinia and thence to Tunis. It made sense to me, as the two journeys were shorter than the long crossing where we risked both pirates and storms.

I had never sailed this sea and when we set sail in September, I was amazed at how quiet, blue and calm it was. Even my vomiting new men coped with it. However, we were the bodyguards and we had to work; we had no time to stare out to see and admire the scenery. My men were employed as extra lookouts and we had our bows ready at all times.

The voyage was inconsequential, and nature fooled us. We landed in Sardinia and then the Blue Sea was wracked with such storms that it was many days before we could sail again.

During our voyage and our time in Sardinia, I found myself growing closer to Lady Eleanor and Lord Edward. In Lord Edward's case, it was merely a softening of the formality with which he surrounded himself. Lady Eleanor, in contrast, became a friend. She would often ask me to walk with her on the ship so that she could use my arm if the ship moved too much, and when we were in Sardinia and wrapped against the wild winds, she asked me to escort her along the battlements of the castle. There, she spoke of her hopes for her children. She was keenly aware that her eldest, Edward, had not turned out quite the way she had hoped and although he was not yet eight, the man could be seen in the boy. She did not blame Lord Edward, but I sensed that he had not shown as much interest in his firstborn as he might have.

"My hope is that he is as lucky as his father and finds an ordinary man like yourself to keep his feet on the ground." She put her hand to her mouth. "How awful of me! I am sorry, Gerald, I did not mean to insult you."

"And you have not, for I know that I am ordinary and quite unremarkable. That I have risen as high as I have is a constant source of amazement, especially to me!"

She laughed at my words and we were very easy with one another. In the dark days of the crusade, that would prove to be vital.

We left for Tunis and the ancient port of Carthage in North Africa. Our ship's captain was keen to make the crossing quickly and he used every inch of sail. We had the biggest and the best ship, the *Henri Grace of God*, and soon we must have been a dot on the horizon to the rest of the fleet. The pirates of North Africa were opportunists and the storms would have left many ships dismasted and ripe to be taken. Two Arab dhows must have put out from the Barbary Coast with just such an intention. The French captain knew his business and he immediately shortened sail to allow the rest of the fleet to catch up with us. I was no sailor, but even I could see that the approaching dhows would reach us first.

Regardless of the captain's actions, I had to protect Lord Edward and his wife, and I gave my orders to my handful of archers. "Will, take half the men and get into the forecastle. The rest, with me!"

Lord Edward had a dozen or so household knights with him, and I heard his stentorian tones. "Squires, guard Lady Eleanor and her ladies. The rest of you, come with me to the mainmast." At the mainmast, he could go to either end of the ship quickly. The two dhows could pick and choose where they attacked us.

While we were not panicking, both of us feared the worst; I saw that as we passed each other. The crew were also arming themselves. When the Moors attacked, the end would either be death or slavery. All of us would sell our lives dearly.

Travelling south had allowed my archers and me to develop a system of defence. We had discussed it on the road and it evolved through the contributions of everyone in my company. We had balanced our archers between us – because I commanded five archers, I had one more man than Will and that was why he had the forecastle. It was smaller, and his archers fitted in more easily.

I hung my arrow bag from one of the hooks in the sterncastle and chose a good arrow for my first. All of our arrows were good, but archers are creatures of habit and if you believed you were releasing your best arrow, then it generally worked. Some of the crew had bows, but they were not archers. It mattered not, for so long as an arrow found flesh, I did not care who sent it.

Glancing astern, I saw the rest of the fleet as they hurried to catch us. I doubted that they could see the Arabs but soon they would – and then they would lay on all sail while the galleys would set about rowing at top speed. The packed pirate ships could sail closer to the wind than any other ship I had ever seen, and the two captains must have often sailed together as they split up to approach the steerboard side and the larboard side.

The glistening bodies of the Moors told me that they outnumbered us. I turned to my men. "Go for the leaders and, when you can, the man steering the dhow!" I realised as I gave my command that I should have told Will to target the steersmen. It was too late now. On the road south we had not envisaged an attack like this. "Ralph of Chepstow, Robin and Peter – go for those on the larboard side. We will take the other." Ralph was another older archer and he could lead. I could happily leave him to control his younger charges.

I saw the greybeard kiss his cross; he thought he was doomed. I did not, for so long as I stood and could draw a bow, then I feared no man. These Moorish warriors looked fierce, but they fought at sea and wore no mail. They were also large men and a big target. I had a good war arrow nocked and its barbed head would cause a terrible wound.

We had the wind with us, and I saw a huge Moor wielding a double-handed scimitar. He was holding on to the forestays as the dhow on our steerboard side tacked its way to us. The wind was behind us and I knew that a well-fletched arrow would fly straight and true. The trick would be to allow for the rise and fall of the dhow.

I aimed at the largest target, his belly. I let out my breath as I released the arrow. So long as I hit him, then I would be happy. It was the sudden shallow trough that aided my strike, and my arrow hit him in the middle of his face. The barbed head had been sharpened and the angle it struck at meant it drove through to his spine. He tumbled into the sea before the dhow, and I saw sharks racing in for the unexpected feast. The knights and the crew cheered. They would see this as almost magic. My men would know that there was luck involved.

"Can we try our hand now, Captain?" Peter asked for all of those in the sterncastle.

"Aye, if you can hit, then send an arrow – but be certain that you can hit!" As I nocked my next arrow, it aimed for the starboard dhow. Will and his men also targeted the steerboard dhow. On reflection, this was a mistake as although we hit eight men, the larboard ship remained undamaged. The French captain knew his business and he turned to steerboard to take us closer to the dhow we had hit.

William of Matlac was another who had been an outlaw and he had great skill. He sent an arrow into the side of the head of the steersman, then the dhow swung under our bows and there was a crunching sound, followed by screams as the dhow was crushed beneath our hull. The low nature of the dhows meant that the second could not see the other ships racing to our aid, and they threw grappling hooks to tie us together.

Lord Edward's voice was loud and clear. "Knights to the larboard side and let us try to emulate our archers!"

For our part, we needed no command – and as black- and brown-skinned arms grasped the gunwale, we sent arrows into their heads. Some were hit by two arrows as we tried to clear the gunwale and the knights severed the grappling hooks.

The rest of the fleet had sailed into view and they were spreading out to benefit from the killing spree.

The dhow's captain realised he could not win and tried to escape. He had the wind, but so did our ships, and our vessel, *Henri Grace of God*, caught him beam on and the warship sliced through the hull of the dhow.

The sharks were now moving amongst those who had not already died, and it was terrible to see. We could do nothing but watch helplessly as the sea turned red, as men and sharks thrashed around until, as we carried on our way, the waters became quiet once more. The pirates had died, to a man. Man might leave survivors; nature did not. With our ships protectively around us, we headed into Carthage.

The voyage had lasted twelve days and yet it felt longer. We descended from our castles to cheers. Lady Eleanor blew me a kiss and Lord Edward shook my arm so much that, had I not been an archer, it would have hurt.

"Just eleven of you and yet you drove off two pirates' ships. Never was a prince served better!"

I smiled. "We are just doing that for which we are paid. It is a pity that their bodies were consumed by the sea and the sharks, for they looked to have bejewelled fingers and good weapons."

"Fear not, when we reach Tunis then there will be riches beyond compare."

His optimism was misplaced, as we discovered when we stepped ashore. A French pursuivant greeted Lord Edward with tragic news. "King Louis and his son Louis are dead!"

"In battle?"

"No, Lord Edward, disease, which has ravaged our camp. We have won the battle and have the peace, but disease took the king, his eldest and many hundreds of our men. King Philip and his uncle, Charles of Anjou, have signed a treaty with the warriors of North Africa. They are to pay us indemnities in return for our departure."

Lord Edward nodded. "And we sail for Acre?"

He shook his head. "The deaths of the king, his son and so many of our men have torn the heart from France and Anjou. We will go home and bury our men in sanctified earth and not this mud."

We were left on the quay, and Lord Edward looked perplexed.

It was Lady Eleanor who saw the light and not the darkness; her voice was calm and reassuring. "This changes nothing, my husband. We can still go to Acre and you can send home for more men. I can understand the loss suffered by the French; we will just find more allies."

He smiled, but even I knew that this was easier said than done. England had been ravaged by civil war and there was not the manpower to send as many men as would now be leaving for France. However, her words and counsel put him in a better mood.

The good mood lasted just three days, for Charles of Anjou refused to share any of the indemnity he had extracted from the Berbers and Moors with the English. He argued that we had arrived too late to be of any assistance to the French and the Angevin. The whole French fleet sailed north, and we were left alone in Tunis where there was nothing for us.

This was where Henry Almain would have come up with some suggestion, which would have had a positive perspective, but he was now dead, murdered by treacherous hands. In the end, Lord Edward set sail for Cyprus. I suspect that it merely delayed the decision he would have to make.

I knew nothing about Cyprus and as we loaded the ships, I asked Hamo what he knew.

In answer, he took me to one side and tapped the side of his nose. "King Hugh of Cyprus is also King of Jerusalem. He is a Lusignan and related to Lord Edward. It is a clever move to go there, for Cyprus is a crusader state and will support Lord Edward. However, do not get your hopes up for even with Lord Edward's men, Cyprus and Jerusalem, we do not have enough soldiers to defeat the Mamluk under Baibars. Still, you and your archers may well cause them some annoyance."

"I thought that we were here to retake Jerusalem."

He laughed. "To do that would take the whole of the Byzantine Empire and every Christian knight in England, France, Spain and the Holy Roman Empire! The best we can hope is that our sins are forgiven and while we live, we make some profit." He clapped me on the shoulder. "I will see you in Limassol!"

It was while we were in Limassol that I learned more about Baibars. Since the time of Saladin, the Mamluks and Turks had been fighting each other; conflict that the likes of Richard of Cornwall and Simon de Montfort had greatly profited from. Baibars was closer in nature to the most famous Saracen of them all than any other leader since that time – and he was eating into Christian lands.

Lord Edward spent longer in Limassol than I might have expected. I suspect he was delaying his arrival, for the Ninth Crusade had been trumpeted throughout England and France. When he arrived in Jerusalem, he would be unable to mount any sort of attack on the Mamluks and I think he hoped for reinforcements.

Lady Eleanor did not waste her time. At one time, Cyprus had been ruled from Constantinopolis and it had boasted an extensive library. Lady Eleanor purchased some of the military writings for Lord Edward so that he could see how others had fared in the past against these formidable warriors, and she also bought maps for him to study. She might not have been a warrior, but she did all that she could to aid her husband.

It was spring when our eight ships and thirty galleys arrived in Acre. Lord Edward had been spurred to action with the news that Baibars was besieging that place. It would not do for the Crusaders to lose their strongest castle while Lord Edward was so close. Such was Lord Edward's reputation, and, I have no doubt, that of the men that he led, that as soon as our fleet arrived in the harbour, then the siege was lifted, and we were greeted like heroes.

I did not feel like a hero.

Acre was a formidable fortress. A line of double walls and towers surrounded the castles and the town itself. As we tacked into the harbour, we saw the huge Templar fortress at the harbour mouth. Even if the rest of the defences fell, the Templars could hold out. I also saw that there were quarters where Italians lived: Venetian, Genoan and Pisan could all be seen. If Acre fell, the Holy Land was lost.

Lord Edward threw himself into action. Until his brother, Edmund, arrived with the reinforcements, we would be limited in what we could do, and we had realised, quite quickly, that the knights of Cyprus were not as committed as us. If we were to show the Mamluks that the English had arrived, then we would have to do it alone.

Lord Edward wanted something dramatic for his first site of action and he chose Nazareth. It was the home of Jesus. It had been captured from Christians and he chose to raid it and to put to the sword every Mamluk he found. Hamo l'Estrange proved invaluable, for he had been there with Simon de Montfort on the Barons' Crusade and it was about this time that Lord Edward came to rely on the mercenary far more than I think he had expected to. Lady Eleanor had listened to me and she had encouraged her husband to involve Hamo.

Hamo spoke authoritatively: "What you need, Lord Edward, is a highly mobile force of horsemen. In a perfect world, you would have mounted archers who could loose from the backs of horses. What have Gerald War Bow, and he and the English archers can outrange almost all of the Mamluk archers. The archers pin them down and then your men at arms and knights sweep them from the field."

"Is there not a castle in Nazareth?"

"Not like the ones you are used to. There is a wall and a tower."

Lord Edward was convinced, and we left Acre to head the few miles up the road to Nazareth. Our intelligence led us to believe that there were more than a thousand men in the small town, and as our force was only slightly larger, I wondered if Lord Edward was taking too much on. However, I was given command of the one hundred archers that had been brought from England and so I set about practising with them. My archers were all mounted and it took some time to procure the twenty or so we needed to be horseless archers. Hamo, who seemed to know his way around Acre, went to find them for us. He was a resourceful man in so many ways, and I knew I could rely on him.

My task was much harder, for I had to manage a wide range of archers brought by the knights who accompanied Lord Edward. The knights had brought archers under Lord Edward's instructions, but some were of decidedly poor quality and seemed to me to be the sweepings of their manor. They could draw a bow, but that was about it. After a morning on the beach, I realised that I had fewer than fifty archers upon whom I could truly rely.

As I sent the archers to recover the arrows from the soft sand, I confided in Will Yew Tree. "I think that we use the poorer fifty as either horse holders or a reserve."

Will nodded towards Richard of Culcheth. "Dick there has been a rock since he joined us. If you gave the poorer ones to him and his son, he might be able to make something of them – for he has a way with men, and he is a good teacher."

I looked at him sharply. "You are saying there is something wrong with the way I lead the archers?"

He sighed at my outburst. "Of course not, but it was obvious to all from the way you spoke to them that you did not rate their ability. A man likes to think he can do a good job, even if he is a poor archer. Dick can coax them. What have we to lose?"

He was right, of course, and I had been a little short with them, but I was their captain! "It means that I have two fewer good archers."

"And yet, if Dick and Robin can make just ten of them into decent archers, then we will have more archers on whom we can rely."

I laughed. "You have a silver tongue, Will. Remind me never to gamble with you."

"You never gamble anyway!"

Surprisingly, not only was Richard of Culcheth happy about the new arrangement but so were the new men. Perhaps Will was right, and I was a hard taskmaster. A man cannot change the way he is, and my nature and character were both set. After seven days of practice, the men were better and there were only ten whom I thought inadequate – they could be the horse holders.

Two of the Knights Templar came with us to act as local guides. Their burnished skin showed how long they had been out here, and Hamo was relatively impressed with them.

"Most are zealots, Gerald, and hate the Turks so much that it blinds them to other choices they might make. Sir Guy and Sir Henry are better than most, and the fact that they are English and not French makes them a better choice as companions."

"And with whom do you fight, Hamo?"

"I have been attached to Sir William's men and that suits me, for he is like you – without a drop of noble blood in his body. Such men are my kind of warrior."

In terms of distance, Nazareth was not too far to travel, but the heat and the road conditions made the journey seem interminable. Lord Edward had no real need to attack the place, except that it had been Christian until the Mamluks took it and it was Christ's birthplace. We reached it at noon and Lord Edward wasted no time scouting it out. He relied on Hamo and the two Templars, Sir Guy and Sir Henry, for advice. While the horses assembled in three lines, he had the archers, commanded by me, rain war arrows into the town. He sent Sir William with two hundred men at arms around the town to prevent the populace from escaping, and then he launched an attack by two hundred of his knights.

As we were sending our arrows to fall from the sky behind their walls, we could not see the whole effect, but I watched men on the walls falling as arrows tore through flimsy mail and flesh. As soon as Lord Edward gave the command, we stopped and followed the horsemen. Slinging my bow over my back, I drew my sword. This would be the first time that I had fought the Muslims and I do not know what I was expecting – except that it was not this. These were not the fierce warriors who had driven the King of Jerusalem from his home. They were fair warriors, but not as good as we were.

I led the archers, but once we poured over the walls, the only men who heeded my commands were my own. Then, the sweepings of the manors showed their true character and all in their path, regardless of age or sex, were slaughtered. My men showed *their* character and we protected the old, the women and the children.

One of the archers who served Sir Hugh d'Aubigny was about to strike down an old man when I spied him. I fetched him such a clout that he fell to the ground and was unconscious. I turned to Peter and Tom and said, "Take him and throw him outside the town. He is no Christian!" What was the point of fighting the Mamluks if we behaved worse than them?

We hurried into the centre of the village. There we found warriors, and these were more like the warriors I had fought before. They knew that they were going to die and seemed happy to do so. They formed a shield wall and I saw that many of them had mail, which was as good as our knights', and they would not die easily. Lord Edward and his knights had the advantage of horses, or else they might not have had the success they did. He and the knights charged into the men on foot, who fought them off as best they could. I led my men to support them and, when I recognised Sir William, Hamo and the rest of Sir William's men fighting some askari, we began to fight our way to them. These were mailed warriors with small shields and long swords. I saw Ralph of Chepstow cut in two and then Hamo l'Estrange knocked from his horse.

"Follow me!"

I led my men to the aid of my friend. I did not wish to lose him in our first battle, especially not for such a mean place. I brought my sword into the back of one askari. Despite his mail, my arm was so strong that the blow broke his back and I used his fallen body to climb so that I could wield my sword at head height. My next blow struck the side of a horsed archer who was turning. My sword sliced into the top of his skull.

It was just then that Hamo was felled by a blow to his helmet. He tumbled to the ground and I knew that he was disorientated. As the askari raised his scimitar to end my friend's life, I leapt between them and used my razor sharp dagger against the hilt of the scimitar. He turned with an angry expression, for it was clear that I was not a knight nor even a man at arms. What he did not know was that I was a fighter – and I hacked at him with my sword. Once again, my natural strength came to my aid and I smashed my sword into his shield, making his arm shiver. His eyes widened at the force of the blow, which made him step back. When

An Archer's Crusade

a warrior steps back then he risks losing his balance – and that is what happened to the askari. I took my chance and drove my dagger into his eye.

Will Yew Tree slew a second warrior trying to get at Hamo. We were unimportant in the eyes of our enemy, but Hamo wore mail and had a good sword, which made him a greater threat and a richer prize. We stood astride his body and those of two other men at arms who had been wounded.

I shouted, "Hamo! Wake!" I kicked his side with my buskin to encourage him to rise.

I heard him chuckle. Then he said, "Aye, Gerald War Bow, but give me your arm, for that blow has made me dizzy." I lowered my left arm and he pulled himself up. He looked at the dead men. "It seems I am in your debt. Now, if you and your men will watch my back, I will try to cleave a path to Sir William."

Sir William and his men were beleaguered. Lord Edward and the knights who followed him had ridden off to end the battle, but we had yet to win this part of the town.

Will and I stood just behind Hamo, who hefted his shield. He said, "If you are going to do much of this type of fighting then get yourself a buckler!"

With his sword in his hand, he stepped forward and I was able to admire his technique. His sword work seemed effortless. While Will and I put every ounce of effort into each blow, Hamo chose the place he would strike and almost stroked his sword into flesh. We had little to do except to stab at those men who came at his side. Within a dozen strokes, we had reached Sir William, who nodded his thanks. Once our two forces were joined, we despatched all of the Mamluks who did not flee. That was the end of our battle. Lord Edward and his knights had the last of the Mamluks concentrated in the square, and they were being butchered.

Sir William took charge. "There has been enough slaughter of those who do not fight. Let us stop the privations of those who pretend to be men."

We began to fetch out the women, the children and the old and infirm. Sir William's men guarded them.

Will and I found a locked door – and that, normally, meant treasure. We opened it and found, instead, a man. He was not a Muslim and he had been treated badly. His face was not Arabic. He looked resigned to his fate and regarded me calmly; I think he thought he would die at our hands.

I sheathed my sword and smiled. "We will not hurt you, for you look to have been a prisoner."

In answer, he spoke a language which sounded like French. I spoke a few words of French but not enough, and his accent made it impossible for me to understand him. I put my arm around him and used my dagger to cut his bonds. "Come into the light and we will see if someone can speak with you."

The bright sunlight made him recoil and while he cowered from the light, I was able to examine him. He was an archer. I say that because he had powerful arms, but he was also very short with almost bowed legs. He had eyes which seemed slanted and narrow while his skin was a different colour from the Muslims'.

Hamo approached and I said, "I do not understand this man, but he was a prisoner. I believe he can speak French, but I cannot understand a word of it."

He nodded and spoke French to him. I did not follow the conversation save for the odd word or two from Hamo, but when he had finished, Hamo grinned. "You have found a prize here, Gerald. This is a Mongol warrior, a noble. He was on his way back from an embassy to Constantinopolis when the Turks took him. He is an envoy of Abaqa

Khan, who rules to the north and east of the land of the Turk. We should take him to Lord Edward."

That was easier said than done, as Lord Edward and his knights celebrated victory long into the night. We kept the Mongol, whose name we learned was Ahmed Tukeder, in our camp. If he was as valuable as Hamo had said, then the last thing we needed was for some drunken Christian to kill him.

As we headed back to Acre, Lord Edward was in high spirits despite the fact that he had lost men. Of course, they were not knights, and so unimportant. We had the Mamluk horses and could field many more men the next time we rode forth. As usual, we were just behind Lord Edward and I nudged Eleanor next to him.

He frowned, and then thought better of it – for I rarely inveigled myself into his confidence without good reason. "Yes, War Bow? I cannot see you being here for praise; it is, thankfully, not your way. Spit out the words that lurk in your mouth. They may distract me from this abominable heat."

"We released a prisoner held by the Turks in Nazareth, Lord Edward. His name is Ahmed Tukeder." He nodded and waited for me to continue. "He is a Mongol from the court of Abaqa Khan. The Mongolians have no love for the Mamluks."

He laughed. "Just when I think that I know you, then you surprise me. How do you know all of this? I assume he speaks Mongolian and you butcher English, so how did you communicate?"

I was not offended, for I knew I had not been brought up speaking well. "He speaks French and Hamo l'Estrange spoke long into the night with him. This khan is married to the illegitimate daughter of the Byzantine Emperor, Michael. Her name is Maria Palaiologina and it explains why he favours the west."

"You have come far, archer, for you devise high strategies."

I shook my head. "It is Captain Hamo – he thought we might send an embassy to Tabriz and speak to him."

Sir John Malton was close by and he shook his head. "Her ladyship showed me some of the books she bought and one of them had maps. Tabriz is as far to the east of us as Paris is to the west!"

Lord Edward was thinking, and he waved an irritated hand. "It need only be three or four men and we risk nothing by trying. The question is, when? Keep this Ahmed Tukeder with your archers and when time allows, we will speak with him. I will consult with my wife for she has a mind for such contrivances." I nodded. "And what does this sword for hire wish from all of this?"

"He has made no secret of the fact that he wishes to be a knight."

"Does he now! And you?"

I shrugged. "I do not aspire to be a knight."

"Good, for we do not give spurs to archers."

Chapter 7

My men quite liked our guest because he seemed so different. With Hamo translating, the Mongol told us how his people were able to use a bow from the back of a horse and still retain accuracy. At first, they did not believe him – but when one of the Mongolian bows was procured from the armoury, they saw that it was possible, for it was shorter than a longbow. The fact that even their great lords used bows interested my men. Archers in England were not held in such high esteem – although it was higher than in France and the Holy Roman Empire.

I know that Lord Edward spoke with the Templars and his wife about the strategy I had suggested. He had not forgotten the mission to the Mongols, but he wanted to build on his success. Ahmed was kept safe in the fortress of Acre and I did not see much of him for a few days. That was a pity, as I was sure that we had much in common.

Lord Edward, King Hugh and the Templars chose St Georges-de-Lebeyne as the next place they would attack. It was close enough to Acre that if things went badly for us, we could retreat back, yet far enough away from the safety of Acre to demonstrate Lord Edward's power, which appealed to him.

Lord Edward was desperate for his brother Edmund to arrive with reinforcements. Until he did, we were limited to what amounted to large scale chevauchée and, as we left for St Georges-de-Lebeyne, Lord Edward spoke with me, Sir John Malton and Hamo – for he had considered the idea we had mentioned to him. "Could the three of you ride to meet this khan and deliver a missive from me?"

It was obvious that Hamo had thought a great deal about this, for he nodded vigorously. "Aye, lord, for we could sail north and use Armenia to begin our journey. If we had Ahmed with us, then he could facilitate the journey."

"And yet I would be without my captain of archers. You are expendable, l'Estrange, as I can acquire ten men like you. We will conduct this raid and then we will consider what we might do."

I could not hide my smile, for I had been paid a compliment while Hamo had been insulted. Hamo and I dropped back to join my archers as we had been dismissed, and I saw Sir John and Lord Edward bend their heads together.

"I need not go at all, Hamo. I have no languages and few other skills."

"You are an archer, and I have no doubt that even though we travel through the lands of the khanate there will be men, sent by Baibars, who will try to kill us. I would be happier to have your bow with us!" He waved a hand at the sky, which was cloudless with a hot sun beating down upon us. "This does not bode well for Lord Edward's army. See how some of those who ride with us are already drinking their precious water. We have many miles to go. You and your archers are doing the right thing and I see that you heeded my words about broad-brimmed straw hats."

Although they felt foolish at first, my men had woven straw into hats and now reaped the reward while others baked under the hot eastern sun. We had also ensured that our horses had plenty of water in Acre, and each of us gave some to our horses when we stopped. Meeting Hamo had already saved lives.

I saw a couple of knights by the side of the road with their squires, whom Lord Edward berated as he passed. This did not bode well. The Templars, in contrast, knew their business and we had even more with us this time. They had enjoyed the success of the raid on Nazareth and saw in Lord Edward the embodiment of the Lionheart!

We did not reach the town until darkness was falling and so we camped. Once again, my archers had brought food and we were also able to hunt a few small animals to put in a stew. The local farmers paid for the lack of foresight of knights, men at arms and even other archers, as their animals were taken without payment.

One farmer made the mistake of objecting when two archers, Peter Red Hair and Paul of Pevensey, who served Sir Hugh l'Ysette, attacked him. Lord Edward showed a hard and ruthless side: he had them tried before a jury of archers, a jury upon which Richard of Culcheth sat. We expected them to be beaten as the farmer had been, but Lord Edward had them hanged.

That they were not very good archers was immaterial. They were Englishmen and they had been executed. It stopped the pillaging, but it created bad feeling amongst the rest of the company.

I was summoned by Lord Edward before dawn. "I want you and your archers on the far side of the town. You can leave your horses here and when I sound the horn, then rain death upon the garrison. I wish you to prevent the enemy from fleeing. I want no warriors to escape."

I nodded, although I was concerned. "We will be exposed, Lord Edward."

"From what we have seen, there is little opposition to worry about. Besides, you are Gerald War Bow and you will cope!" He nodded firmly, saying, "Leave now so that you are in position by dawn." With that, I was dismissed.

I gathered my men – and that included every archer. I had each of them carry an extra war bag of arrows. We had lost men and I had not begun with many. I needed every archer to become my man. If we were attacked, then I wanted us to be able to defend ourselves.

As we marched around the town, looking down to the ground to avoid the spiders, scorpions and snakes we had been told emerged at night, I sensed disquiet amongst the men. They had not liked the hanging but then again, I had disapproved also. If he had waited until we were back in Acre, then we would have had less risk of desertions – but Lord Edward could be ruthless! I would try to get these archers back on Lord Edward's side before desertions began.

I led the line of archers and I watched for the shadows that were the walls of St Georges-de-Lebeyne. As its name suggested, it had been built by Christians and the Templars had chosen to attack it to punish the Mamluks for taking it. The low curtain wall around the town was Christian-built and, as such, of better quality than the mud used by the locals. I sought the road leading from the town and we easily found it. We retraced our steps until we were just two hundred paces from the walls. We would have to close with the walls when we began our attack, but I did not want to give away our position too soon.

Richard of Culcheth and Robin were with the poorer archers behind us.

"Richard, you will use your arrows against St Georges-de-Lebeyne, but you must also watch for Mamluks coming from behind you. If we are attacked, then tell me first and then turn to face the threat."

"Aye, Captain." He lowered his voice. "The hanging was not well done, Captain. Those two archers were piss poor, but they did not kill, and Lord Edward did."

"The carrot is out of the ground now, Richard, and we cannot replace it. We must try to heal the rifts, but let us wait until we are back in Acre."

Nodding, he went to give his orders. I stuck a handful of arrows in the ground and then strung my bow. Will Yew Tree and my men were with me but before the battle started, they would spread themselves out amongst the others to stiffen their resolve. This was a strange land. There was not just the heat, there were also alien smells and strange sounds. It was as different from England as it was possible to be. I hoped that I would not make a poor judgement because of the land.

I looked east and saw the sky was growing lighter. Lord Edward would be preparing his knights. No matter how much care they took, the squires would still make a noise as they saddled the knights' horses and fitted their mail. Those in the small town would know that someone was there, and they would be prepared.

On the other hand, they might not know what or who was making the noise. That became evident when Will pointed to the town. The gate had opened, and a rider was heading out. As he galloped towards us, I realised that I did not speak any Arabic and would have to use an arrow to stop him.

I tried, in my abysmal French, to shout "Stop!" but the rider ignored me – and so I pulled back on the bow and sent an arrow into his chest. His dead hands locked on to the reins and I hissed, "Will, grab the horse!"

I wondered if those in the town had heard the noise although the only sound was the neigh of the horse as Will grabbed its reins and soothed it by stroking its muzzle.

I looked around and saw that the men were all alert, and each had an arrow ready to nock. Even the ones unused to me were becoming better.

The sky was a little lighter when Lord Edward sounded the trumpet. "Draw!"

I looked down the line and said, "Release!" We sent our arrows high into the air to clear the curtain wall and most of the buildings. We heard shouts and cries, but I ignored them. You could not picture your arrow slaying an innocent, for therein lay madness, but every archer knew that doing as we had been commanded would result in such deaths.

"Release at will!"

I knew that the different bows and the nature of our archers meant the arrows would fall over a large area, and that suited us for there was unpredictability and men could not hide from random arrows. For those in the town, the only safe place would be in a building. However, when the knights and men at arms arrived, then they would become death traps. I had seen the dark side of crusaders. Hamo had told me that the Templars could be cruel, which I found strange as they were supposed to be warrior priests.

Dawn broke and our arrow rate was slowing as arms ached and strings slackened. When this was over, I would have men search for undamaged arrows and shafts. Only those arrows whose heads and fletch had been destroyed, and which had a broken shaft, would be left. No one wanted to dig an arrow from a body. We had brought spare arrowheads and I hoped we would have enough time to make new ones, although if Lord Edward continued to have us raiding so regularly, we soon would run out.

I am not sure if the Berber horsemen had always planned on travelling to St Georges-de-Lebeyne or if they were nearby and heard the battle, but whatever the reason, when I heard Robin, son of Richard's voice shout out, "Captain! We are under attack!" I knew I had to do something.

The threat from the horsemen was greater than the threat from St Georges-de-Lebeyne, and so I gave the command. "One archer in two, change targets to the horsemen!"

Will Yew Tree and Martin glanced me and when I turned, they continued to send arrows into the town. There were about one hundred horsemen heading towards us, although it was difficult to estimate numbers accurately. The whirling horsemen were sending arrow after arrow towards us and while we were emptying saddles, it was worrying that they were also decimating my archers. When an arrow clanked off my own helmet, I realised how good they were. However, our arrows and our yew bows appeared to be more powerful and the Berber archers were suffering more than we were.

Will Yew Tree shouted from behind me, "Captain, they are trying to come out of the town!"

"Then try to hold them!" While we had had enough to hold them within the town, the attack on our rear meant that we would struggle to survive. All that we could do was nock, and release as fast as we could. I was glad that we each had two arrow bags. Looking around I saw spent arrows that we could send back to their owners.

"Captain, we are not holding them!"

Will would not make such a statement unless it was true, and we had broken the backs of the Berber archers.

"Yarpole, turn!"

I would use my ten best archers to bolster the defence from the town and when I turned, I saw why I had been summoned. There were mailed horsemen trying to get by us. I sent a hurried arrow into the chest of a mailed askari; I had checked to see what kind of an arrow it was, but at a range of fifteen paces I could not miss and even a war arrow could pierce mail.

Then I saw Lord Edward leading the knights to run down the fleeing askari. Soon, we would not be able to use our arrows, for if we did then we might hit our own knights. I knew my men and they would keep drawing and releasing almost as though some machine was working them.

The worst thing to do would be to worry and panic. Even when a mailed warrior seemed about to run me down, I kept aiming and loosing. Disaster almost came when Will hit an askari at such close range that the warrior fell from his horse and his dying hands dragged the horse down. It missed harming any of my men but struck two archers behind me, and the Mamluk's boot knocked my bow from my hand. Leaping to my feet, I grabbed my sword and held it two-handed. A warrior who was not wearing mail saw the gap created by the falling askari and rode for it. I do not think he realised that an archer could use a sword. He made a lazy swing with his sword and I ducked beneath it, swinging my own weapon as I did so. I hacked into his leg and my strike was so strong that it sliced into his horse's flank – not deeply, but sufficiently to make the horse rear and throw him.

And then the Turks had passed us, and it was our knights and men at arms we had to avoid.

As soon as they were gone, I turned to find my bow and then to assess the damage. We had lost over thirty archers and that was a grievous loss. I was just glad that none had been my men, although I was now closer to all of the archers who had come with the lords and masters. We had not been as potent a force before the battle as I might have hoped, and now we would be lucky to hurt the enemy. I saw that my men, my Yarpole archers, were whole and that we had survived unscathed.

"See to the wounded and then let us see what treasure these barbarians bear."

I began to take the mail from the two askari I had killed. They both had ornate swords that might be worth selling and coins in their purses. The leather reins and saddles were also well made, and I took them. One had a tijfaf, which was a sort of quilted mail for horses. I took it. I sent Tom and Peter back to our horses with the booty while I sent others to search out arrows.

It was late afternoon by the time Lord Edward and our horsemen returned from their chase. There were bodies draped over saddles – our men at arms and knights. It had not been one-sided.

Lord Edward did not speak as he and the knights passed but Hamo did and, reining in, he shook his head. "They fought hard and we lost these archers unnecessarily; Lord Edward could have offered surrender, but he wants a great victory."

I had to defend Lord Edward. "But it is a great victory!"

He gave me a sad smile. "He has burned crops and he has defeated some local lords' men, but Baibars has an army that could swallow Lord Edward's whole and spit out the gristle. I fear that, unless his brother brings a mighty army, this crusade will just annoy the Mamluk and do little to win back Jerusalem."

With those sad thoughts ringing in my ears, we headed back to Acre. More men died on the way back due to the heat and the fact that some had taken booty when they should have taken water. My men and I had taken treasure, but we had also made sure we had water for ourselves and our mounts.

It was a weary and depleted army that crawled into Acre.

We did not see Lord Edward for five days, but then I was summoned, along with Hamo. Our Mongolian friend had been Lord Edward's guest since Nazareth and when we reached the quarters he was using, we found both of them there with Sir John Malton. Lady Eleanor followed us into the large room, and she had with her a priest who carried some of the books and maps she had bought. She smiled disarmingly at me.

Lord Edward looked happy, which was always worrying. "Sit, gentlemen. There is wine and food. Before we begin, can I thank you all for your actions thus far in this campaign. While others may have let me down, you have not."

Hamo poured the two of us large goblets of the excellent local red wine, and he quaffed half of it in one. He smiled at Lord Edward, who rolled his eyes.

Lady Eleanor laid out the maps and weighed them down with a pair of daggers. It was she who spoke and not Lord Edward. "I have spoken with our Mongolian friend here, Ahmed." The Mongol inclined his head. He had understood his own name, at least. I suspected that anyone who was an emissary of a Mongol khan needed skills in languages. As we soon discovered, he was truly gifted.

Lady Eleanor continued. "Lord Edward and I believe that the khan will bring his army to attack Baibars if we ask." I was about to ask a question but thought better of it. "Lord Edward proposes that the three of you – Sir John, Gerald the Archer and Captain l'Estrange – accompany Ahmed back to the khanate. We have procured a vessel for you, which will drop you in Armenia. You will deliver the letter to the khan and bring back his answer."

She made it sound so easy that I believed her. Lord Edward had chosen her to give us our instructions – and for a reason. It made the dish more palatable. I looked at the other two. I was a lowly archer and if they would not ask a question, then neither would I.

In the end, it was Hamo who spoke. He finished off the wine and poured himself a second helping. He said, "It might have been better had we been asked, Lord Edward, rather than told that we were appointed to this task." He held up a hand as Lord Edward reddened: he was unused to being addressed in this manner. "I am not saying I will not go but, for myself, I would have a reward which is in keeping with the magnitude of the task."

Lord Edward said, through gritted teeth, "And what would that be, mercenary?"

Hamo smiled, for he was not insulted. "Why, a knighthood of course. It is a small thing for you and will cost you nothing, for I do not expect a manor. With a title, I can marry a rich woman!"

Hamo was a simple man in many ways and endeared himself to me by his openness and honesty.

Lord Edward asked, "And you two, what do you wish? Windsor Castle?"

I spoke first, for I would not go cap in hand to beg for something I did not really want. "Lord Edward, I am your captain of archers and your man. You ask me to go and I will do my best, although I go into a land which is neither Christian nor, so far as I can see, civilized."

Mollified, he nodded and looked over to Sir John who said, simply, "I was your squire and owe all that I have to you. Like Gerald, I will do this, but I will not take my squire, Richard, for he is young, and I believe we may lose our lives in this venture."

Lady Eleanor put her hands on mine and Sir John's. "And that, I too, fear is a danger. Ahmed here has told me that Baibars tried to buy him from the Emir of Nazareth. He will send men after you for, no matter what we do, they will know that we have sent men north. There are many spies in Acre. He has told me of some men called the assassins who are deadly killers from the region through which you will pass.

Even Ahmed is afraid of them. It is said that if they say they will kill a man, then he is a dead man walking. That is why you will travel overland to Beirut with some Hospitallers who will be escorting pilgrims. At Beirut, you will leave them and slip aboard the ship that will take you north. The ship belongs to an Arab and he has been paid well. You will have to buy horses when you land at Iskenderun. It is still, thanks to the marriage of the Emperor's daughter, Byzantine, and for that reason relatively safe – for they keep it guarded well. We will give you a letter asking for safe passage, but it will not reveal your mission, which must remain secret." She squeezed our fingers and sat down.

Lord Edward smiled and kissed the back of her hand. He was a different man in her presence. "When you return, Captain l'Estrange, we will, reluctantly, accede to your reward."

Hamo looked delighted.

We spent some hours discussing the route and the various problems that might occur. It was obvious that Lady Eleanor had done much of the planning but, in the end, we would have to use our own minds and survival skills, for there would be problems we had not even thought of.

Sir John wondered why there would be danger inside the khanate. It was Ahmed who explained, although I heard it second hand when Sir John translated. "It seems there are factions inside the khanate who are opposed to his western sympathies and, of course, there are still places where there is opposition to the Mongols." He looked at me. "This will not be easy, Gerald."

I had never thought that it would be!

Lord Edward, who would not have to make the journey, seemed very optimistic. "You are small in number but you each have great skills. I feel confident that your mission will succeed."

When I returned to my men, I could not tell them the details as it would put the four of us at risk. I had good men and loyal men, but when they drank, they were loose of tongue. Sir John and I made up a story about having to meet some ladies from England who were coming to join Lady Eleanor and would land in the north of the land. I hated the deception, for they seemed to believe me.

Lord Edward had assured me that my men would not have to participate in any fighting while we were away, but I could not rely on that and so I put Will Yew Tree in command. I made it quite clear to him that they were not to undertake any raid.

When we left, the next day, I think they were suspicious when Sir John and I did not ride our best horses, but all they had was speculation. We rode as the locals, encased in voluminous robes. I had just one war bag of arrows, bow, my sword and my daggers. I had my helmet, but that could double as a small cooking pot if we needed it to. We were quite literally heading into an unknown country. Ahmed and Hamo appeared to be enjoying the experience for, although Ahmed's face rarely changed, I saw the ghost of a smile at the corners of his mouth and in his eyes.

We joined the Hospitallers and the pilgrims north of Acre. There were ten sergeants and four knights. Something must have been said about us to the knights who led us, for we were placed close by them rather than the baggage and they did not ask questions. It was not a particularly long ride to Beirut, under seventy miles, but it would be long enough and the last thing we needed was questions that we could not answer.

The rest of the pilgrims were rich Frenchmen. It explained our escort for the Hospitallers and the Templars would often act as hired escorts. The Hospitallers frequently escorted poorer pilgrims for free, but the Templars were keen to make money for their order. With money came power. I learned from Hamo, who listened in to the conversations of the French merchants around us, that they had come on pilgrimage because of King Louis. Now that he was dead, they did not feel safe. There was talk of making him a saint. To me, that seemed strange. The man, although he was a king, had died of dysentery! It had not been a noble death.

Apart from mumbled conversations, we remained silent. This would be the easy part of the journey. Once we boarded the ship, we would have to be alert to danger all of the time. One of us would need to be awake when we were on the boat and when we travelled through the khanate. Ahmed would have to stand a watch and I was not yet certain if we could trust him.

Of the four of us, I was the most fearful. The other three had more languages at their disposal and they had all travelled more than I. Apart from my first journey to France, I had never been abroad. Sir John, when he was Lord Edward's squire, had travelled in Spain and even Germany. What if the others died and I was left alone? Could I carry on and complete the appointed task? I knew that I would try, but I would probably die in the process.

With that cheery thought, we spied the imposing walls of Beirut. We had been instructed to wait until the pilgrims were all safely within the walls of the hospital before we slipped away to the harbour. I was impressed with the timing, for we reached the port as darkness was falling and there was much coming and going before the gates were barred. We would, hopefully, be unnoticed.

Sir John was speaking with one of the Hospitaller knights when I was aware of a figure in the shadows opposite the guarded entrance to the Hospitallers' home. He was watching us, that much was clear.

Hamo said, "Let us dismount. Mounted men will stand out more than four who merely lead their mounts."

As we dismounted, I said to Hamo, "We are being watched!"

"I know. Have your hand ready on your sword but we are safe here. Remember that we have but forty paces before we are on the main thoroughfare. Let us see what our watcher does."

Sir John had finished speaking with the Hospitaller knights who had gone inside the gates. He dismounted and came over to us. The gates of the hospital slammed shut and the small street seemed inordinately empty and sinister. Hamo said, "Sir John, we are being watched." He nodded towards the shadowy figure.

Sir John was no longer the callow youth I met in Aquitaine. He had carried Lord Edward's banner in battle, and he was confident in his own ability. He merely nodded and said, "Keep Ahmed in the middle. Gerald, take the rear. We do as was planned and walk to the port. One man cannot harm us, and Gerald has quick reactions."

I knew that I was expendable. Our Mongolian friend was vital, and I dropped to the back. We had not moved above five paces when the shadowy figure suddenly leapt out and scurried to the side of Sir John. My dagger was out even as he passed me. Hamo placed his huge body before Ahmed and Sir John had his sword pressed against the man's chest as he stopped.

What saved his life was that he spoke English. "You must come with me, for you have been compromised!"

We all knew that this could be a trick. If the assassins were involved, then we could expect all sorts of plans and ploys to make us deviate from our task. Sir John showed quick thinking. "You mistake us, my friend. I know not who you are, but let us be on our way."

"You are Sir John Malton, with Captains Gerald War Bow and Hamo l'Estrange. I knew you, Sir John, when you were a squire in France – and you, Gerald War Bow, were a young outlaw seeking a paymaster. You are escorting an important Mongolian to the east, are you not? Now, you must heed my words, for there are killers watching for you. I have been sent by the Lady of Beirut, Isabella Ibelin, and she awaits us in her castle. There, you will be safe."

Sir John said, "Come and stand before me. You will lead us and at the first sign of treachery you will die for my sword will be in your back."

Everything in me screamed that this was a trap, but I was a lowly archer and so I obeyed Sir John's next command: "Gerald, watch our back and be alert for others following us."

"I speak the truth, Sir John, but I will walk before you."

I would have preferred to be leading Eleanor, for she was a clever horse and might have alerted me to danger. As it was, I risked a serious neck injury as I swivelled my head back and forth. We crossed the main thoroughfare leading to the port and passed large numbers of people, and then we passed into alleys and narrow streets that seemed, to me, perfect places for an ambush. The man who led us would, of course, die as soon as an ambush began – but we would all soon follow.

We passed through Muslim sections of Beirut and I wondered why, if the man was here to help us, this route had been chosen. And then we were at the gates to the citadel and we had not been attacked, yet we did not enter by the main gate. The man led Sir John around the high wall to a small sally port. He gave a special knock and the gate opened, then we were ushered in. It slammed behind me and I felt both relief and, at the same time, fear – for I wondered at our new predicament.

As we were led to a stable, I tried to remember all that I had heard of Lady Isabella. She had been married as a child to King Hugo of Jerusalem, but he had died soon after the marriage. Her affair with Julian of Sidon had shocked even the Pope, and I had heard rumours that she was favoured by Baibars, the Mamluk leader. This could all be a trap, and we might be delivered to our enemies before our quest had even begun.

We were helped to unload our war gear from our horses and then our mysterious shadow led us to a mean door leading to the kitchens. We were hurried through a labyrinth of passages until we found ourselves in a chamber. There was a table with wine, bread and ham and four straw-filled sleeping sacks on the floor. The man bowed and said, "You are safe for now. Wait here and all will become clear."

The man smiled and dropped his hood. He had a long white scar running down his tanned face. "You shall not see me again, but the next time you see Lord Edward tell him that his old man at arms, Godfrey of Goole, serves him still." With those enigmatic words hanging in the air, he departed.

Hamo took off his cloak and dropped it onto one of the sleeping sacks. "Well, that was interesting. Does either of you know the fellow? He said he was Lord Edward's man."

I shook my head. "I did not recognise him, but then there have been many men at arms alongside whom I have fought. He certainly seemed to know us."

Sir John spoke in French to the Mongolian, who merely nodded. He had such an impassive face that I never knew if he felt fear. I knew he was trying to learn English, and I yearned for the time that I could speak with him. I knew that he was an archer and I was keen to discover his skills.

I walked over to the wine and food and sniffed it. "Is this safe, do you think?"

Hamo laughed. "We are prisoners here and if the Lady of Beirut wished us dead, then we would be. Let us just see what the morrow brings. For myself, I will eat and drink!" He looked around and saw a large clay pot. "And as there is no garderobe, I will relieve myself."

I had a sudden thought and I went to the door. I opened it and found myself facing an armed man at arms. He merely closed the door. I turned. "We are guarded but the door is not locked. This is a strange situation."

I looked at Sir John, for he was a knight. He shrugged. "Like you, Gerald, I am at a loss. Perhaps Hamo is right and, hopefully, a new day will bring answers – although this is an inauspicious start to our quest."

Although I did not think we would be murdered in our beds, I did not sleep well; each sound and movement had me awake instantly. I had been up for some time – and added to the clay bowl – when the door opened, and a servant appeared. He looked to be a Muslim and was both cultured and polished; I felt like a piece of rough-hewn timber next to him. "If you gentlemen would care to rise, the Lady of Beirut will grant you an audience."

Sir John and Ahmed were already up, and so I nudged Hamo with my foot.

"I am awake – although as we are prisoners, granting an audience seems a little grand a title to me!"

We went to pick up our gear when the servant said, "You can leave your war gear here. You will return hence when the audience has ended."

I looked at Hamo, who shrugged. We were still prisoners, and that fact was emphasised by the two armed guards who preceded us and the two who followed us. Once again, we followed a labyrinthine path and entered the main chamber through a small door. We were obviously not using the main entrance. When we were ushered before the throne and Lady Isabella, I saw that we were alone save for the servant. Even the four guards disappeared.

We turned to face the woman; she was something of a legend and I confess that I was under her spell the moment I saw her. I had met powerful women before. Lady Maud was such a one, as was Lady Eleanor, but in a completely dissimilar way.

Lady Isabelle had a different sort of power. Her eyes seemed to bore into you and devour you. I found that I could not hold her gaze and looked down. Sir John, despite his noble upbringing, was the same. With Ahmed, it was hard to see the effect, but Hamo not only held her gaze, he also held her attention. It gave me the chance to study her briefly. She was beautiful, more than that, she was stunning and even in a room filled with the most beautiful of women, she would stand out. I had thought Lady Eleanor to be the most attractive of women, but it was like comparing a daisy with a rose. Indeed, there was no comparison. Lady Isabelle's skin seemed to glow, and her dark hair cascaded down her shoulders to be almost cape-like. Around it, she had a simple coronet denoting her power. I would have tried to guess an age, but I truly had no idea. Her lips were coloured red and, to me, appeared like the petals of a red English rose.

When she spoke, it was as though a spell had been broken and spun at the same time. Her voice was mesmerizing. Someone had once used the word alluring and I had had to ask what it meant. That morning in Beirut, I truly understood the meaning of the word, added to which her voice had a hypnotic quality. Although she spoke to all of us, her eyes never left Hamo, nor did his eyes leave hers.

"I apologise that I had to act the way I did, gentlemen, but had you followed Lord Edward's orders then you would now be dead, for the captain of the dhow had orders to throw you overboard whilst at sea. The Old Man of the Mountain and his assassin brotherhood seeks you."

Sir John was our leader, and it was he who spoke. "But how did you know of our mission and of the plot to kill us, my lady?"

"I am a woman who rules a small county. I keep a network of spies who let me know what goes on. And I heard of the assassins who were travelling from their mountain lair to kill the three Franks and the barbarian. I remain neutral in most things and that is why Baibars lets us survive, but I was married, albeit briefly, to the King of Jerusalem and Cyprus and despite what others think of me, I am a Christian. As for the Arab captain, he was already known to us as a servant of the assassins, and when we heard that the four of you were to travel on his ship, then I sent men to discover the truth."

"And the captain?"

Her voice was chillingly cold. "He will send no more men to a watery death."

Silence hung like a dagger in the room, but Lady Isabella and Hamo seemed bound by an invisible thread.

It was Sir John who broke the silence. "We thank your ladyship, but where does that leave us? Are we all prisoners here?"

She smiled. "I thought the words of Godfrey of Goole would have allayed your fears, but to answer you from my lips, I will say that you are safe here and what is more, I will facilitate your journey – for the longer you stay here, the more danger you will be to my city and my people."

"Then what will happen?"

"You were due to sail to Iskenderun and you will still do so. Today, at noon, a shipload of Armenians will be returning to their home-land. They are Armenian Christians and have been on a pilgrimage to Jerusalem to visit Golgotha. You will join them; my guards will accompany the Armenians for their own protection and so you will be safe until you board the ship. The captain knows nothing of you and will believe that you are Armenians. He is not a stupid man, however, and it may well be that when he returns, he will talk – for knowledge is worth coins, and so this trick merely buys you a two- or three-day start."

Hamo spoke for the first time. "In truth, my lady, it may not even buy us that. If the dhow captain knew where we were going, then these killers will be in Iskenderun already."

She smiled. "They tell me that your name is Hamo l'Estrange and the price for your participation in this hazardous venture is to be knighted."

If the Lady of Beirut thought to embarrass Hamo with her words, then she was wrong. "Aye, my lady, I have served kings and princes enough to think that, like Gerald War Bow here, I deserve the honour. Lord Edward does not seem to think so."

"You do not think he will keep his word?"

Hamo laughed. "I think he will do all that he can to ensure that he does not have to!"

Lady Isabella laughed. "I like you, Hamo l'Estrange, for such honesty is refreshing and you seem to have a healthy attitude." They held each other's gaze briefly and then she continued. "When you return to your cell there will be food and drink waiting. I apologise for the conditions, but you are hidden there. Only my steward and Godfrey know your true identities. My guards think that I have kept you prisoner as I believe you are spies. Let them think that. When you reach Iskenderun, there is a horse dealer called Guilbert of Nogent. He was a crusader but now he raises horses. You will find him a mile east of the town. He knows the land through which you travel, for he was taken as a prisoner briefly and it ended his life as a warrior."

I was intrigued but I said nothing.

Sir John said, "We thank you, my lady, how can we repay you?"

Once more, she was looking at Hamo when she said, "Return here if you are able, to tell me the tale – for if you succeed, then this will become one of the greatest stories ever told."

"I promise you that we shall."

"Now, you had better go, for time is pressing and you must be ready to leave with the real pilgrims. The clothes you have chosen were selected wisely. Continue to use your minds and you may well survive. I will pray that you do."

For some reason, Hamo had fascinated her and I, for one, was grateful.

Chapter 8

We said little once we were back in our cell, and I think each of us was wrapt in his own thoughts. The Mongol was a complete enigma to me, and I could not tell if he was happy or sad as his expression never altered. The fact that he was also so short amused me. If it was not for his beard and moustache, his size and stature would have suggested he was a boy rather than a man!

I knew that Hamo was thinking of Lady Isabella and Sir John was just worried about failing Lord Edward. I was going through my war gear to see if I had forgotten anything.

We did not have long to wait for the door to open and the sentry to gesture for us to leave. The steward escorted us and our war gear. We went, once more through the back passages and narrow servants' ways. We came to a door and he said, "Cover your faces now and until you are in Iskenderun. I would advise you to speak as little as possible. If you do have to speak, make it French. The assassins know that Lord Edward has sent Englishmen."

That meant I would have to remain silent. I swore then that I would learn French, if only to make my life easier.

We stepped out of the side door in the castle to a cacophony of noise.

There had to be sixty people buzzing around like angry wasps. They were mainly men, although there were women too. The steward gave a signal, but it was so subtle that I think few of the Armenians realised. The leader of our escort shouted something, and the gates were opened. Those assembled cheered, and we found ourselves propelled by this small sea of humanity towards the harbour.

I could smell the ocean as soon as we left the castle. I saw the cunning of this plan, for in such a noisy mass of people we were anonymous. We wore similar clothes to the Armenians and the only thing that might have identified us was our size – but the warriors who marched next to us were also large men and, standing close to them, we blended in.

As desperate as I was to speak, more out of nerves than anything, I was mindful of the words of Lady Isabella's steward and I kept my peace. The smell of the sea and the port became more obvious and I saw the masts of ships ahead of us. The leader of our guards headed towards a large vessel and I saw that this time, we were going on a galley. I had never travelled on one before, although I did know that they were rowed by slaves. We shuffled aboard and I followed Hamo, who had the Mongol and Sir John before him. It seemed my lot was to be the tail of this secret horse!

Sir John cleared enough space so that we were close to the larboard bow and had the side of the ship and part of the forecastle as our domain. Using our bags, before us we were able to make a protective barrier which would mean we did not have to risk speaking with others. In the event, it proved unnecessary, as those around us also formed their own family groups and we were left alone.

Once we left the land the slave-propelled galley powered through the water. I was not certain if such vessels could cope in the harsher waters close to England, but I could see that they were perfect for these more benign seas.

It was dark as we approached the harbour of Iskenderun. Our forward position on the ship allowed us to appreciate the port built by Alexander the Great. He had constructed it so that he could march his mighty army through the Syrian Gates when he went to conquer Darius. The master of the ship had his officers form the crew so that they funnelled us as we headed towards the gangplank. I had my precious bow and my arrows to cling to as we wobbled down the gangplank. I kept a tight hold, as I knew we would need them at some point, and I did not want to lose them in this harbour!

When we reached the quay, we just followed the sea of humanity as it flooded through the town. We were in the hands of Sir John, but we had the words of the Lady of Beirut in our heads as we kept moving east along the road, long after the last of the pilgrims had left us to find inns or seek friends. Assassins could be watching the port, and so we left the city and, in the dark, headed east seeking the former crusader and the horses he would hopefully be willing to sell to us. We now knew that our opponents were deadly killers who cared not for their own lives, and I did not relish meeting up with them.

When we were no longer passing any buildings, I strung my bow and nocked an arrow. I had not sought permission, nor expected for the others to wait for me. I had a job to do and I knew that I would be able to catch up with them. I turned and peered back towards the distant lights of the city of Iskenderun. We had only just managed to get out of the city before the gates were closed, and I hoped that meant there would be no one following us. There was but one way to find out, and so I would have to wait a while, listening and smelling the dark. Even if men are barefoot, there are still noises which can be heard. Cloaks and other items of clothing can move next to one another and make a noise. Leather creaks and men, especially those who are rushing, can breathe heavily. I heard none of those noises and so, after I was sure we had not been followed, I turned and ran up the road.

The others had not waited for me, but they had slowed and when I caught up with them, we were almost at the horse farm. I could smell the horses and the neighs and the clattering of hooves on stone confirmed it. We had reached our first objective and now we had to see if the Lady of Beirut knew this knight as she thought.

Sir John looked at me and I nodded to confirm that we had not been followed. He waved his arm and we headed down the track, passing lumps of horse dung that confirmed that we had reached the right place. We moved silently, but I knew that the watchers within the walls would have heard us and when we neared the closed and, no doubt, barred gate we heard a voice shout something in Arabic. Surprisingly, it was Ahmed who answered. The responding voice answered in French and Sir John spoke.

My lack of languages was beginning to irritate me.

Hamo must have sensed my frustration for he said quietly, "They have asked us to wait for Guilbert of Nogent to inspect us."

Lights appeared on the walls and I saw armed Armenians line the fighting platform. There were bows aimed at us.

Sir John said, a little nervously, "Let us hope that the Lady of Beirut was correct, or this could be a short journey!"

Hamo was protective towards the Lady of Beirut. I knew, even then, that he was smitten. "Fear not, Sir John, she struck me as a lady a man could trust and, besides, we would have had to procure horses in any case. At least this way we buy them from a Christian and may not be robbed!"

A voice from above spoke English. "That is very kind of you, but a little bold if I may say! There are Christians in these parts who would slit your throat as soon as a bandit would – and less efficiently! Who are you, and what brings four such strange travellers to my home after dark?"

The lights from the burning brands were in our eyes and I could not make out the features, save that the man had a grey beard.

"I am Sir John Malton and I am here to buy horses." There was a pause and it was clear that Guilbert of Nogent was waiting for further information. "Lady Isabella of Beirut directed us to your gates."

I heard commands and the gates were opened. We stepped into a large courtyard which had, to my surprise, a cobbled surface. I had expected something cruder. There were stables opposite the gate and a large hall, which looked like a French fortified hall. I glanced around and saw the fighting platform ran around the stone wall. It was not a high wall, but it could be defended. Guilbert of Nogent came down the steps and I saw that he limped.

He shook his head. "Had you told me that first, Sir John, then I would not have had to leave my hall and you would have been admitted. I am Guilbert of Nogent. I see that you are the only knight. Introduce me to your companions, for I am interested in why three Englishmen should be travelling with a Mongol!"

Hamo snorted. "Two Englishmen, for I was born in the Welsh Marches and my name is Hamo l'Estrange."

Guilbert of Nogent laughed. "And you, I can see, will reward the offer of a free meal with some interesting tales, the veracity of which will be in doubt."

"I am Captain Gerald War Bow."

"And you are an archer, more than that, an English archer. You have me intrigued, gentlemen."

Sir John said, "And this is Ahmed. He is our translator, for we wish to travel through the khanate."

Guilbert of Nogent nodded. "It is after dark and too late for me to turn Christians away. There is an empty stable in which you can sleep, and if you would join me when you have deposited your war gear then you can tell me what you want, and I will feed you." He smiled. "I am guessing it is horses, and the price of your food will be added to the cost." He shrugged. "A man must make a living."

One of his men showed us to the empty stable. What he had meant was an empty stall, for we were in one of the largest stables I had ever seen. His man waited without.

Sir John said quietly, "Once we are inside, I want no mention of Ahmed's true identity nor of the mission. Nor do we mention Lord Edward, for if the assassins know that Lord Edward has sent men then it would not take them long to piece together our movements. Do not drink too much, and be guarded."

Hamo snorted. "No matter how much I drink, Sir John, I know exactly what I say."

The hall showed that it was a male only establishment. It was entirely functional in its design and its furniture. The table was solid and plain, as were the chairs. The platters were made of polished wood without adornment. The food, when it came, was simple. It was bread with a rustic mutton stew. The wine was a coarse red wine and I smiled when Sir John wrinkled his nose as he tasted it. Hamo and I downed it happily.

Guilbert of Nogent did not converse until he had finished eating. He was a plain man and he liked order in his life, that much was obvious. The stables had borne the mark of a man who knew where everything was, and everything was in its place. So with his house and, it appeared, with his eating habits.

"Let me guess what you want. Six horses to take you a long way east of here. The horses need to be hardy and fast. I can see that the Mongol will have no problem riding one of my animals, but your Welshman, Sir John, might need something a little different."

Hamo growled, "I am lighter than I look."

That made Guilbert of Nogent laugh. "Aye, keep telling yourself that. I might sell you the horses, but you should know that the name of Lady Isabella gains you entry and no more. There is no discount for knowing the finest lady in Outremer!"

Sir John said, "I hope you do not mind me asking, Guilbert of Nogent, but what is your connection with the lady?"

A frown appeared and then cleared on the former knight's face. "Let us just say that Julian of Sidon was my lord and leave it at that."

The three of us nodded. Ahmed's inscrutable face looked the same as it always did. I had known him since his rescue and yet I do not think his expression had ever changed.

"You know you have an almost impossible task ahead of you? The land is hard enough for men on peaceful missions, but you four have assassins and Mamluk killers on your tail."

Sir John needed to take lessons from Ahmed. His face registered surprise immediately. Guilbert of Nogent laughed. "I knew who you were as soon as you appeared at my gate. Three Franks and a Mongol are sought by killers. Three days hence we heard that rumour, and I thought it a nonsense for four such men would stand out in this land." He held up a hand. "I do not want to know more, for I gave up the politics of war and intrigue when I... Let us say it is in the past, and that is a different country and another knight. I admire you for what you do, but except for selling you the horses then I can do no more."

Sir John stiffened. "Nor do we ask more. You were a knight and you know that when a knight gives his word, then he keeps it."

"Some knights keep it. Let us leave the Mongol out of this; the other two are not knights, what is in it for them? Are they being richly rewarded?"

Hamo said, openly, "For me, I get spurs. That is reward enough for the risk and I believe we shall succeed."

Guilbert of Nogent nodded towards Hamo and said to Sir John, "His optimism helps, and the Mongol arrows are more likely to hit him than you – but what of you, Captain War Bow? What is your reward?"

"My lord commanded me to go and I did, but I would have gone anyway, for Hamo is my friend and I have known Sir John since he was but a squire. A man fights for his friends."

"Good, then you are all committed and none are forced. I will sell you the horses as well as food and extra waterskins. I will not rob you out of respect for the lady, but my horses are not cheap, and I regard them all as my children. If, by some miracle, you return, then I will buy back the horses from you. It will not be that which I charged you, but the archer may make enough profit from the venture to line his purse. And now, gentlemen, entertain me with tales of your wars, for I am starved here!"

We all spoke of battles in which we had fought. Although we tried to be discreet, I knew that he would know we followed Lord Edward, especially when we spoke of Evesham. He shook his head when we described the death of de Montfort. "I knew him a little from when he came on crusade. He was a man driven to gaining power. He saw himself a king. He was not a bad leader, but misguided. A man should choose his targets wisely in life. It is like our archer friend here. He knows the range at which he can hit and does not try to risk a valuable arrow by loosing too far."

At the end of the night, he had his man take us to the stables. As we made our own beds, Ahmed surprised me by saying, "Bow! Ger-ald, I need bow!"

I was surprised, on many levels. Firstly, that he had picked up enough English to speak with me, secondly that he knew my name – even though he pronounced it strangely – and finally that it was to me he spoke and not Sir John.

I nodded. "Aye, you do but we need a heathen bow for you, eh, Ahmed?" I accompanied my words with gestures. Hamo and Sir John looked on bemused at our little tableau.

"*Heath an bow*?" He struggled with the words, although he recognised 'bow'.

"Aye." I strung my bow and handed it to him. "Draw!"

He did so, but he held the bow horizontally and not vertically. I took it from him and when I drew, he saw the full extent. I realised then that he had never seen me draw a bow before. His narrow eyes widened, and he felt my bicep. He used the French word: "Fort!"

I nodded and unstrung my bow. "Aye, bloody fort!" I put it back in my bow bag. "He is right. We may need another archer and even if we had a longbow, he couldn't use it."

Sir John was smiling. "I don't care, Gerald. That was the first conversation initiated by our friend and I think it bodes well. His English has improved and that can only help. Well done, Gerald."

As I rolled into my blanket, I wondered what he meant. I had done nothing.

We rose before dawn but that was not of our choosing. The heat of the day in this part of the world meant that the men who worked for

Guilbert had to start work in the cool of the day and then rest again when the sun was at its hottest. We would not have that luxury. We bathed at the water trough and one of Guilbert's servants brought us food and ale. The ale was preferable to wine.

The former knight limped over and greeted us warmly as the sun began to rise above the distant Syrian Gates. Guilbert had told us that it was also known as the Belen Pass and, after we had entertained him, had warned us that the fortress of Trappesac – known in Turkish as Darb-i Sak Kalesi – had been retaken from the Mongols and was now in the hands of the Mamluks once more. As I stared towards it, I realised the immensity of our task.

We put all those obstacles from our minds as we walked with Guilbert to choose our mounts. To be fair to the man, he was honest and sold us six mounts that were as good as we could have bought elsewhere. They were hardy and strong. Rather than selling us the two spares to just carry our war gear, all six could be ridden – for who knew what might occur? If we lost a horse we could still maintain our speed, at the cost of our equipment.

Guilbert had done all that Lady Isabella had said he would. Not only were they the best horses, he had not skimped on the horse furniture. The saddles were not the ones we normally used, with high cantles to hold the rider in place. There were instead four projections, called pommels, which performed the same function as the high cantles, but I saw that they could be used to hold equipment. Guilbert told us that they were based on those the Roman cavalry had used, and he thought they might be more useful to us as we would have more places from which to hang war gear.

Sir John agreed on the price readily and while they were being saddled and prepared, I asked, "My lord, have you an Asian bow for Ahmed here?"

His eyes twinkled. "I can do even better, my archer friend. I have a Mongol bow and a sheath of their arrows. There is no arrow bag, but—"

"I will buy it!"

He looked at me in surprise. "You are the one with the least to gain from all of this, and yet you would spend your own coin to buy someone you barely know a bow. Why?"

The answer was blindingly obvious – but I was a guest, and so I was polite. "He is an archer and needs one. If he has a bow, then we double the power of our most effective weapon."

He clapped me on the back. "Well said, Gerald, and you may take it as a gift. None of my men can use the damned thing, anyway!"

When I gave it to Ahmed, I saw – for the first time since I had met him – a change of expression. I saw joy. The man was an archer!

We mounted and Guilbert said, "I will have six of my men ride with you for ten miles or so. It may sow confusion, for if there are watchers then they will be looking for four men and not ten. I still do not know how you will get over the pass. If you are fearless men, then you can try a night crossing, but you would have to pass within one hundred paces of the walls of the castle that guards it. The one on this side is small, but Trappesac was built by Templars! The only alternative is to become mountain goats and climb them."

Sir John nodded. "Thank you for your help. I know not how long the journey will take, but we will bring back the horses. I can see that you are a man who loves his horses."

As we headed towards the pass the three of us were able to talk, for we had six men to watch for danger. "From the maps, we should be able to camp just short of the pass and do as Guilbert suggests. At its narrowest it is three hundred paces wide and, so far as I can see, a daylight approach would be impossible."

We all nodded, and I smiled when Ahmed did so too. He had understood at least some of the words. He might still be learning the language, but each day his skills improved. I said, "If Ahmed and I have our bows ready then we can deal quickly with any challenge. At night they will not have too many guards."

"That would mean pursuit!"

Hamo laughed. "Sir John, they will pursue in any case. This is now the border and we must make noise passing through. Gerald is right. We are prepared to be discovered and then we ride as though the devil himself is behind us." He looked ahead and said, "And I am guessing that himself will not be giving us a warm welcome when he finds us!"

Our guards left us at noon, and we adopted a new formation. Ahmed rode at the fore, for this was his land and, for the first time, he looked the part. His horse suited him and the bow he carried was almost an extension of himself. Sir John and Hamo each led a packhorse and I brought up the rear. It was almost as though the roles had been reversed. It made sense, for Ahmed and I had the ability to keep enemies at a distance. Should they close with us then Hamo and Sir John, encased in mail as they were, would be crucial but for now, Ahmed rode forty paces ahead and I rode forty paces behind. It meant there was no conversation, but the two of us scanned the land ahead and behind for enemies.

However, the enemies were not just the Mamluks and the assassins, for the land was cruel and appeared to have been carved purely from rock. I saw no sign of habitation nor evidence of farming. Perhaps there was richer land on the other side of the pass, but the land through which we travelled seemed to be warning us to stay away. Yet, we had to travel further in this land than I had travelled in my homeland.

If they had sharp-eyed sentries, then the sun, which would set behind us, would highlight us. We stopped well short of the fort, which guarded the entrance at one of the many crossroads we found. We were on the main road, but smaller roads crossed over ours and by stopping at a crossroads we hoped to confuse any watchers on their walls. We made a cold camp and rested our horses whilst eating fruit and drinking water. Ahmed seemed determined to communicate with us in our language.

"Fort has watchers. Tie sacks around hooves when we close to pass." Ahmed was still using many hand gestures and signals. As archers, we were used to them, and I wondered if the reason we understood each other so well was that we were both archers.

We should have thought of that, but I was not a horseman and I am not sure that either of the other two had identified the problem of hooves clattering on rocks. We had sacking, which covered our war gear on the spare horses, and we took the time to prepare it. We would not need to fit it until we began the climb.

I strung my bow and hung it from one of the pommels on the saddle. The war bag of arrows hung from the other. For an archer, these Roman saddles were much more useful than the ones we normally used.

We left after a very short rest, by which time it was dark, and we would not be seen. Ahmed rode not on the road, but in the dust to the side, which dampened the sound of hooves. I was so far back that I could not see him, but I knew when he stopped, for the horses before me slowed. By the time I reached them, Ahmed had skilfully fastened the sacking around the hooves of his horse. Sir John and Hamo were riders but Ahmed was a horse warrior. Since he had been given a saddle and horse that he could use, it was as though man and beast were one. We had all come to know our horses, but the Mongol was almost able to talk to his through his body. We, in contrast, took longer to complete the task and that allowed the Mongol to go ahead of us, on foot, to spy out the fort.

He returned, seemingly satisfied, and leapt onto his horse. He nocked an arrow and nodded to me. I did the same. I was a good archer, but using my bow horizontally, as was required on a horse, would limit my range and if I was to do my job, I would need to be very accurate. It was unfortunate that Guilbert only had one such bow.

This time, we would be riding nose to tail. When we stopped, we discussed how we would get through this most imposing of barriers. That we might be seen as we camped was obvious, but even if they expected us to come by, they would not know when. The fact that some hours had passed since the sun set meant they might not be as vigilant.

The second fortress, the former Templar castle, worried me most, for this first, small fort would not have a large garrison. It was there to tax those passing through. The second fortress, Trappesac, was there to stop the Mongols invading.

Ahmed signalled and we began to climb. He knew this pass and we did not. The whole venture would have been impossible without him. I nocked an arrow and held the bow in my right hand. Guilbert had given us good horses and my left hand was enough to keep the reins just taut enough to tell the horse that I was in command. I let him pick his own way up the rocks. They were all careful horses and I heard nothing, save the occasional creak from the leather on the mounts ahead of me.

The walls of the fort loomed ahead but Ahmed had taken a path on the opposite side of the pass. Our dark clothes and horses, and the shadows from the cliffs, all hid us. I let my horse follow the others and stared at the walls of the Mamluk fort. I saw nothing – but that did not mean there were no watchers. Would the first sign that they had spotted us be an arrow that plucked us from our saddles?

The enormity of our task hit me. What was Lord Edward thinking?

How did he expect two Englishmen and a Welshman to pass through many hundreds of miles of inhospitable and enemy-held land to deliver a message? And why did he expect the Mongols to agree to his request? Even as I thought this, I had my own answer. We were expendable. Lord Edward gambled with three lives that a Mongol army coming to his rescue might give him the victory he wanted. If we failed, he would be no worse off than he was before.

While all these thoughts raced through my head and I stared at the small fort, I realised that we had almost passed it. Amazingly, we had avoided detection and were now heading through the narrow and imposing Belen Pass. Of course, we had to pass a more formidable fortress at the far end – but the fact that the first one had been relatively easy gave me confidence. On the other hand, we were now trapped between two Mamluk strongholds. If they came for us, we had nowhere to go.

I relaxed my hand on my bow and loosened the nocked arrow. My eyes had become more accustomed to this almost tunnel-like pass and I could see Hamo and his packhorse more clearly. He occasionally turned around to see if I was still there. I turned around too, but my search was for an assassin coming with a deadly blade to end my life.

As we neared the end of the pass, my heart sank. The Templars built good castles and Trappesac had been not just a refuge, but an armoury. The towers and the walls faced east, for that was where the enemy had come from. I hoped that any watchers would be watching there and not down the pass.

I saw the road descend to the plain on the other side, although the plain itself would be many miles away. The castle walls were at least one hundred and fifty paces from us, but that felt too close for me. It was almost as though they would hear us breathe. I tightened the grip on my bow.

We had almost passed the castle when we were spotted, or rather, we were heard. Hamo's horse made an uncharacteristic mistake – or it may have been that, carrying the largest load, he was the weariest. The shout from the wall was rewarded with the thud of Ahmed's arrow as he killed the sentry, and then the other three took off. I stopped my horse and stood in my stirrups. It meant I could almost use my bow properly. Drawing back, I aimed at a man I saw pointing at the other three. The arrow flew straight and true and knocked him from the fighting platform.

Even as I smacked my horse's rump with my bow, I knew I would have caused confusion. My arrow had come from a completely different direction to that of Ahmed. Horns and drums sounded inside the walls and I hurtled after my companions. That we were doomed was clear. Our horses had had little rest and although they were good ones, the Mamluks who would pursue us would have better. Our only hope lay in putting as much distance between us while we could.

The single arrow I had sent allowed the others to make a gap of almost four hundred paces, and I wondered if I would be the sacrificial lamb that allowed them to escape. Perhaps I could hold them off long enough. It would mean one of two things: either my death or life as a galley slave.

So, Hamo's voice from the side came as a complete surprise. "Gerald, here!" I saw that Hamo was in a side gully and I wheeled my weary horse in. He led me along a twisting rock-lined gully, taking twenty paces towards the others. It was a dead-end and I wondered at the wisdom of the decision, but it had been made and I heard the thundering of hooves as the Mamluks galloped down the road after us. The bend in the gully stopped me from seeing them, but I estimated there to be at least twenty riders.

I turned to speak but Ahmed, who was close to me, put a finger to his lips. It was clear who was in charge now. We had been protecting him, now he was protecting us. This was his land and we were strangers; we had to trust him and put our lives in his hands.

We seemed to wait far longer than I expected; indeed, it was bright daylight when he urged his horse from the gully. He said, "We go first. Bows!"

I followed him and expected to see Mamluks waiting for us, but there were none. I saw that a curve in the road hid us from the fortress, which lay some distance away, and the road itself seemed empty. Our horses had rested, but I knew it had not been for long enough. We might be able to carry on, but they would not – and without animals, we were dead men.

We rode down a road that twisted and turned. We were still in the shadow of the pass and paths and gullies led from both sides of the road. Ahmed had me confused, for he rode down a couple of side trails and gullies and then retraced his steps. After half a mile, he suddenly took one which lay on the left of the road, the opposite side to those he had previously taken. It was clearly a path and it twisted around and beneath unscalable rocks. We rode for perhaps five hundred paces and came to a pool of brackish-looking water. Despite its appearance, our horses gratefully drank as Ahmed explained his plan. He did not speak in English because he did not have all the words he needed.

Hamo and Sir John nodded and then Sir John explained. "Ahmed says that the men sent after us will soon discover that we turned off the road. They will split up to examine every gully and path. We will wait here to ambush them."

"And if they do not come here?"

Hamo laughed. "Then we have won, and they will have lost us, but

I think they will. Our hoofprints were quite clear – but they will need to examine every gully in case we hid our hoofprints."

Sir John continued. "Hamo and I will wait here as bait while you and Ahmed climb the sides and attack them at the rear. The only way they will be able to get at you is if they eliminate us first."

It was a plan, but it sounded risky to me. Strapping on my sword and carrying my bow, I walked to the end of the pool and began to climb up the rocks. Ahmed followed me. He went along one side and I another. I found a little cleft where I was hidden from the path that we had taken, and I was a good twelve feet above the path with a wall of stone behind me. If they had bows, they could hit me, but they would be riding away from me and I would have the initial advantage.

I looked at the twenty arrows which remained to me. I had more war bags of them, but they were in Acre. Ahmed was on the other side of the path and he was slightly further back. I saw Hamo and Sir John just fifty paces from us. They were eating and the horses, having drunk their fill, were now grazing on the grasses around the pool. Every moment that they were able to do so meant we had more chance of escaping.

I was still unsure of the plan and I worried as we waited. My worrying had a curious effect, for I began to look for positives in our course of action. Had we tried to escape as soon as we had been discovered, we would have been caught. True, we would have killed many of them, but we would have died, and our quest would lie in the dust of this dry and desiccated land. If we had left our first hiding place and continued east, we would have bumped into the Mamluks and the result would have been the same. Ahmed's plan meant there would be uncertainty in their minds. How many of us were there? Had we split up? Had we been ultra-cunning and made a false trail whilst hiding our real one? They would have to leave men on the main road while sending smaller parties to search for us.

I ceased worrying. Ahmed's plan had the best chance of success. I could see why the khan had sent him as an ambassador; he was clever.

I heard the horses in the distance. I glanced around and Ahmed nodded. I saw that he had an arrow nocked, as did I. I had three others close to hand. The horses appeared to come closer and I waved to attract Hamo's attention. He nodded and, after donning his helmet, hefted his shield and his sword. The Mamluks would see the two men and the horses. I doubted that they would even pause. The worst thing that Ahmed and I could have done was to peer around – and neither of us did. We both drew back on our bows. It was what I called my three-quarter pull; the last, back-breaking pull would be just before I sent the deadly missile into an enemy.

The gully we had ridden down was wide enough for three, but I doubted that the Mamluks would risk that, for it was too restricting, and when I saw two Mamluks with spears heading towards the pool, then I knew that Ahmed was right. I glanced at Ahmed, who shook his head. We would wait until the two men were almost at the pool.

We had to use our bows to send arrow after arrow before the Mamluks realised that they had been ambushed.

When I saw the Mamluk on the left of the pair pull back his arm, I sent an arrow into his back and nocked a second to hit the Mamluk following him. Ahmed was even faster than I was, but his bow was shorter and drew back more quickly than mine. It would be interesting to see which one could send an arrow the furthest.

Six Mamluks were hit before they realised that they were being ambushed. The next two held shields above them, but it merely made us send our arrows into their legs, to pin them to their horses. Maddened horses bucked and reared, ripping the arrows from their riders' legs. In the case of the Mamluk I had hit, the effect was to tear a hole the size of my fist in his leg. The last two tried to turn and my arrow merely embedded itself in one man's shoulder.

I saw Ahmed take off and run back to the horses. He was fast, and by the time I reached the horses, he had mounted and was driving the riderless animals along the gully. I followed with a nocked arrow and Hamo and Sir John brought up the rear. This part of the plan appeared to carry the greatest risk. What if the men who had first followed us had been reinforced?

We had killed at least seven and wounded four more. In theory, that should have given us an advantage.

All I could see, as we twisted and turned down the gully, was the back of Ahmed and his horse. Ahead of him were five horses, maddened by the smell of blood and Ahmed's Mongolian curses. And then I saw the wall of rock on the opposite side of the road and knew that we were nearing Mamluks.

That was when I saw the skill of the Mongol. As he neared the end, I saw him send an arrow at a target as yet hidden from me, and then a second and a third. As I emerged, I saw that there were at least twelve Mamluks and three had bows. I stood in my stirrups and sent an arrow into the head of a horsed archer. The range was fewer than ten paces and the broad head of the war arrow punched a huge wound into the side of his head. I sat as an arrow flew over my shoulder. I was relying on my horse, and as I guided it with my knees, it obeyed me. I nocked another arrow as Ahmed slew the archer who had sent an arrow at me. These Mamluk archers were good, but Ahmed was quicker and better. Three Mamluks with spears came at me as I stood and, calmly, sent my arrow into the last horsed archer.

I was saved from certain death by two things: one was Ahmed's skill, for he kept sending arrow after arrow into the Mamluks whilst riding around at seemingly impossible speed, and the second was the arrival of Hamo and Sir John, whose swords slew two Mamluks and drove the survivors back to the fortress. I was a foot archer and here I needed to be a Mongol! If Ahmed had not been with us, then our quest would have already ended.

We wheeled our horses and headed down the road. I took the opportunity to grab the reins of the horse of a dead horse archer. There were two war bags of arrows hanging from it, and I was running low. I kept glancing over my shoulder as we rode east. Would our bold attack result in a pursuit into Mongol lands? I did not know, but I had to trust in our continued good luck – and the amazing Mongol who had, undoubtedly, saved us.

Chapter 9

We did not ride hard, for we were unable to, but I deduced that by the time the Mamluks reached the fortress and more men were summoned we would have at least an hour's start. It was obvious to me that there were many routes we could take, and the longer the start, the further the Mamluks would have to travel in Mongol land. I had seen what one Mongol archer could do, and I had no doubt that the Mamluks would be reluctant to risk more men.

Ahmed stopped well before dark. He found us a small stream which, once again, was brackish – but it would serve the horses and the greenery around it would augment the cereal we had brought. He scurried up the nearest high piece of ground as we unsaddled the horses.

Hamo shook his head. "I thought no one could release faster than you, Gerald, but you have met your match in that one."

I nodded. "The man was born to ride and to loose arrows from the back of a horse. I can only dream of such skill and I am glad that he is on our side. I would not face a Mongol army."

We would not light a fire until Ahmed told us to, but we prepared all else. I went to the captured horse and removed not only the arrows

148

but also the curved sword that hung from the saddle. The horse was a good one and I had a rich haul.

Sir John prepared a fire. He remembered his training when a squire. "We would have failed without Ahmed."

Hamo said, "If it is was not for Ahmed, we would not need to be doing this. Which came first, the chicken or the egg? This was meant to be, but you are right. We owe our lives to him, though his strategy at the pass seemed irresponsible, rather than bold."

Just then, Ahmed ghosted into the camp. He smiled. "No follow. Light fire!"

Sir John stood and held out his arm. Ahmed seemed confused. Sir John said, "Thank you, Ahmed, we are in your debt."

The poor man looked totally bewildered. I said, slowly, "We owe you our lives!"

He nodded and grinned. He grasped Sir John's arm. "We are one or we die!"

Hamo laughed. "Aye, you are right there."

I made the stew, for I was neither a knight nor a gentleman.

Ahmed came to join me, and he patted me on the back and grinned at me. I had gone a long time without seeing emotion and now I saw the full range. "You good." He mimed pulling a bow.

I nodded. "Archer. But you are better!" To emphasise my words, I bowed.

"Your bow…" I could see him seeking the word and, in the end, he puffed out his cheeks and made an explosive sound.

I laughed. "Powerful! Aye."

Ahmed shook his head and, pointing to his horse, said, "No good for…"

I nodded. "No good. When we fight, we stand and all loose together."

He frowned and I mimed an arrow loosing many times. I made the sound of arrows, too.

He watched me stir the stew and said, "We…" and he mimed whipping a horse and loosing arrows. "With many men."

"Do you ever lose?"

He nodded. "Mongol fight Mongol, it is not good."

And that was the start of our communication. It gradually improved, for we used common ideas and eventually had longer conversations. It helped that he was a quick learner and had, unlike me, a natural skill with languages. As we headed east, we understood more every day. I devoured the words I was learning, for I was desperate to talk to this archer, who was so much better than me.

After the meal, I was excluded, for the other three spoke French while I cleaned the cooking pan and saw to the horses. It was necessary, for Sir John needed to know the plan. When they had finished, they waved me over. Sir John, speaking very slowly and enunciating every word clearly, said, "Ahmed is keen to learn English. He asks that we use it and he will ask, in French, when he needs it to be explained."

I bowed. "Thank you, Ahmed. I appreciate it." He looked at me blankly and I shook his hand and said, "Merci!" That I had butchered the French with my pronunciation was immaterial – he grinned.

Sir John continued. "We should have an easier journey for a while, but there are few Mongol garrisons this far west. When we find one, we shall have an escort."

Hamo nodded and he also spoke slowly. "I am worried about these assassins and so is Ahmed. It is one thing to rid ourselves of Mamluks, but these killers have been paid and they like to deliver."

Sir John said, "To that end, we will take it in turns to watch. To make it easier you will have the first watch, Gerald, then you will wake me, I will wake Hamo and Ahmed will watch until dawn." It was a generous offer, for Sir John and Hamo would have a disturbed night of sleep, but Ahmed and I would sleep continuously. I could think of few other knights who would have done what Sir John did.

And that was our routine. I watched and used the stars and the moon to gauge the time. I studied the harsh landscape and I spoke with my horse. He was a good beast and he, as much as Ahmed, had saved me. I also examined the Mamluk arrows. They were longer than mine, but I would be able to use them. They were better than nothing and my arrow bag was almost empty.

Over the next few days, Ahmed and I learned more words of each other's language and were able to converse more easily. We were archers and, as such, had a common language. He was fascinated by my bow and on the third day, when we rested early because we had found water, we tried each other's weapons. He found it hard to draw mine and I think that showed which weapon had the greater range. While I could use his, I preferred my longbow. However, I wanted a bow like his; I saw the advantages of using it from horseback. Of course, an archer needed a good horse – but with bows used from the backs of horses, then whole battles could be decided.

I also learned about Ahmed. He was well educated and a Mongolian noble. The khan had chosen him to be his messenger because of his skills. His people, it seemed, valued archery above all else.

We had kept up our night-time rituals, but we varied the order so that each of us had the opportunity to get a decent stretch of sleep. Ahmed commented, as we ate around the fire, that he was surprised at the lack of activity on the road. He had expected both Mongol and Mamluk to use it. We three could not know if it was quiet or not. Certainly, we had seen fewer people on the road than in the Holy Land.

I had the early morning shift and it was Ahmed who woke me. Something about the way he woke me made me wary. Normally, he would say something, but this morning he just shook me and handed me my bow. I strung it and, after nocking an arrow, jammed two more in my belt. In truth, I wanted to make water, but Ahmed was suspicious about something. When we had discussed the lack of activity, Hamo had seen it as a good thing, but it worried Ahmed and I wondered if this was merely a symptom of that worry. He also nocked an arrow. The sky was cloudy and the moon was hidden. We had camped on a slightly higher piece of ground and, as was our practice, spread spiky plants around the perimeter. I saw him staring intently at the plants and wondered why, when I realised that there was a gap. Someone, or something, had moved part of the boundary.

Immediately alerted, I pulled back on my bow and as I turned, saw something moving at Ahmed. I had just released the arrow as a second figure rose from almost beneath Ahmed's feet. I sent another arrow at the figure, at the same time as Ahmed, but the man I had hit was still alive and I saw him stumble towards me.

I had no time to nock another arrow and so I whipped the bow across his throat. This had never happened for me before, but the end of the bow tore out his throat and he gurgled to death at my feet.

"Awake!"

I nocked an arrow, aware of sticky blood slipping down the bow. Hamo and Sir John awoke as Ahmed and I scanned the area for more killers.

"What the…?"

I nodded towards the dead bodies. "I am guessing assassins." I had never seen them in our time on the road, but these small, almost emaciated-looking men seemed to fit the description given to us by Guilbert of Nogent.

Ahmed had quickly recovered his composure, having slain the second killer. "You watch and I look!"

Hamo fetched a light so that we could see the bodies better, and we had just finished searching them when we heard Ahmed return with two horses. That confirmed that there were no more… for the present.

Ahmed found what we had not; the two killers each had a small phial containing poison and the two blades were covered in it. We put the daggers in the flames to burn it away. After that, we were even more careful about our camps.

Ahmed thanked me for saving his life but, in truth, I had just reacted. The poisoned blades terrified me. The arrow I had sent into the first killer should have ended his life and yet he was strong enough to come at me. My bow had saved me, for any cut with the blade would have ended my life. The incident brought Ahmed and me closer together.

It was two days later when we approached a Mongolian castle. Ahmed told me the Mongols did not build but they were happy to utilise the fort, which may well have been Roman. The Mongols used such sites as bases from which to attack and plunder their enemies, whilst also guarding important roads. This one guarded not only the main road to the east, but also a major crossroads leading from the south of the khanate to the north.

The horde of horsemen left the castle and reached us so quickly that my head spun. We were surrounded by twenty Ahmeds, each of whom had an arrow aimed at us. Even Hamo looked intimidated. I had not heard Mongolian spoken and its harshness and aggression took me by surprise. It sounded like a violent argument!

After a short interchange, Ahmed turned and smiled at us. " Messenger will ride to the khan. We sleep here tonight!"

It became clear, by the deference he was shown, that Ahmed was an important man. The commander of the garrison bowed. Once we entered the castle, Ahmed was whisked away and we were left to fend for ourselves. But we were in familiar territory inside the castle, for it was adapted from an old Roman fort and as such, followed the traditional design. We took the horses to the stables and after unsaddling them, carried our own war gear.

Hamo pointed to the building that housed the warriors. "Let us see if there is room in there."

To our surprise, the barracks were empty, and we later learned that the Mongols preferred to sleep in the open when they could. It suited us, as we had plenty of room. We had just laid out our war gear when Ahmed found us and took us to the outdoor cooking area.

He greeted us with good news. "There was a battle recently and one of our generals defeat the Mamluks. Now I see why we did not see more of them on way here. We can eat and sleep soundly this night."

The Mongolians were most intrigued by us, for they had seen few Franks. Perhaps unsurprisingly, it was my bow that attracted the most attention. Ahmed took great delight in inviting the Mongols to draw the bow. That none could match my pull made my friend grin from ear to ear. From that moment, I gained more respect than either of my companions. Mongols like someone who has more skills than they have, for it gives them a target and they kept trying to outdo me!

We learned, as we ate, that the Mongolian warriors were restless and that a war with the Mamluks appealed to them. They believed, in Ahmed's case passionately, that their horse archers were better than those of the Mamluks. They were keen to prove themselves better warriors.

The next day, six of the Mongols acted as an escort as we continued our journey east. The three horses we had gained meant that we could now travel faster and, of course, in greater safety.

That there was still danger was shown when we were just two days away from the khan's yurt. Ahmed had told us the yurt was the traditional home of a Mongolian warrior and was preferred to a building. It was an enormous tent. The khan's was the largest, but the whole encampment was like a large town. I do not think that either Ahmed or myself had grown careless, for we had come close to death. One cut from the poisoned blades would have guaranteed our demise, but I think the others – the Mongol escort, Hamo and Sir John – were more relaxed. It was probably our fault, for the four of us had stopped taking turns to watch. With six Mongols, we thought we had no need. But we did have.

We had made our camp as usual and taken all of the normal precautions. Ahmed had the six Mongols take turns as sentries. I had not made water before I turned in and that was a mistake. I realised that I would have to get up and, as I opened my eyes, I heard the soft sigh of a man dying. As a sound, it can be barely discernible, but I had heard it often from men who had died at my hands and others – friends – who had died in my arms. Once you heard it, you never forgot it.

I saw the assassin lower the sentry to the ground and I shouted, "Alarm!" Grabbing my sword, I ran towards the killer, knowing that I had to avoid his blade. I saw that there were two assassins and the second was running towards Hamo and Sir John. Ahmed rose, and he had his sword in his hand as a second of our sentries ran at the assassin. Mongols are deadly warriors; assassins are deadlier, and the lithe little killer ducked below the swinging Mongolian sword and slashed his dagger across the Mongol's throat. I would take no chances and, as Hamo and Sir John rose slowly to their feet, I pulled my dagger from my buskin and raced towards the first assassin. I swung my sword – not at his head, for I knew he would duck, but at his middle. He could not duck beneath my blade, nor could he jump over it. All he could do was block the strike with his dagger. I ensured that his blade came nowhere near my flesh and I rammed my dagger up under his ribs. I kept pushing as the dagger twisted and grated on bone, and my fingers found flesh. I turned the knife and used my superior strength to keep his dagger away from any part of me. I felt his broken skin with my dagger hand and pushed my hand inside his body. This was one tough killer and he would not die – until the tip of my dagger found something vital and his dagger fell to the ground from lifeless hands.

The second killer lay with his body separated from his head, and Ahmed was wiping blood from his sword. He raised it in salute and then turned to the other Mongols.

The Mongolian language sounds aggressive at the best of times, but the look on the faces of the surviving men showed the power of his words. He gesticulated at me three or four times and, when he stopped, the four men came to take away the bodies.

I smiled at him. "What did you say to them?"

He shook his head. "That you have proved that you are worth any four Mongol warriors and that I am ashamed of them."

"These were assassins, Ahmed, and the best of killers."

He shook his head. "I thought that Mongols were the best of killers, but I can see that it is just you and I who can be relied upon! Until we reach the khan, the two of us will watch."

And so we did. I am not sure if Sir John and Hamo were offended, but we took each watch for the days it took us to reach the khan's yurt. I did not mind the lack of sleep, for I had the respect of a great warrior and that was enough for me.

The khan lived in a sea of tents. His was the most magnificent and the largest I had ever seen. Around him, his various clans camped protectively. The riders sent from the Roman fort had warned him of our arrival and, I suspect, that was why he met us at his yurt. I later found out that he often stayed in the palaces of the cities he had conquered, but that was mainly for the sake of his wife, who was Greek.

The khan had massed his warriors and they made an impressive show as they rode in huge blocks, crisscrossing before us in a meticulous display of horsemanship. He was trying to impress us, and I did not know why – for we needed his help! I deduced later that Ahmed's message had told the khan what our mission was.

The khan's wife was beautiful and as we approached, I was deeply aware that I stank and was dirty. I had been riding a sweaty horse for more days than I could count, and I had dried, stinking blood on my clothes – and yet I was being presented to a beautiful queen! I felt ashamed and hung back behind Hamo and Sir John. At least they had no blood upon them.

Ahmed approached the khan first and their embrace told me all that I needed to know about their relationship. The khan must have been angry that his emissary had been taken. They spoke at length, and Ahmed's words were punctuated by gestures towards the three of us and occasionally towards our escorts. As the escorts' heads hung low, I guessed that Ahmed was yet to forgive them. The four were dismissed by the khan, who then approached us. He spoke to the others in French and Hamo and Sir John bowed.

Then, Sir John turned to me and said, with a bemused look on his face, "The khan wishes you to approach him." I gave him a questioning look and he just shrugged.

They parted and I walked forward, keenly aware that Ahmed had a smile upon his face. The khan, who was much shorter than I was but broader, threw his arms around me and hugged me. When I heard the roar behind me, I feared for my life. He then turned me so that his horsemen could see me and began to shout. I did not understand one word, but the reaction of the warriors was incredible. When he stopped, he turned and smiled.

I said, "Thank you, Khan," and felt a complete fool.

He then turned to Sir John and spoke in French again, before gesturing to his senior generals to follow him. Sir John and Hamo also followed.

I was about to join them when Ahmed said, "You need not go, my friend. You wish to bathe. I will take you to a bath where we have slaves to bathe you. You are now an honoured guest."

His English had improved dramatically over the course of our journey. Almost six weeks on the road meant we had grown incredibly close. I had been close to Sir John already and now Hamo felt like a brother. As for Ahmed, I had now begun to uncover the secrets of the Mongol archer and, I suppose, wanted the journey to last even longer.

"What was all that about?"

He shrugged. "I told the khan about the journey and the fact that the lowliest of the three men who escorted me was the greatest warrior and slew more men than even me. When he heard that you had slain assassins, he told his warriors that Gerald War Bow is now a Mongol warrior and to be accorded the status of leader of a hundred."

I had been accorded a promotion by strangers, of a type Lord Edward would never have given me!

The slaves who attended to me were a mixture of Mongolian, Muslim and Christian, as well as some darker brown-skinned slaves who, Ahmed later told me, came from a hot land to the south and east of his homeland. There were also some Chinese slaves. The Mongol empire was vast. I confess that I was uncomfortable with the treatment, as it felt strange to be undressed and then washed by young women. As slaves, they did not seem unhappy and in the brief time that we were with the khan, I never saw them mistreated in any way.

Having said that, the Mongol warrior is fierce-looking, as are the Mongol women. I saw that many of the Mongol warriors had concubines who were not Mongol.

I was dressed in Mongol clothes so that my own clothes could be washed. The clothes I was given were not the rough, hardwearing garments that Ahmed and the other warriors wore to war. These were beautifully cut, soft robes of bright colours. When I came out of the bathing tent, Ahmed was not to be seen and I wondered what to do.

A Chinese slave approached me and spoke to me in English. "Please to come with me."

I followed him and asked, "You speak English here?"

"My job is to learn all languages."

I knew then that I had to learn French, for I was embarrassed that these barbarians could speak more languages than I!

He took me to a large yurt guarded by six Mongolian warriors. They saluted me as they stood apart to let me enter. I found myself in the presence of the wife of the khan, Maria Palaiologina. She was beautiful and seemed almost to be carved from alabaster, so perfect were her features. As with all such wives, she was guarded by two eunuchs and surrounded by a sea of slaves. Close to her were four other Greeks and I guessed that they were a Mongolian equivalent of ladies of the queen.

The Chinese interpreter hovered behind me. The khan's wife spoke, and he interpreted.

"Lady Maria is called Despina Khatun by the tribe, for she is now the spiritual leader of the tribe and she welcomes you to her yurt. She asks you to sit."

I saw that there were pillows covered with furs and I chose one, although I did not find the position that I had to adopt comfortable. "I thank the Lady Maria."

"Lady Maria thinks that you, Gerald War Bow, were sent here for a reason."

As the words were translated, I looked at Lady Maria. I had thought I was here to have a meaningless talk with her, but I could see that she had something more serious on her mind.

"Lady Maria had a slave of whom she was very fond. Her name was also Maria. She looked enough like Lady Maria for her to be used in her place."

"What for?"

When my words were translated it brought a smile to the face of the alabaster lady.

"Lady Maria says that you are an honest warrior and she can see no guile in your eyes. There are times when enemies of the khan must be deceived. It has been six months since such a deception was needed. A strong force of warriors escorted Maria on a journey to the south of the khanate. They were attacked and the warriors were slain." There was a pause before the Chinese translator spoke and I could see that he had been affected, too. "Maria was taken as a slave by the Mamluks."

That he would be close to the women of the court, slaves and ladies alike, was no surprise and I sensed real emotion in that yurt. This slave, Maria, had been popular.

"I am sorry, but I still do not understand. What has this to do with me?"

Lady Maria spoke directly to me and said, in English, "Maria was English!"

I had thought that she must have been Greek, for Maria is not normally used by English mothers. Mary is more common.

The Chinese interpreter took over again. "We have tried to buy her back, but to no avail. It seems that one of Baibars' lieutenants, Salar, has taken a fancy to her and she is held at the fort that you passed when you came here." I frowned, and the translator said, "Darb-i Sak Kalesi, Trappesac."

Now I saw what she meant by 'sent for a reason'.

"Does she wish her slave returned to her?" I confess my question was to buy thinking time.

Lady Maria shook her head and the Chinese man interpreted her words. "She wishes her former slave freed and released. Lady Maria feels guilt that the deception resulted in such cruel treatment, for Salar is a vicious man who likes to inflict pain."

"She may be dead already, Lady Maria."

The next interpreted words came as a complete shock to me. "Salar served my father when he was a young man and he was besotted by me. He fled my father's service after I rejected his advances. She is alive because she looks like me, and he knows that her captivity will hurt me." I noticed that the interpreter now gave Lady Maria's words directly and that, somehow, made the story more personal.

"I am at a loss as to how I can help."

She smiled and clapped her hands. A fermented drink mixed with milk was brought. It was an acquired taste, but I did not mind it. When I had drunk some, she spoke again.

"You should know that Khan Abaqa is already agreeing to the request made by your Lord Edward. Your journey to Armenia will be swift, for you will be escorted by many warriors. The fort of Darb-i Sak Kalesi will be taken. However, there is a danger that Maria might be executed when the castle is attacked. You will rescue her."

My face fell. How was I to get inside the formidable fortress while a battle raged? The Chinese interpreter allowed the hint of a smile to crease his features. Lady Maria did not speak these words, they came from him.

"The fortress was in our hands for some years and we know it well. When the Mamluks captured it, the reason was treachery. There is a passage cut from the mountain and there is access to the inner bailey. One or two men could manage to get inside. Ahmed Tukeder has said that if you will be the other, he will enter the castle and rescue Maria. Lady Maria would have you swear an oath that you will do so."

I was stunned and merely nodded. I took out my dagger and, holding it like a cross, kissed it. "I swear that I shall do all in my power to rescue Maria from the Mamluks." The delight on Lady Maria's face was obvious. "And if by some miracle, we do rescue her, will Ahmed bring the young woman back here?"

"Oh no. Maria is to be given her freedom and you will return her to England, where she can have her own life. I owe that much, at least." Was there a hidden message in her words? One of the ladies of the court came over to me and handed me a purse. Inside, I could feel a number of coins. The interpreter continued. "You will give this to Maria so that she can start a new life as a lady."

I had been briefed and I was then interrogated by Lady Maria and the ladies of the court. It was not just England that fascinated them, but me. Ahmed must have told them of my prowess and I think that some of the slaves who bathed me had spoken, for some of the questions were quite personal. When a messenger came to take me to Sir John and Hamo, I felt a sense of relief.

The two of them were beaming, but the sight of me in Mongol clothes made them both burst out laughing. Hamo put his hands on his hips. "And what are you? Some performing monkey?" He sniffed the air. The slaves had used scented oils on me. "You smell like a high-class whore!"

I smiled. "And you smell like a horse. Who do you think has the more appealing smell?"

He sniffed himself. "A fair point! We have succeeded. The khan is sending an army."

I nodded. "I know. His wife told me, but I know something that you do not. We are to take Trappesac, and Ahmed and I are charged with the rescue of a slave."

I took great satisfaction from the stunned looks upon their faces. I told them all that I had been told.

Sir John said, "I do not like this. We have a duty to return to Lord Edward!"

I nodded. "And, should I fail, you and Hamo can return to our lord and tell him that we succeeded and that he has his Mongol army. We all know that I am expendable, and, in all honesty, we cannot refuse. For this request, no, *order*, comes from the khan's wife. What do you think Lord Edward would say?"

Sir John was an honest man. "But I do not like it!"

"Nor do I, but we are not the masters of our own destiny, Sir John. This quest has altered all of our lives." I gave Hamo a sly grin. "My friend here, for example, has had his life turned upside down by the Lady of Beirut, and I do not think that he will return to serve Lord Edward."

"How so?"

I smiled. "I have watched you and heard you for a long time Hamo and I saw the change after you met the lady. We are brothers in arms and there are no secrets. You are besotted by her!"

He gave a sheepish smile. "But she is so far above my station."

Sir John said, "Gerald is right, Hamo, and I believe that Lady Isabella knows her own mind – any decision that must be made will be made by her, and she will not care what others think."

Hamo nodded. "You may be right about all of these things, but the fact is that we need to return as soon as we can."

"And do you think that we will be able to sneak through the pass as easily a second time?"

"No, and that means delay for we will need Mongol support."

"And it is in place. As I said, a thousand men will accompany us and reduce the walls. The general who will lead the khan's army is Samagar, and he is considered one of the best of their generals."

Sir John laughed. "We discuss matters of great import with the khan and you take a bath and chat with his lady, yet you know more than we!"

I was the one who felt the most comfortable when we dined with the khan, his lady and his generals, for I had bathed and been dressed as our hosts. I know now that Ahmed had done all of this, for on the journey east, we had grown close. He could have spoken more easily with Sir John and Hamo, yet he had chosen the harder task of learning my language. I was seated next to him and I saw a new Ahmed. He was dressed like the other Mongolian nobles and his high status was obvious. I felt as though I was the guest of honour rather than Sir John, as both Lady Maria and the khan's generals all spoke to me as they entered to take their places. Of course, I had no idea what they were saying, but I smiled and bowed to them all. It seemed to be the accepted way here in the east.

The food, when it came, was mainly mutton and lamb. It was, as Ahmed had warned me, heavily spiced and I heeded his advice and drank the sheep's milk to cool down my mouth. I smiled as Hamo and Sir John attempted to cool their mouths with water. As Ahmed had warned me, that did not work. While we ate, I questioned him about the journey back for, like Sir John, I was aware that Lord Edward needed his answer.

"It will be two days from now, my friend, and we will make the journey west in half the time. A Mongolian warrior has two horses and we will all change mounts as we ride. You and your friends are lucky that you have captured horses already. You will be able to keep up and, who knows, you may grow legs like mine!"

I lowered my voice. "And is this plan, to enter by a tunnel, possible?"

He was still learning words and he frowned and repeated "possible?"

"Can it be done?"

He smiled. "A short word which says much! It can be done, and the men who go with us will be the best of men. We do not fear death and the chosen ten warriors all expect to die to carry out the wishes of Despina Khatun. She is the spiritual leader of the tribe now that she is the number one wife of the khan." I nodded. "We will not be using our bows but you have good skills with your sword and your dagger. Our hope is to make Salar look at the main gate while we enter. You and I will see to Maria while the other ten take and open the gate."

I knew that could not be achieved without great loss of life and he saw it in my eyes. "Yes, my friend, most of them will die."

Chapter 10

The day we left the camp, the khan came with a gift for me. It was a Mongolian bow and a war bag of their arrows. They were longer than ours. It was a fine gift, for there was silverwork and engraving on the bag. I had learned a few words of Mongolian and I butchered them as I gave him my thanks. He laughed and clapped me on the back.

Ahmed translated his words for me. "He says it is an honour to meet a man who can pull his bow as far as you can."

The day before, Ahmed had invited all of the generals and the khan to watch me send my arrows further than any of the Mongols. When none of the generals had been able to pull the bow back as far as I could, my star rose even higher.

I did not speak with Lady Maria before I left, but she held my gaze and waved me off. She was a lady who impressed me. She had left the comfortable world of Byzantium and exchanged it for a yurt – and yet she wielded more power than any other woman I knew. She was quite remarkable.

That my view of her became coloured was a lesson to me, as I had believed all of her words – and while she had not lied to me, not all of them were the truth.

I had warned Hamo and Sir John of the riding arrangements, but I do not think they believed me. I had my horse and one of the captured Mamluk mounts. I would do as the Mongols did and, when we stopped, change horses. There were servants charged with leading the spare horses with our baggage and I knew from Ahmed's words to them that they would watch my war gear and new bow as though they belonged to the khan himself. This time we had no fear of an assassin's attack, for there were two thousand warriors with us. Ahmed had doubled the force we would be using to take the castle. Samagar would bring the rest of the army once it had mustered. By my estimate, if we reached Acre and Lord Edward's army a couple of weeks before the Mongol army, then we would be lucky.

We moved at an astonishing speed. I asked Ahmed, when we camped each night, about the cost in horseflesh. In answer, he pointed to the horse herd that followed us. "If any die, we have replacements and we eat well. Tomorrow, I shall show you an old Mongol trick to make the meat tender."

I wondered what he meant. The next morning, he showed me. There were sides of old beef we had brought with us and he sliced off two thick steaks. They were obviously tough. He placed one below his saddle and one below mine. He grinned. "The old ones would have had it next to the horse itself, to season it with horse sweat, but we are more cultured and put it between the saddle and the sheepskin."

I had no idea what he would do with the steak until the evening. He took out the steaks and I saw that both had been flattened. He showed me how tender they had become by teasing a piece from one. "The old warriors who followed Genghis Khan would have eaten this as it is!" I shook my head and he laughed. "Do not worry, we will cook them, and I know that you will use this when you are back in your cold home in the west."

He was proved correct, for despite the smell of horse sweat on the steak, the meat itself was so tender it did not need to be chewed. I tried to persuade Hamo and Sir John to try it, but they refused. It was their loss.

The hard riding took its toll. Our bodies were unused to such continuous riding and we had chafed, raw skin and more aches and pains than I thought possible. The Mongols did not seem discomforted in the least by the rides that lasted from dusk until dawn.

We picked up more men at the crossroads with the Roman fort and they were used, because of their local knowledge, as scouts. It proved to be a wise move, for they surprised a Mamluk patrol. There was little love lost between the two peoples, but Ahmed had demanded a prisoner and they brought one back. He was more dead than alive. They began to torture him, and I left – for I did not enjoy seeing men suffering, even if they were enemies.

Ahmed returned wiping his bloody hands and he looked pleased. I had learned to see the slight nuances of expression that told me how my friend felt. "It is as we expected. Salar has reinforced the garrison and there are now one hundred more Mamluks inside the fortress. It is a waste of his efforts, for we do not intend to attack the high walls. We have also learned that Baibars in is Egypt, putting down a rebellion there. This means he cannot stop us once we take the pass! By the time Samagar arrives, we will be able to help your Lord Edward to defeat these Mamluks. The only thing that might stop us is that I heard before we left, the Golden Horde to the north of us is causing problems on the border."

I had learned that the Mamluks had connections with the Mongols. They were descended from some of the Golden Horde who had settled far to the north. They had come south over many years and they had similar skills to the Mongols. A battle between them would be interesting, for their weapons, style of fighting and character were similar.

Victory would go to the better general and talking to the men with us, they felt that Ahmed was a better general than Samagar. His enforced absence had let his rival gain power and influence. Ahmed was pragmatic about it. "If he wins the battle then all will be happy. If he loses then he will lose his influence and perhaps his life. I will then be able to show the khan what I can do!"

We camped before the pass and I thought back just a few short weeks to the time we had fled in fear of our lives. That seemed like another lifetime and another man. I had changed during the journey. I could now speak a little Mongolian and I had even begun to improve my French.

When our camp was set up, I spent that first late afternoon with Hamo and Sir John. I was aware that I might not survive this attempt to rescue the slave. "Sir John, if I fail in my mission then give my weapons, bows and my purse to Will Yew Tree. He will see that they get a good home."

Sir John looked appalled. "You will come back, Gerald, you must!"

"Let us be realistic, Sir John, we have already overused our luck, have we not? I do not say that we will not take the castle, although that seems improbable at the moment. But I will be doing something for which I have not trained."

Hamo said, "Ahmed has great faith in you."

"And he is a good man, but I know what I am capable of. Do as I ask and then, if I return, you can mock me all that you like, and I shall not care – for I will be alive!"

"You have my word, Gerald."

Ahmed came to our camp just after I had delivered my message to Sir John. He had with him the ten men who would be entering the castle. They took out some pots containing a black, greasy concoction and he proceeded to smear it on my face and hands. "This will hide our features." When that was done, he handed me a thick hide vest. "Wear this over your tunic. It will deflect blows almost as well as your mail." He saw my helmet on the ground. "You will wear your helmet?" I nodded. "Good, for the tunnel was built for Mongols and not giants like you, War Bow!" When I had donned it, he straightened my vest and said, "Let us ride, we have a night in the dark ahead of us and tomorrow our men will begin their assault at dawn."

Hamo knew strategy. "They have seen your men preparing their assault. They know you will be coming."

Ahmed answered, "And they know when, Hamo. They will watch through the night in case we try a sneak attack. They will be tired, and tired men make mistakes."

I mounted the Mongolian pony and followed the others. Our route took us well north before we swung to head west. Darkness had fallen when we finally stopped at a flat place just before the steep mountain began to climb. The Mongols tied their reins around their saddle pommels. I did the same, wondering what we were going to do with the horses. The answer surprised me. They slapped the rumps of their ponies and the animals took off, back towards the Mongol camp. I did the same with mine and gave Ahmed a quizzical look.

"They may have heard us riding north – they will wonder where we are until they hear the thunder of the animals' hooves. They will think we sought another entrance." I learned much from Ahmed, who was a clever and cunning leader.

I followed the others as we took an almost invisible path, which twisted and turned as it climbed the mountainside. We climbed higher and walked further than I had expected. Eventually, the man before me, Ogedei, stopped.

171

Ahmed came back to me and led me through the men. He pointed to an impossibly narrow cleft in the rocks. "This is the entrance and, from now on, there will be no words. I had forgotten how narrow it was and I fear that you may be too big to fit. You will go last and if you cannot get through, then make your way to the castle and await our assault."

He left me to squeeze into the cleft and the others all grinned as they passed me. Ogedei patted my belly and said something. I guessed it was Mongolian for 'fat'. He squeezed through and I was alone. I sucked in my stomach and went to the gap. I had seen the Mongols bend their bodies. No matter how much I tried, I could not do it and I cursed the vest.

And then, it came to me. I took off the vest and tried again. It was better, but not good enough. I took all of my clothes off apart from my helmet, buskins and breeks. Holding my clothes, I tried again. The rocks tore and scratched my body, but I was through and, after eight paces of squeezing, I found that it was wide enough for me to walk without ripping my body to pieces. I did not risk donning my clothes in case it narrowed again, and I followed the tunnel, which was clearly man-made, towards what I hoped would be a door.

Ahmed had told me that the first objective was to get to the door and then we would wait until the castle was silent. He wanted us inside the castle an hour before dawn. I could not see how he could manage that trick. I was still thinking about it when I almost bumped into Ogedei. He turned, saw my half-naked body and put his hand to his mouth to prevent him from laughing out loud. I saw Ahmed nodding proudly and others began to pat my back. I saw the ancient wooden door and began to dress. Ogedei helped me. I winced as the leather bracer on his arm caught one of my bleeding wounds, but I did not utter a sound. I would not let my new comrades down.

When I was dressed, I squatted on my haunches like the others and closed my eyes. Ahmed had taught me that this was meditation. The Mongols had learned it from the Chinese, and he told me that it was a technique as valuable as pulling a bow. It was a way to empty the mind of worries and fears and it helped a man look deep within himself. It was a way to reflect on oneself.

I closed my eyes and felt each cut, bruise and graze – and then dismissed them as unimportant. With my mind emptied, I was able to fill it with positive pictures. I was a strong warrior and I could use a knife and a sword. I had killed assassins and avoided their poisoned blades. I could lead men and I knew that, back in Acre, my archers were desperate for me to return. All of these thoughts drove away the fear of failure and instead, gave me a picture of me leading Maria through the Syrian Gates to freedom.

Ogedei tapped me on the shoulder and I rose. I drew my dagger, for the space was too confined to use my sword. The door opened and, infuriatingly, creaked. Ahmed had said that there was a possibility of this happening, but in a huge castle there would be many such creaking doors and it was not as though the castle was asleep. Most of the garrison would be on the fighting platform and only the servants and women were abed.

After the darkness of the tunnel, the dim lights from the corridors above us seemed almost bright. Ahmed began to climb up the rough rock. He had told me that we had twenty feet to climb and then we would find ourselves near the cesspit, into which the garderobes were emptied. I could smell the shit and piss as we climbed. Fortunately, there must have been recent rain for the pit was only half full and we could use the sides to brace our feet as we pulled ourselves through the soiled entrance. I was lucky that I was last, as Ahmed and the others almost cleaned it for me as they pulled themselves through.

Then, I saw that we were in the castle. I saw the huge keep ahead of us and in the distance detected movement, for I could see the fighting platform. The brilliance of the plan now became apparent. All eyes were looking towards the Mongols who were gathered outside, and so only two walls were manned. The wall beneath which we stood had a mountain behind it and needed no sentries. Similarly, the keep only had men watching on one side; the side that faced the gate.

Of course, we still had to get inside the keep and I knew that there would be guards there, but Ahmed had planned well so far, and I knew he would have thought this one through. One by one we ran the forty paces to the unguarded north wall of the keep. We then worked our way around the wall, and I took the opportunity to draw my sword; it was the one I had taken from the Mamluk. When he reached the end of the wall, Ahmed held up his hand and then tapped Agadai, another of our Mongol comrades, on the shoulder. They disappeared. Eventually, Ahmed returned and signalled to us. This was the most exposed part of our route, but the men on the fighting platform were nocking arrows and I heard horns from without. The Mongols were preparing to attack.

There was a wooden staircase leading into the keep and I saw, as we entered, Agadai's body along with those of three Mamluk sentries. I was amazed that all four had died so silently. Agadai's friends passed his body without a second glance. That was the Mongol way.

Ogedei and Mongke took two bows, which had belonged to the dead sentries, from the floor, and stood on either side of the doorway, arrows nocked. We had protection for our backs.

I was in more familiar territory now, for this was a Christian-built castle and I could work out which way to go. Inside was a wooden staircase which climbed to each floor. Just seven men and I followed

Ahmed to that first floor. I knew that he was counting on finding it devoid of soldiers. Even Salar would be on the walls, but his concubines and wives would be guarded. I saw Ahmed open the door slowly and peer through. He shut it suddenly and stepped to one side.

The door opened and a Muslim stood there. Ahmed's mighty fist reached in and pulled the man over the side of the staircase. Even as the man fell with a sickening crunch onto the hard stone floor, Ahmed and the rest of our men were rushing through the door.

I was the last one through and I saw that we were in the concubines' quarters. I recognised Maria immediately, for she was indeed Lady Maria's double, although her blackened and bruised face told me that she had been beaten.

Ahmed ran to her, and I saw him speak urgently in her ear. She nodded and then whispered back. He pointed to me and then back to Maria. I was her protector. No matter what happened next, I was to guard her. I nodded.

Ahmed pointed to two men and to the stairs which led to the next floor and, ultimately, to the fighting platform on the top of the keep. He then led the others back down the stairs. As he passed me, I held out my hand for him to clasp.

He nodded – and that nod said many things, for it was a goodbye.

He and a tiny group of men would now try to do the impossible: open the main gate. My job was to keep watch from the keep and hope that the other two Mongols could clear any warriors from it. If Ahmed failed, then I would have to take Maria and retrace my steps through the cesspit and the tunnel. My orders had been quite clear.

I sheathed my dagger and took Maria's hand. Putting my mouth to her ear, I said, "I am Gerald and Lady Maria has sent me to guard you. Trust in me and we might survive."

"You are English!"

"It is why I was chosen. Now come, for the hardest part is not yet here."

When we reached the crumpled body of the guard she said, "Wait!" She took the dagger from the man and drove it through his right, dead eye and then she spat on the body. She needed no words, for I read a whole story in those few simple actions.

I spied a second bow in the guard room and after sheathing my sword, I grabbed it and a sheaf of arrows. I walked to the door and opened it so that I could see what was going on. Mongol archers were attacking, for I could see men on the fighting platform were being hit. I also saw the Mongols, led by Ahmed, as they used the cover of the buildings to get closer to the gate which was guarded by at least twenty men. The two Mongols left in the keep must have cleared the top of it, for neither arrows nor shouts greeted the movement of Ahmed's party.

Daylight was breaking now. The sun might have been up a little while, but the nature of the castle's design and the cover of the mountains delayed the light in the bailey. I nocked an arrow.

Maria appeared next to me and I said, without turning, "Keep out of sight."

She nodded. "And now I have a knife, they will not make me a slave again!"

"If this works, then you shall never be a slave again. Lady Maria has given you your freedom."

She began to weep, and I cursed myself for opening my mouth. There had been no need, that news could have come later. But before I could do anything, Ahmed and his men came into view. The alarm was given but, thanks to the noise from the fighting platform, it took some time for it to be noticed. Ahmed and his men were one hundred and fifty paces from me. They were further away from the two Mongols on the keep's fighting platform, but I saw two arrows hit two of those trying to kill Ahmed and his men. I raised my bow in assistance, and my arrow slammed into a Mamluk who was racing to Ahmed with a spear in his hands. As I nocked another arrow I said to Maria, "See if you can find me more arrows!"

I think she was pleased to be doing something and I found it remarkable, even as I slew another Mamluk, that despite what had been an obviously traumatic experience, she had kept her strength of mind and purpose. She wanted to live! We had just three bows sending arrows at the Mamluks, but it was helping, for Ahmed and his men were whittling down the guards. As others tried to hurry down the stairs from the fighting platform, I switched my aim to them. I hit one man, who tumbled down the stairs, knocking three others from their feet. I also saw more of those on the fighting platform falling to arrows from the attackers.

Maria arrived with a sheaf of arrows and she shouted, "Salar! That is Salar!"

I looked to where she pointed. "Which one!"

"The warrior with the red shield and the plume on his helmet."

I saw him ordering men to finish off Ahmed. He was hidden from the two men on the keep by the corner of the gatehouse, but I had a clear target. I pulled back the Asian bow and aimed at his chest. Had I had a bodkin arrow, then he would have died but even so, I knocked him from his feet and all eyes switched to me. Another warrior pointed at me and I just managed to close the door as half a dozen arrows struck the wood.

Nocking another arrow, I said, "Maria, when I say 'now', pull open the door and take shelter behind it."

I stood at an angle and tried to remember where I had seen Salar. I closed my eyes and focussed. Opening them I said, "Now!"

As the door opened, I saw Salar rising to his feet. At the same time, I saw four men, all mailed from head to toe, racing towards the keep and finally I saw that Ahmed and the last two Mongols, Ogedei and Temur, had managed to lift the bar on the gate.

I released the arrow and it flew straight and true. This time, I had not aimed at Salar's body but his head and as he was moving slowly, my aim was exact. I pinned his head to the wooden stairs.

I nocked a second arrow and sent it at the nearest Mamluk; it hit his shoulder and spun him around. The other three were fewer than forty paces from me. My next arrow went into the mouth of one of them and I managed one more arrow, which penetrated mail and tore into the shoulder of the penultimate warrior, before I had to relinquish my hold on the bow. The sword which came for me never reached me, for I used the composite bow like a club and swept the sword to gouge a hole in the side of the door instead. He turned to flick the sword at me. I was bending as he did so, and the tip of his sword scored a hit along my face. I reached into my left buskin with my hand and drawing my bodkin, I drove it into the eye of the mailed askari.

It was at that moment that I saw daylight, as the two doors were opened. I pushed the dead askari outside and slammed the door shut.

"Help me with the bar." Between us, Maria and I fitted the bar into position. There were just three of our men left in the keep. There were me and two more on the top; we could not hold the keep against the Mamluks. This way, they would have nowhere to run and the Mongols would end their lives from outside.

Maria said, "You are hurt. I will clean it for you." She reached for the vinegar skin, which they used here just as we used it in England. I knew it would hurt as she wiped the wound. I looked for the honey pot, which we would have used to seal it, but I saw none.

She had just begun to dab away the blood when the first axe smashed into the door. She flinched a little and then carried on wiping away the blood with the vinegar-soaked cloth.

I found the action, despite the acid, quite soothing. "Lady Maria has asked me to take you back to England. Where were you born, Maria?"

She said, "Hold this cloth while I see if I can find some honey." The axe on the door continued and I wondered if she was afraid. I was not, for the Mongols outnumbered the Mamluks many times over.

She returned with a pot. "There is a little in here."

"You didn't answer my question."

She smiled. "Firstly, it is Mary and not Maria. Lady Maria called me Maria because it suited her. I was born Mary, but I know not where I was born or even in which country. I was born on the road, for my father took the cross and my mother accompanied him. He died somewhere in the lands to the east of Italy, and we were taken as slaves by the warlord who slew my father and his men. We were sold in the market at Constantinopolis. My mother served in the palace kitchens and when I was old enough, because I was pretty, I was allowed to play with Lady Maria. Her father had a fancy that we looked alike and so I was dressed like her and had my hair grown like hers. I did not like it, but I had a better life than most of the other children of slaves. My mother was executed when I was fourteen. Someone was poisoned and as no-one owned up, all of the kitchen staff were executed. I was lucky that, by then, I was living in the palace as a companion of Lady Maria. So you see, Gerald War Bow, that I do not regard Lady Maria's act as one of kindness. Her family took my mother from me. More than that, I was deliberately sacrificed and other slaves, not to mention the warriors who guarded me, died. I was left in the hands of Salar." She shivered. "I thought to take my own life on more than one occasion. I will let you take me to England, but I know not *where* in England."

I nodded as the banging on the door stopped. "And there is money for you. Lady Maria sent a purse."

She smiled. "Good!"

I heard Hamo's voice. "Let us in, Gerald!"

I went to the door and managed to lift off the bar. Hamo and Sir John greeted me. "You live! I was worried when I saw that only Ahmed and two others had survived."

I shook my head. "Two more are upstairs. This is Mary."

"I thought her name was Maria?"

I said, firmly, "Her name is Mary. This is Captain Hamo and Sir John Malton. We travel together and serve Lord Edward."

She smiled. "I will find food, for I know what Mongols are like and I know where the kitchens are." She hurried off. She was resourceful.

Ahmed, Ogedei and Temur had survived the battle but they had been wounded. Temur had the most serious injury and I doubted that he would have the use of his right leg.

He seemed philosophical about the whole thing and Ahmed explained why. "He can still ride and draw a bow. He will still be a warrior." He gave his toothy grin. I had learned that this look equated to his purest joy. "And I owe you a life once more. You slew a Turk who was about to kill me and ended their resistance when you slew Salar. You impressed every one of my warriors. It is what I have always thought. You are a master archer!"

I nodded. The Mongol healers had worked on Ahmed and he was able to stand.

"And what now?" I asked.

"We take the small fort. I think they will flee when they see us and then we take you to Iskenderun."

Sir John said, "Will that not alert the Mamluks to your khan's intention? Baibars is in Egypt. Surely it is better that he stays there?"

"It may be, but I want Gerald safely on a ship before I return to the army."

"Ahmed, just take us to Guilbert's and do so with no more than ten men. It will attract less attention."

I saw the Mongol rub his beard. "Perhaps you are right. And now, let us eat."

I smiled. "We have food being prepared by Mary."

"Mary?"

"You know her as Maria. I fear that Lady Maria was misguided in her interpretation of the relationship. Mary thinks she was used."

Ahmed nodded. "That she was. It was a trick to send her south, for the khan wished to draw out an enemy and it worked, but the men with Maria… Mary… paid the price." He shrugged. "It is our people's way, for the tribe is all and one man does not matter. I know, from speaking with you on the long ride home, that for you it is different. You worry about each man who dies fighting for you. We do not!"

Chapter 11

As we headed south and west, away from the pass, Mary became more relaxed. I had tried to make her smile and laugh. She had seemed so serious. Now I saw her realise that at last, she was free. I was also gentle with her. When we stopped, I always helped her from her horse. In the short time I had known her, Mary had changed my life for she was the first woman I had known. I had lived in the world of men for so many years that I did not know how to be gentle. Mary was teaching me that.

We were on the last part of the journey and had been on the road for a couple of months. The Mongol horses had made our return slightly quicker than our journey east. The small fort was empty by the time the horde of Mongols reached it. No doubt the garrison would head for Baibars in Egypt to tell him of the disaster. Leaving others to patrol for Mamluks, Ahmed chose ten of his best warriors to ride with us to Iskenderun and Guilbert of Nogent. It was a journey of fewer than forty miles.

We were spied and recognised as we approached, and the gates swung wide to admit us. Guilbert's face was a mixture of incredulity and joy. "So, Sir John, not only do you bring back my horses, you bring back extras too. Quite remarkable! And a lady! This hall has not seen a lady since… forever. Come inside and we will hear your tale."

Ahmed shook his head and turned to me. "I am sorry, my friend, but I must return to my men. I may see you on the battlefield or I may not – but know that you will always be here," he tapped his head, "and here," he tapped his chest.

I nodded and clasped his arm. "We are friends and we are archers. There is no closer tie! Farewell."

I waved as the Mongols mounted their horses and disappeared east. I was touched by their emotion. Archers were a kindred spirit, regardless of nationality.

Guilbert shook his head. "He could not speak a word of English – and yet now he converses easily. What magic has there been?" He turned to one of his men. "Robert, prepare a room for the lady. Gentlemen, my lady, let us go inside – for who knows what spying, prying eyes are watching us?"

Although there were no women in the hall, Guilbert had a kind old retainer and he saw that Mary had all she needed. I saw the gratitude in her eyes as she was treated gently by the old man. While she cleaned the dust from herself, Guilbert opened a jug of wine and we told him all.

"So, war will come. That means higher prices for my horses and, perhaps, danger."

"Danger?"

"Yes, Sir John. You seem on good terms with the Mongols, but if they win against the Mamluks then they may turn their eye north, to us, for when they first came they swept over Armenia – and if they had not had internal discord, we would be part of their empire."

To me, that seemed unlikely for I had not seen that side of the Mongols; but Guilbert had more experience than I did.

I realised that my priorities had changed in the desert. I had sworn to take Mary home, and yet I was still bound to Lord Edward. Until he returned to England, I could not. We also had still to achieve our end, or rather Lord Edward's; he wanted Jerusalem! All the conversations I had enjoyed, and all my experiences, told me that was impossible. Even with the Mongolian army, we did not have enough men.

When Mary joined us and sat at the head of the table, we changed the conversation and Guilbert told us his own news. Lord Edward's brother, Edmund, had brought more men to Acre and the King of Cyprus had also sent men. When Samagar came, there would be enough men to attempt clawing back some of the lands lost to the Mamluk.

Surprisingly, Mary did not seem interested in the empire where she had grown up. As the others chatted about the likelihood of success, I spoke to her about that.

"Are you not interested in the empire? I would have thought that having grown up there, you would have had concerns."

She smiled and put her soft hand on mine. "I can see that you are a kind man, Gerald. The words spoken by Ahmed and the high esteem in which you are held tell me that – yet you know nothing of life as a slave. Even if the cage in which I lived was gilded, it was still a cage, and a silken tether is still a leash. I had no will of my own and I made no choices." She waved a hand down her shift which, while it might have once been lovely, was now dirty and torn. "I have never chosen my own clothes. I wear that which Lady Maria chose for me. I was selected to be her mirror and her plaything. A slave is not a person, it is an object that someone owns and discards on a whim. When my mother was executed, they knew she was innocent; but it cleared the air and prevented resentment."

I nodded. She was right. I was a warrior and knew little of anything else. "Then tomorrow, while Sir John seeks a ship to take us to Beirut, you and I shall visit the bazaar in Iskenderun, and you will choose all the clothes that you wish."

She smiled and shook her head. "You say there is a purse of coins for me, but until we reach England, I would not spend it – for that has to last me a lifetime."

"I agree and I will not be touching your purse. The clothes you choose will be paid for by me." I saw a frown cross her face and knew that she was extrapolating a different meaning. I shook my head. "There are no ties. When I take on new men, I equip them. It will be my gift to you."

Even though I had expressed myself badly, I saw that she understood the meaning. I was out of my depth when speaking with ladies.

She nodded. "And I believe you. I can see that you are different from most of the men I have known." She sipped her wine. "Tell me, Gerald, what will we do until we take a ship to England? I know that you are a warrior and…"

"Do not worry about that. Lord Edward's wife, Lady Eleanor, has ladies with her. They are not servants, they are friends, and I shall ask Lady Eleanor to include you in her group."

"She would do that?" I heard the doubt in her voice and, knowing what Ahmed had told me about Lady Maria, I understood her misgivings.

"Lady Eleanor is one of the kindest ladies I know, and she is a mother. She has sons and daughters. She will see the pain that lies within you. I may be a rough and crude archer, but I believe Lady Eleanor may be your salvation."

My words seemed to lighten Mary's heart and she became animated. She told us amusing stories of life at the court of the eastern emperor and when she retired, all of us felt better.

Now that we were alone, we could focus on the task in hand.

Guilbert pushed a purse across to Sir John. "Here is half the money you paid for the horses. You have done well."

Hamo said, "Aye, but we are not out of danger yet. There are still assassins out there. Gerald might have slain some but that, I think, will merely make them more determined to succeed. We will need you to escort us to the quay and to find a berth in a ship heading south – it must be going to Beirut. The assassins will be watching the ships that sail directly to Acre."

I smiled, for I knew Hamo's secret. He wanted to get to Beirut, and he would not return to Acre.

"And Mary needs clothes. I will go to the market with her," I said.

Sir John shook his head. "That is too much of a risk and I cannot allow it."

I laughed. "Allow, Sir John? I am not yours to command." I saw in his face that he did not like my words. I had changed and was no longer the pliant archer who obeyed every command. "I will take care. You and Hamo secure the ship and I will see to Mary, for Lady Maria charged me with her care."

"That promise means nothing, Gerald, for we know that Lady Maria was less than truthful with you."

"Just because you are a knight and I am an archer, does not mean I do not understand the meaning of an oath. It matters not the circumstance of the oath; God knows I made it and I will not stand before him on judgement day with a broken oath in my mouth!"

It was Hamo who became the peacemaker. "Guilbert, your man Roger, the old greybeard, seems to know what he is about."

Guilbert nodded. "Aye, he was a Templar sergeant and is still fitter than most men."

"He will know his way around the bazaar. If he goes with Gerald and Mary, then all will be well, and it will not take long for them to choose clothes."

Guilbert nodded, then I did, and finally, Sir John. But I saw in his eyes that our relationship had changed. It was nothing to do with being warriors, we would still fight side by side, it was more subtle than that. There had been an illusion of equality before, but Sir John's order had brought matters to a head. I was my own man and I was Captain Gerald War Bow. I was now glad that I had not been knighted, for had that happened, then there would have been an obligation from me to obey Baron Malton. As things stood, I was still a free man.

Guilbert himself led his men to escort us through Iskenderun's busy streets. As well as Roger, I had Peter and Raymond, two more of Sir Guilbert's men. If I thought choosing clothes would be quick, then I was wrong, for where I would have chosen the first outfit that fitted, Mary went through each and every item four or five times. Sometimes, she returned to an item she had discarded at the start!

Roger chuckled at my frustration; I was looking around nervously the whole time. "Fear not, Captain, this is women for you. I had a wife for ten years and when she shopped, I went to an alehouse for an hour or so." I nodded. He lowered his voice. "And do not worry about assassins here, for they would stand out like a blackamoor in King Henry's court."

He was proved right and, eventually, with arms laden, we headed to the quay. I saw an irritated Sir John pacing up and down. It was clear that he had managed to get us berths and had been waiting for us. Hamo merely seemed amused.

"Where have you been? We could have sailed an hour ago!"

I shook my head. The meditation I had practised helped me; I emptied my mind of anger and smiled. "We were buying clothes. If you were buying clothes for the rest of your life, Sir John, you would take time to do so and besides, there are no tides here. We are safe and we can now board." I turned to Roger. "Thank you for your help."

He beamed. "It was an honour."

"Get those bags aboard!" Sir John snapped his words out. It was another sign.

Mary gave him a bemused look and, after thanking the men who had guarded us, she strode aboard as though she was the Queen of Sheba! I clasped Guilbert's arm. "We are indebted."

"Good luck, archer. Meeting you has made me wish to travel again."

Hamo had already said his goodbyes and I strode up the gangplank, where he waited. He said quietly, "You have certainly upset Sir John. I do not think he likes this argumentative archer. The one who left Acre jumped when Sir John spoke."

"And you?"

He put a mighty paw around my shoulders. "You are the same fellow I met after Evesham and I know that you have not changed much. It is just that now, you know who you are. The journey east and then west has changed you. Some men are changed by the Holy Land, but it was the east changed you and there is no going back." He looked to the south. "I also know who I am and, for the first time in my life, I know what I wish to do and who I shall be. Poor Sir John still seeks himself. He is just an extension of Lord Edward's will and that is not a good place to occupy."

As it had happened, the only ship we could hire, the one we had boarded, was going to Beirut, but I had wondered what would have happened if the only ship had been going Acre. Hamo had rejected that idea.

"Lady Isabella asked us to return to Beirut and it would not do to make an enemy of such a woman."

The journey south was peaceful, and the weather benign. The three-day voyage was pleasant. The busy Beirut harbour looked intimidating, but the galley captain negotiated his way through with skill and a few shouts and curses. We had had Guilbert's men to carry Mary's purchases aboard and as we had our war gear to carry, we hired men from the port to transport them to Lady Isabella's palace. Once the men discovered where they would be carrying the bags to, their shoulders slumped. If the Lady of Beirut was our friend, they would not be able to steal from us, nor would they be able to overcharge.

News of our arrival spread to the palace so quickly that the steward was waiting for us as we arrived. That fact also made me nervous, for it meant our enemies knew where we were. At sea, we had been safe, in the khanate guarded by the Mongols we were safe, but we now had an uncertain journey down the coast to Acre.

The steward's face had an impassive expression. "Lady Isabella asks that you hurry inside." He glanced at Mary. "We did not expect a woman!"

"It is not a problem, is it?"

"No, sir, but it is unexpected."

I took pleasure in the man's surprise, for when we had first met him, he seemed aloof and almost arrogant.

Our bags and war gear were taken by Lady Isabella's hired men and the steward watched Sir John count out the coins until he put his hand over them and said, "Enough!" I did not blame those who waited near to the docks for work. I think that in their circumstances, I might have tried to gain an extra few coins.

Despite the steward's words, there was a chamber for Mary and even a couple of servants to help her with her clothes.

The steward turned to us, for we would all share one large chamber. "My lady invites you to dine with her. If you need to bathe, we have some baths inside the palace."

We all nodded. Hamo would be trying to impress the lady. I had my Mongolian outfit, which I would wear, and I knew that Mary now had some fine clothes with which to impress the Lady of Beirut. We were taken by a slave down to the bathhouse. I knew that it was Roman, as I had seen one in England. I knew also that I stank. Since my last bath, I had ridden so far that I had felt I was a centaur and not a man. I had crawled through a cesspit and sailed from Iskenderun. I gave off so many smells that they had all amalgamated into one great stink. I think it was only the fact that we all had similar issues that made us able to tolerate each other.

The slaves who took us to the bathhouse carried our clothes away. I think I would have been tempted to burn them, but I knew that they would make them as good as new. We lay in the tepidarium, having enjoyed the caldarium and the strigils of the slaves, then we braved the frigidarium before relaxing with chilled wine.

"The Lady is a kind hostess."

I chuckled. "Aye, Hamo, and you hope that she finds you equally attractive."

"I did not say that, merely that she offered to knight me!"

"You did not have to, for I saw the looks you exchanged before we left."

Sir John was still distracted, and he asked, "What do you mean, Gerald? Lord Edward has promised Hamo his spurs. It was a kind offer from the lady, but Hamo would rather be knighted by his future king."

Hamo bridled a little. "Firstly, Sir John, I care not who gives me my spurs and as for my future king – that is only true if I return to England."

"You mean you will not?"

"I may not. I have found parts of this land that I like, although I think that if I am to live here, I might have to make accommodating arrangements with the Mamluks."

"Lord Edward will not be happy."

Hamo's face clouded over. "I have paid back the paltry sum Lord Edward paid me many times over, as has Gerald here. Do you honestly think that there are any other men who could have done what we did? Gerald is single-handedly responsible for the support of the Mongols. But for him, we would lie with our throats cut. If we do no more fighting, then Lord Edward is still in our debt."

Sir John was Lord Edward's man and I could see that he was not happy. I felt honour-bound to support Hamo. "Captain Hamo is right, for the Lady promised him spurs and I believe that she will deliver. Lord Edward is free with his promises, but less so when it comes to delivering them."

Sir John rose. "I shall dress and see you two when we dine."

He left us, with a towel draped around him. He would have to walk through the castle to reach our chamber and would lose all dignity while he did so. For Hamo and I, although we would have the same ordeal, neither of us would worry what others thought.

"You are right, Hamo. You will become Sir Hamo... if you stay here."

He gave me a sharp look. "Then you know I will not be returning to Acre with you?"

"I have known since you first laid eyes on Lady Isabella. When we reach Acre, I will have your horse and war gear sent to you – although the Lady Isabella may well buy you better."

"You think so?"

"Unlike Sir John, I use my eyes and I saw the looks Lady Isabella gave to you. Now we had better leave and prepare ourselves. I wish to impress Mary and you wish to impress the Lady Isabella."

"Mary?"

"Unlike you, I have no romantic hopes – but she is the most beautiful creature I have ever seen and if I am to escort her back to England, I do not wish her to be embarrassed about me."

The slaves began to dry us while others prepared the toga-like cloaks we would wear to get back to our rooms. Hamo lowered his voice. "She is damaged, you know?"

I nodded. "I am not a fool. Salar abused her, as did some of the others. In fact, she may never be able to abide the touch of a man. You misunderstand me. You wish for much from Lady Isabella and I believe you will attain it. Lady Maria was right, I was sent to the khanate for a purpose and that was to rescue Mary. Now I am bound to protect her until she tells me that she no longer needs my protection. She is a clever woman, and thanks to the Byzantine court, she is well educated. She will not need me for long after she reaches England. I have yet to touch the coins Lady Maria gave me and they will make Mary a rich woman. I shall ensure that, while I live, she remains rich."

He put a mighty arm around my shoulder. "You may not have your spurs, but you have nobility within you."

With servants to help us dress, the atmosphere in the chamber was frosty for Sir John, I think, thought that Hamo and I were, in some way, taking sides against him. We were not and had merely been honest.

Lady Isabella brought down a radiant Mary. The former slave was resplendent in one of the finely-made gowns we had bought for her. For my part, I knew that I would impress the ladies. The Mongolian gown had been fit for a noble.

Lady Isabella twirled Mary beneath her arm. "Mistress Mary has told me her story and it is quite remarkable. I had thought that Sir John would have been the guest of honour, for he did what his lord commanded, but I have decided that it shall be Mistress Mary who sits at my right hand and Captain Hamo, you shall be at my left."

I did not mind, for I would be on Mary's right. Sir John looked unhappy to be on the periphery.

Lady Isabella took her seat and then gestured for us all to sit. As the wine was poured, she said, somewhat cheekily, "So, Captain Hamo, do you wish your spurs from me or from Lord Edward?"

Sir John began, "I think—"

Without even looking at him, Lady Isabella said, "I asked Captain Hamo the question."

"If you would dub me, my lady, then I would spend my life serving you."

This time, she glanced at Sir John as she said, "And leave the service of Lord Edward?"

He nodded. "I am like Gerald here; I take Lord Edward's gold and follow his banner, but I am not his liegeman. If he were my king and I had knelt before him, then I would have to obey his commands. I shall, with your permission, dear lady, stay here in Beirut and forego any gold that is due to me."

I saw that they only had eyes for each other and communications were flying between their gazes that none of us heard. For the rest of the meal, their conversations with the rest of us were short or functional. Lady Isabella was interested in how we managed to avoid the assassins.

When I spoke of the poison she nodded, and I had her complete attention for those moments. "It is a deadly poison they use, and it has many names. The most common one, which you no doubt know, is wolfsbane. It is an aconitum. There are other names and varieties:

aconite, devil's helmet, queen of poisons, women's bane, leopard's bane, mouse bane, monkshood, blue rocket. Some are less deadly than the one assassins use."

Hamo laughed. "Gods, but you know your poisons!"

She was still serious. "This close to the Old Man of the Mountain, it pays to be an expert." She took a phial from her belt. It was so small that I had not even noticed it. "This is the antidote. I have it made here, and it is active charcoal. I should have had some made for you, and I will remedy that before you leave." She replaced the phial. "The brotherhood has not forgotten you, no, it is the opposite. You have become, Gerald War Bow, a worthy enemy – for you have slain some of their best killers and when they know where you are, more will follow."

I stopped mid swallow. "Then I bring danger to you all!"

The seriousness of the matter was made clear to me by the concerned expression on her face and she said, "Aye, and the sooner you leave us the better." Then she smiled. "A ship arrived today with Hospitallers and I asked the commander to wait until tomorrow so that he could escort you back to Acre. The assassins do not fear death, but they want you dead and if you are protected by Hospitallers, then they will not get close to you. My advice, Gerald War Bow, is that you take this young lady and board the first ship for England once you reach Acre." I nodded. "But you will not do that, for you are loyal to your Lord Edward." I nodded again and sipped some wine. "Do not forget your promise to this young lady – for you cannot take her to England if you are dead!"

With that sobering thought in my head, I turned to speak with Mary. "Perhaps you regret that I am to be your protector, now?"

She laughed. "No, Gerald, for the more I see of you, the more I get to know you and I have yet to discover a trait of which I disapprove. You have heard my story. What is yours? I am sure that it will be worth the hearing."

I began with the story of the time I held the reins of the four horses while the other archers attacked the castle of Iago ap Mordaf. That seemed more than a lifetime ago and as I told the tale, I did not recognise the boy I described. I told her of my time as an outlaw and crossing to France. By the time I reached the battle of Evesham, the platters were empty, and we were enjoying sweet wines. I think I would have carried on, but Sir John rose, somewhat unsteadily, and he said, in a slurred manner, "I believe I will retire, for we have a long day tomorrow. Good night, ladies."

I think he thought to make a dignified exit, but his feet decided otherwise and as he turned, he tripped over them and landed face first. His nose erupted and I ran to his side. Although covered in blood, he lived.

Lady Isabella, to my surprise, could not contain her laughter. "And the evening finishes with a jester and entertainment!"

I hoisted him and supported him with my right arm. "I will put him to bed. Goodnight, ladies."

Mary stood. "I will help you, Gerald, for I am tired. Thank you for all your kindnesses, Lady Isabella. I have learned much in my conversation with you."

I was more than capable of carrying Sir John, and Mary just had to open doors for me. "What did you mean, conversations? You were speaking to me before we ate!"

"Lady Isabella came to my room shortly after we arrived, and while you were bathing, we spoke, and her ladies bathed me. She was interested in you all, but especially Captain Hamo."

"And what did she say?"

Mary laughed and opened our chamber door. "Ladies have secrets from gentlemen and that is very right and proper. You know all that you need to know, and if you were privy to all of our words, then you would have such a high opinion of yourself that you would not see the doorstep that trips you up! Goodnight."

She pecked me on the cheek and I felt disappointed. It was like the kiss of a sister and I cursed Sir John. Had he not fallen, then we would still be talking.

His nose had stopped bleeding and I undressed myself first, grateful that none of the blood had spoiled my Mongolian clothes, and donned my sleeping breeks. Then, I undressed him and washed as much of the blood off as I could. He would have blackened eyes when he woke. I had put enough drunken archers to bed, and so I lay him on his front with his head and mouth hanging over the edge. I put the night soil pot beneath him. I knew that Lady Isabella had servants, but they should not have more work because Sir John could not hold his wine.

When I rose the next morning, I saw that Hamo's bed lay undisturbed while there was a smell of vomit, which told me that my precautions had been wise. I dressed in my travelling clothes and while Sir John slept on, I packed my other gear. We would need horses and a wagon. I doubted that Sir John would think of that and so I decided to organise them – once I had eaten.

Hamo was in the hall and sitting in the same position he had occupied when I had left. The difference was that he was eating freshly-baked bread with ham and cheese, as well as figs, grapes and nectarines.

I poured myself the lemon and orange drink that the Muslims enjoyed. "You did not come to bed?" He looked guilty. "You did not sit here all night, did you?"

He shook his head. "I will not be coming back with you, Gerald. The Lady and I…" I nodded. "I am to be knighted on Sunday. Apparently, it is within the remit of the Lady of Beirut to do that, but the Bishop will also be in attendance. This is my new home."

"Will the title be legal? I thought a knight had to knight another."

He laughed. "You know, I care not. There was a time when I thought the acquisition of a title was everything. You have taught me it is not. Lady Isabella is giving me the command of her armies and… well, that is for the future."

"I wish I could stay, but the assassins… the sooner we get to Acre the better and this means that you will be safer. Besides, any delay would really annoy Sir John."

He laughed. "Last night was the funniest thing I have seen in a long time. It was as though the bottom half of his body rebelled against the top." I laughed, for it was true. "Gerald, I have learned much from you so take some advice from an older man. Do not let Mary slip through your fingers."

"It is not like that. I am sworn to protect her and, as we both know, she was hurt, and she is vulnerable."

"Not as vulnerable as you might think. Lady Isabella had a long talk with her, and Lady Isabella is wise. Speak with Mary."

By the time Sir John rose, I had arranged to hire a wagon for Mary and our gear, and the steward had loaned us two horses. They would be returned when I sent my men north with Hamo's horse and war gear. Sir John's parting was stiff and awkward, but that was not so with the rest of us. Mary and Lady Isabella parted as though they were old friends, and Hamo and I held each other longer than I had held any other man at a parting. I did not see much of him after that, for he became famous. He was knighted and married Lady Isabella, who promptly gave him Beirut so that he became Lord of Beirut. Many, no doubt jealous, men said that he had set out to win himself a fiefdom. I was the closest to him and know that was a lie. He was a good man, and he fell in love. The fact that he fell in love with such a powerful and infamous woman was immaterial. It was love – and that is the way it happens sometimes.

With the black and white of the Hospitallers surrounding us, we headed south to Acre. I patted the phial of antidote in my belt. I had been given many gifts on this journey and I wondered if this one would be needed. I knew that the assassins were good at what they did, but we would be in the heart of the Christian Holy Land.

Chapter 12

We were ushered directly into the presence of Lord Edward. I left Mary under the protection of my bemused men, who had raced to my side when we entered the gate of St Antony. I saw that they had many questions but all that I said was, "Guard Mistress Mary and the wagon."

I recognised the younger brother of Lord Edward, Edmund. He later became known as Crossback, for he was a crusader. There were other senior lords recently arrived from England. They were recognisable by their reddened skin! I had felt pale amongst the Mongols but now, as I saw the newcomers, I knew that they would see me as a tanned veteran.

Lady Eleanor reserved a smile for me and, no doubt, Sir John – but he did not look at her. His bruised face was staring intently at Lord Edward.

When Lord Edward saw us, a slight frown crossed his face as he realised that Hamo was not there. But he saw the parchment in Sir John's hand, and he held his own out for it. "The heart of it! Give me the heart of the matter! Do the Mongols come?"

Sir John nodded. "They will be here hard upon our heels, for we heard that Baibars was in Egypt and it seemed a good time to strike. They will come through Aleppo."

The lords looked at each other and Lord Edward smacked one hand into the palm of his other. "Then we have them! When they strike at the Mongols, then we can fall upon the Turcoman who are at Qaqun. The door to Jerusalem will be wide open for us!" He turned to his younger brother. "Have all the men prepare, for we strike within the week."

Sir John said, "Lord Edward, although the Mongols are swift, their army will be at least four weeks behind us."

"And when the Muslims begin to flee south, then we know that our allies are coming, and we use the confusion of flight to launch our attack. You and your companions have done well, Sir John."

Although my scar had healed somewhat and was no longer red and angry, it was still visible. Lady Eleanor said, "My lord, where is Captain Hamo and how did you and your men earn such wounds?"

Lord Edward seemed to see the bruises and the scars for the first time. "I have had worse injuries at the pel! But I am intrigued, where is Captain Hamo? Is he dead?" He did not seem overly worried about the prospect.

I wondered how much Sir John knew. I knew that Hamo and Lady Isabella would be married, perhaps not immediately, but soon.

Sir John was diplomatic – or as much as he could be. "Captain Hamo is to be knighted and has been given command of the army of Beirut."

I had known Lord Edward for many years and the surprise on his face was obvious. "It isn't much of an army, but even so. Do they fight alongside us?"

Sir John looked at me and I saw the desperation on his face. "Captain Gerald here spoke more often with both Lady Isabella and Captain Hamo." It was a cowardly thing to do and Sir John fell even lower in my estimation.

I smiled. "He was given the command but a day or two ago, my lord, and it will take him some time to organise them. From what I could see, they were mainly palace guards but, in the fullness of time they will, I have no doubt, fight alongside us." I did not think it was true, but I believed it to be immaterial. When the Mongols defeated the Mamluks we would be able to go home and Hamo would not be called upon to choose sides.

Lord Edward almost snarled. "And we do not have time!" He waved a dismissive arm. "You two shall be rewarded, for you are loyal and your wounds do you great credit."

Sir John had the good grace to bow his head, but Lord Edward took that for modesty. "Come, my lords, let us to the map room! We have a battle to plan." They turned, and Lord Edward said, "Are you coming, Sir John? We would value the opinion of such a fine warrior!"

I was left alone with Lady Eleanor. She patted the seat vacated by her husband. "Come, Gerald and tell me all." Her eyes met mine. "*All*, do you understand?"

"My lady?"

"Sir John did not earn those bruises in battle. You did – but not he! And Captain Hamo, there is more to that tale than we were told. You know I am your friend and that you can trust me, so begin at the beginning."

I took a momentous decision. "First, my lady, I must fetch someone for you to meet and then you might understand all."

"I am intrigued, but I trust you. This is too public a place; bring this *someone* to our chambers. There we can use the antechamber."

I knew it well, for it was where I slept each night. The only other access to Lord Edward's chamber was to scale a forty-foot tower and squeeze through a narrow arrow slot. I hurried back to Mary and my men. They were all laughing, and I felt jealous. I do not know why, but I also felt angry. "Mary, come with me, you are to meet the wife of Lord Edward, Lady Eleanor."

"But I have not washed, and I am covered in dust."

Tom said, "You are lovely, my lady!"

As I took her arm and guided her up the stairs, I knew that Tom was right. The bruises on her face had faded and Lady Isabella had shown her how to apply creams and colours to mask those that remained. Her time at court had given Mary the skills and poise of a lady. I had been fooling myself to think that I could mean anything to her. I would take her to England and, when she was settled, return to Yarpole.

The sentry on the door had been forewarned but he knew me anyway and nodded as he opened the door for us.

Lady Eleanor patted a chair, which had been pulled around so that it was next to her. "Sit here, my dear; Gerald is a strong boy and he can stand." As Mary sat, Lady Eleanor smiled at me. "I knew from your words that it was a lady, Gerald." She poured three goblets. "And while the two of you tell me your tale, we will enjoy this chilled wine."

Between us, we told her Mary's story and that of her rescue. Unlike her husband, who would have been bored, Lady Eleanor showed not only genuine interest but also, at the relevant points, real emotion. When I told her how we had gained entry to the castle, she patted my arm. "What a brave warrior – and I hope you have bathed since then!"

Mary laughed, for Lady Eleanor had a glint in her eye.

I emptied my goblet when I had finished. "And there you have the tale, Lady Eleanor. Within these walls, I will add that Sir Hamo will, probably, end up wed to the Lady of Beirut. I am happy, as he is my friend. I know that will not endear me to Lord Edward, but…"

She waved a hand. "Pah! I love my husband dearly, but he is the most single-minded man I know. That is probably a good thing in a king but you, Gerald, have qualities that I admire just as much as my husband's driving ambition. You are as loyal a man as I have ever met, whilst also being true to your beliefs. It may cause you your downfall, but it is to be admired, and to have taken on the protection of this lady is most noble and, dare I say, chivalrous."

She turned to Mary. "Now, to practical matters. It is obvious to me that you cannot stay with Gerald and his archers. They are good fellows, but it is simply not done and as much as Gerald may wish to whip you off to England, we both know that my husband will not allow it. Until Lord Edward's crusade ends, then the two of you, like me, are stuck in Acre." She took Mary's right hand in hers. "Now answer me truly, Mary, how do feel about being one of my ladies in waiting? In truth, I only brought two and the duties I have mean I need more. You would be doing me a favour. Who knows, when we are back in England you could be at court?" She looked over at me. "Edmund brought the news that King Henry is unwell. I may be queen already and not know it." I was stunned by the confidences. She turned back to Mary. "Well, child, what say you?"

"Of course, it would be an honour. I saw the ladies at court in Constantinopolis and know how to act, but what would people say? What if my story was to become common knowledge? I would be embarrassed if others knew what had happened to me; I would be ashamed."

"There are three people only who know the tale and I am sure that Sir John is a gentleman and will respect your privacy. But I will, in any case, speak with him. So, are you happy?"

"Oh yes, my lady."

Lady Eleanor stood. "Good. Gerald, she will share the room with Lady Anne and Lady Maud. Bring up her bags."

"They are ladies?" I heard the fear in her voice.

"Of course, they are… just as you are, Lady Mary!"

"But…"

"You are what I say you are, for this is my court and Lord Edward will be too concerned about war to worry about a title. Now, off you go, Gerald, and send Sir John to me. I need to have words with him."

Lady Eleanor was a force of nature and I was glad that she was behind the future King of England.

By the time I had done all, I was exhausted, and it was a relief when I found my men with the wagon driver, who asked, "Captain, what about me?"

"You spend the night with us. Tomorrow, Will, I want you to take four men and return with this wagon driver to Beirut. You will take Sir Hamo's horses and war gear."

"*Sir* Hamo?"

I realised that I had not told them anything and so, while we unpacked the rest of the gear, I gave them a version of the events further north. I would not lie to my men, but I could not allow a hint of Hamo's secret out, just as I had to keep Mary's. This was harder than fighting in a battle.

The driver ate with us and proved to be good company. A Frank, he had served under Lady Isabella's father until a lamed leg stopped him. He added to my knowledge of the Holy Land and its politics.

"All this about Muslims and Christians, it is not as clear cut as you might think, Captain. A lot of folk live close with neighbours who are of a different religion. It is the leaders who cause the bother. This Baibars wants to rule Egypt and the south, but he knows how important the north is. We never have any trouble from the Mamluks. Baibars seems to respect Lady Isabella. Of course, that might be because we don't fight him, but we have no need to. He leaves us well alone. We have more trouble from other Christians. Between you and me, I am more than happy that your Captain l'Estrange is in command of the army."

That night, as I made my way to my usual place inside the antechamber of Lord Edward's room, I had so much information racing around my head that I thought it would burst. Once I had ascertained that Lord Edward and his wife were within, I barred the door and lay on my sleeping fur. I used the meditation I had learned with the Mongols, and all the mist and fog in my mind dissipated. I began to see what was important and what was not.

I sent my men off just after dawn and was then summoned into the presence of Lord Edward, his brother Edmund and Sir John Malton.

"I gave you time yesterday for I can see that you and Sir John have worked hard for me and I am grateful, but that is all the rest you will have. We leave in three days' time for Qaqun and I wish you to command the archers."

"Very good, my lord. And do we know where Baibars and his army are to be found?"

"As far as I know, he is still in Egypt, for there are few refugees spreading south. I have riders to the north watching the roads to let us know when the flight begins. The last time the Mongols came it was a bloodbath and the civilians will not stay to be slaughtered." He rubbed his chin. "I am disappointed in l'Estrange. He was your man, War Bow. Why did he abandon me?"

"I introduced him, Lord Edward, but I thought he gave good service and he did not leave until we had achieved that which we hoped. He wished for advancement."

"I promised him spurs!"

"The Lady of Beirut did not just promise, my lord, she delivered."

He glared at me. "And do you feel the same? What is it *you* want of me?"

I smiled. "I want to go home, Lord Edward, to Yarpole, just as soon as you have achieved that which you wish to achieve. He nodded absent-mindedly. "What is it we hope to achieve, my lord?"

My voice was neutral, but I had hit a raw nerve for he jumped up. "You are an archer and not my military adviser. Go and organise the archers and ensure that they all have horses!"

I had had my answer. He did not know what he wanted to achieve and, as a result, men would die needlessly. I bowed and left.

Sir John hurried after me. His face had almost healed, unlike mine, which still had a scar. I suspected it was a scar for life. "Gerald, you must curb your tongue. He will lose patience with you!"

"And what? Send me back to England? Good!"

"He will remember all these hurts and insults – and when you are back in England, then there may be repercussions."

I turned and looked Sir John in the eye. "I would that he remembered all that men did for him so easily, but they flit and out of his memory, do they not, Sir John? I thought that our quest to the Mongols would have been enough. It seems that I was wrong."

I saw in his face that he agreed with my judgement, but he was Lord Edward's man and could not bring himself to say the words. Instead, he said, "Lady Eleanor spoke with me. You have no need to fear. Mary's secret is safe with me."

It was on the tip of my tongue to say that, from a knight of the realm, I expected nothing less, but that would have been less than respectful. "Thank you, Sir John. Where will you be when we fight?"

"I shall bear the standard of Lord Edward and Lord Edmund will bear the standard of the cross."

"Then be very careful, for that will be the most dangerous part of the battlefield."

He laughed. "Says the man who dismounts to fight and wears just leather!"

"Perhaps, but the enemy does not seek out archers. They look for standard-bearers and lords. There is much to be said for anonymity."

We had reached the outer bailey and I was heading for the stables when Sir John said, "I miss him, you know."

"Miss who?" Although I knew to whom he referred.

"Hamo, of course! I felt safer fighting with him on one side and you on the other."

There was no more to be said and I nodded and headed for Eleanor. I now had a second bow and that needed a different arrangement on my saddle. I had managed to buy a Roman saddle from Guilbert, and I spent a fruitful day adapting it to carry my bows and my arrows. I also had a Mamluk sword to accommodate. The archers who had not gone to Beirut joined me and studied the saddle.

"That is a strange-looking thing, Captain!"

"It is, Martin, but look at how much I can carry."

"And that, Captain, is that a Berber bow?"

"No, Alan, it is a Mongolian one and tomorrow I intend to see if I can use it as they do, from the back of a horse."

I had not seen Mary that whole day. It was the first time since her rescue that I had not done so, and I missed the sight, sound and the smell of her, for all three were comforting. I was heading for my chamberlain duty and feeling weary when I passed the door to her chamber. As I did so, she slipped out – and I confess I felt energy and joy race through my body in equal measure.

She took me to an empty corridor. "I have had the most wonderful day, but I missed you. I thought I would see you every day."

"I have duties, but it is good that I see you now. What was good about your day?"

The words came out in a torrent. "Lady Eleanor is the very opposite of Lady Maria. I have never met a woman so thoughtful, since... well, ever. At least, not since my mother died. And Lady Anne and Lady Maud are also good ladies, and kind. They are older than I am, and I think they find I talk too much." She was suddenly aware that she had not shut up. "I do talk a great deal, do I not?"

I laughed. "Do not stop on my account. I love it."

Just then, Edgar the night sentry came around the corner. "Captain, I am sorry, but Lord Edward is seeking you. He wishes to retire, and you are not in place."

Mary cheekily stood on tiptoe to kiss me on the cheek and then scurried back to her room.

"Sorry, Captain."

"It is not your fault, Edgar."

I closed the door and had just barred it when Lord Edward's head appeared from the inner room. "You are supposed to be ready at all times!"

"Sorry, my lord."

Then the real reason for the reprimand emerged. "I believe you sent Hamo l'Estrange's war gear and horses back to him?"

"Yes, my lord, he needed them."

"You should have asked me – and I would have refused! A man abandons my service at his peril. Remember that, War Bow!"

He was being unreasonable, as the horses and war gear belonged to Sir Hamo.

Lady Eleanor's hand appeared and pulled him back. "I am

sorry, Gerald, Lord Edward had some fish that disagreed with him. Goodnight."

"Goodnight, Lady Eleanor, we have all suffered from such ailments. The Mongols have milk which has fermented, and it seems to help them sleep."

I heard her laugh as she shut the door. "We should try that, then!"

I lay down on the fur and, for once, I was not downhearted at the reprimand. Mary had kissed me – and all was well with the world.

Luckily, my men arrived back before we departed for the raid, and I did not have to endure more criticism. I was, however, kept busy from dawn until dusk with barely any time to eat for more archers had arrived with Lord Edmund and I had to send my men to buy horses for them and then organise them.

Richard of Culcheth had learned much from his first command and while I had been in the khanate, neither he nor his son had been idle. They had continued to train the other archers; Martin told me that his experience in the forest as a bandit had helped, as he used his fists to establish his authority and the archers respected that. Now tanned, like my other archers, the pale-skinned English archers took him for the veteran that he was and obeyed his orders instantly. I hoped that this time we would have more archers, and I would have more control. I had not enjoyed being so isolated in our first attack.

The day before we left Acre I was summoned, with the other captains and leaders, to a council of war. Refugees had been streaming south for two days and so we knew that the Mongols were coming. They were probably still north of Aleppo, but their reputation preceded them. When my men returned from Beirut, they had also brought news from Guilbert of Nogent. There were only ten thousand Mongols coming to the aid of Lord Edward. That was less than the number promised and would not be enough for a decisive victory. I knew that something must have happened to prevent Abaqa Khan from delivering on his promise.

I had, of course, told Lord Edward how many men were coming to our aid, and he dismissed my fears.

"Gerald, the Mamluks fear the Mongols and the ten thousand will appear many times that number! See how many refugees flood the roads! It is good that you are cautious, but I command the army, and this battle will show the world my skill. The Templars, Hospitallers and Teutonic orders have all offered me men, to lead."

At the council, his plan was quite clear. He would surprise the Turcoman garrison before they could flee to the castle. He saw this as an opportunity to lead knights to a glorious victory over the Muslims. Thus, my archers and I were relegated to supporting the knights and preventing the enemy from entering their castle as a refuge. Bearing in mind the problems we had had the first time we fought, at Nazareth, I had the blacksmiths make caltrops for us so that they could not simply ride us down. This time, there would be no foot soldiers.

While Lord Edward went through the details of the attack with the leaders of the knights, I studied the map. The town of Qaqun was important, as it guarded the only route to Nablus and was not far from Jerusalem. I could see that it needed to be taken, but if I had been Lord Edward, I would have had men ready to take the castle. He seemed to think that they would capitulate once he destroyed their army.

Compared with the Mongols, we were ponderous. We had forty miles to travel and that distance would have been covered in just over half a day by Ahmed and his men. Part of the problem was that Lord Edward wanted a raid just after dawn and so we left one day and travelled twenty-five miles before building a sprawling camp.

My archers were given the task of guarding the knights and their horses. I arranged a rota so that every archer managed to have at least six hours of sleep. I had less, but they were my men and I remembered the assassin attack. Until we had been attacked a second time, I had thought that there was safety in numbers. I now knew that was not true, and I stressed the need for vigilance. The targets would be Lord Edward, Sir John and me. From what we had learned, my actions had attracted their attention.

Richard and Will were my deputies and we patrolled our lines together. Both were good archers and keen to know our opposition.

"I think that most of the men we face will not wear mail for these are animal herders. The ones with mail will be in the castle, but if they summon help, then it will be emir-led askari who come, and they will wear mail. Have your men use our bodkins judiciously. We do not have an unlimited supply."

Will said, "When we were in Beirut, we saw that there were many crusaders taking ship for home. Is our quest doomed for failure, Captain?"

"Some will be those who were here with the French and finally chose to go home, while others see this is a war that can never be won. The Lady of Beirut has the best idea. She tries to live with her neighbours rather than fight them."

He grinned. "It is rumoured that Sir Hamo and the Lady are to be wed! He has done well for himself."

"A man takes chances where he can." I nodded to Richard of Culcheth. "Richard and Robin made the right decision when I gave them a choice. When we go home, God willing sooner rather than later, we will all go back as richer men."

"How so, Captain?"

"Lord Edward promised us a payment and the men we fight have full purses. Already, most of our men have what amounts to a small fortune. When I spoke with those in Beirut, I discovered that a small amount of spice can be bought for next to nothing here in the markets and sold for one hundred times its value in England and France. Tell your men that when the time is right, we will buy spices, which are easy to carry and will make us all rich men."

I was aware that I was talking to myself as well as to them. I had promised Mary I would take care of her and I knew that would need a larger purse than Lady Maria had provided. Mary was a lady, although born a slave, and she was used to a life which richer than mine in Yarpole, where we made do and used wooden bowls and spoons. I had been frugal with my money and I had a share of the horse money coming to me. I would use it well.

We roused the men well before dawn. We were lucky that we were on the coastal plain and there had been few night creatures to eat us alive. We mounted our horses and took our position ahead of the army as Lord Edward and his one thousand knights and members of the religious orders prepared for battle. Bishops blessed us all and men kissed crosses and other lucky charms. It was Sir John who rode to me to tell us to advance. There would be neither trumpets nor drums.

"It is time, Gerald War Bow. Lord Edward reminds you to position yourselves where you can cover the castle."

He had no need to remind me, but I nodded, and I waved my arm to take my mounted archers down the coast road the last few miles to Qaqun. This was a road filled with tiny farms and the homes of men who fished the sea. The people who lived here were practical, for they had been conquered many times before. They viewed us with indifference. Had we stopped, then they would have worried.

They took the left fork and the more direct route to the castle we would attack. At the small village, we took the smaller road which gave us a longer route. We were in Muslim country now – although just twenty years earlier it had been Christian – from now on, all that we met would be potential enemies. Baibars was the most successful Muslim since Saladin. Saladin had taken Jerusalem and now Baibars was uniting Turks and Mamluks. He had the people behind him and that was dangerous.

I led my column, with Will next to me. Richard and his son were with the pale-faced archers who had recently arrived with Lord Edmund. There were no towns, but there were huddles of huts and the people fled ahead of us. It was pointless to slay them, for there were too many to guarantee that we would get them all. The enemy would know we were coming, but as we were heading down the coastal strip and Lord Edward down the main road, it would not be an accurate report. In addition, we were travelling faster than the mailed knights and we would be in position long before they reached the Turcoman warriors. The Romans had been in the Holy Land for many years. I might have struggled with languages, but I had learned to read the stones Romans had placed every mile along their cobbled roads. I knew, just by counting them, how many miles until I needed to make the turn to the east. Once we turned, our speed would slow, for we would leave the road.

Dawn was just breaking over Nablus, many miles east of us, when I ordered the turn. We changed from a column formation to a triple line. It would, perforce, be a ragged line, but we would halt before we strung our bows.

I took my Mongolian bow from the sheath, which hung on the pommel, and selected a Mongolian arrow. I had had time to practise with the bow and now I did not find it so awkward to use from a horse's back. The hardest part was holding it horizontally, for it was an unnatural position. My own men were more than interested in how it performed. I had told them that the yew bow gave a better range and more accuracy used from the ground, but all appreciated the advantage of loosing from the back of a horse, and they were keen to see how I got on. We heard horns and trumpets from ahead when still a mile or so from the castle, which was a shadowy lump in the distance.

We were not galloping, but we were travelling quickly, and animals and herdsmen fled before us. The first opposition came at a small farm which had a wall and a flat roof. A couple of hopeful stones and an arrow flew at us and I heard a cry as one of my archers was struck. In an instant, I had reined in Eleanor a little and drawn back my bow.

I saw the enemy archer, who was just forty paces away on the roof. Next to him were two youths. The Mongolian arrow flew straight and true, striking him squarely in the chest and throwing him over the back. The two youths ducked. I was pleased that I had practised, for it was a good hit and the men behind appreciated the strike and cheered. I slowed, for if we were attacked in numbers, then we would need to dismount to clear the opposition.

When dawn came, it came suddenly, and the sunlight flared behind the castle. I could hear the clash of arms to the north of us as Lord Edward charged his mailed ranks at the Turcoman defenders. I could not see the battle, but I could hear it, and I slowed even more as I sought a good defensive position.

We were too far from the castle yet, as I needed my archers' arrows to make the castle entrance a death trap. I nocked another arrow as we entered the outskirts of the town. The men I had brought from Yarpole acted as leaders, and they spread the archers through the town. A spearman raced from a building just twenty paces away and raised his spear to hurl it at me. Once again, the Mongolian bow came into its own and the spearman's face disappeared into broken bones and blood, as the broad-headed arrow smashed into his skull.

There was too much danger now for ambush and so I shouted, "Halt! Horse holders!"

Richard had assigned the twenty least experienced men who had come with Lord Edmund, and they rushed up to grab our horses. The exception, as all my men knew, was Eleanor, who would stay by me. Now that I had my Mongolian bow, I could use Eleanor as an elevated position from which to direct arrows while still sending arrows at the enemy.

I slung my bow from the two right-hand pommels and took my yew bow from its sheath. I had my bow strung and ready by the time my men began to join me. I nocked an arrow and, holding my bow in my right hand, led Eleanor with my left. We were moving more slowly now, but my men had arrows nocked and the odd warrior who tried his luck was soon felled.

The clash of steel and horses to the north of us was now much closer. That Lord Edward would rout them was never in doubt, but that, alone, would not give us victory. I found an open space just one hundred paces from the walls and a Mamluk arrow thudded into Eleanor's saddle, telling me that the walls were manned.

"Take cover! Will, get those walls cleared!" I led Eleanor into the courtyard of a shop and house. It looked to be a butcher's shop, as there were hooks and the floor was covered in sawdust. I wrapped her reins around the gate and then joined my archers. Here, we would not be loosing our arrows in a mass; instead, we would target those on the walls and those who were trying to gain entry to the castle.

I drew back my longbow, aware that it took more effort than the Mongolian one. An emir was encouraging his men through the gate, and my arrow slammed into his back and knocked him from his saddle. His frightened horse reared, clattering two warriors who were close by with its hooves. It then took off and galloped into the castle. My men joined in, and it took just twenty arrows to clear the throng at the gate.

I heard Richard of Culcheth organising his new archers. "Aim for the fighting platform. On my command! Release!" Fifty arrows flew, while my more experienced archers sent our missiles at the faces on the walls. The effect of the dual attack was dramatic. The arrows coming in our direction ceased and when more of our arrows struck the handful of men attempting to gain entry, the gates slammed shut.

"Martin, take twenty men and get around the other side of the castle. There must be another gate. Stop them using it. If you need more men, then let me know."

"Aye, Captain." As he turned to go, he said, "I like the Mongolian bow. It would be good to be able to use a bow from the back of a horse."

He was right, and I entertained thoughts of acquiring a number of them from Ahmed. If I had ten or twenty men in England who could use such weapons, then we could swing the balance in many battles. Static lines of archers were vulnerable.

The fact that we had stopped them using their own fighting platform gave me the chance to move men to support Lord Edward. "Richard, keep your men here and shower death on their fighting platform. The rest of you, come with me." This battle was nowhere near over and I needed to use all of my experience if I was to take more than a handful of archers back to Acre. Lord Edward's plans to make a swift and successful raid were now dust and we had a battle just to stay alive.

Chapter 13

I went to the butcher's shop and grabbed Eleanor's reins. Swinging myself up onto her back, I suddenly had a much better view of the town. The houses were definitely made by locals and the flat roofs would make good places from which to use archers. I saw, three hundred paces away, Lord Edward and the Christian knights. The battle had already swung in our direction. I stopped when I spied the open place just two hundred paces from the rear of the Turcoman line.

Still in my saddle, I turned and shouted, "Will, have half of the archers climb on the roofs of the buildings. Make barricades."

I found a small enclosure at the rear of what looked to have been a grand house and wrapped Eleanor's reins around a post. Nocking an arrow, I ran to the front. I directed the archers as they came. I sent some to the roof and some to stand by me. As Richard had the less experienced archers with him, I was confident those with me had the range. "On my command, I want five flights in rapid succession. We clear the rear ranks of horsemen."

I heard a chorus of "Aye, Captain!" and I drew back on my bow.

I heard the creak of yew as my men drew back and, without looking, I said, "Release!" My command meant that my archers would each send five arrows.

I drew my next one and sent it high. I was the fastest of my archers and watched the last of the flights as they descended amongst the enemy. Struck in the back, few had any protection against the deadly missiles. Those with mail had it on the front and the Turcoman warriors – who had yet to be engaged – never got the chance to fight. Those who were not hit, turned and fled. Some would escape, for there was a limit to the number of arrows we could send, but there were more horses without riders than with them. We stopped sending them when I saw Lord Edward's banner, held by Sir John Malton, gallop past.

"Back to the castle!"

I quickly mounted Eleanor and exchanged bows, nocking a Mongolian arrow into the khan's gift as I rode Eleanor with my knees and followed some Teutonic Knights. I did not look around for my men. They would join me and if Richard had done as I commanded, then the castle would still be under attack.

By the time I reached Lord Edward, he and the knights had reined in out of arrow and crossbow range. He was conferring with the masters of the three orders and his brother as I nudged my way close to him.

Recognising my horse, he looked up. "Yes?"

"I have men watching the other side of the castle, Lord Edward."

"Good man! Your archers did well! Have them be ready in case we receive the wrong answer. Ready when you are, Commander."

The Knight Hospitaller rode forward and, raising his voice, shouted in Arabic for the enemy to surrender. Four arrows sped from the walls and slammed into his chest and his helmet. Although he was wearing mail, he would have been hurt and his men formed a protective wall of shields around him.

Lord Edward was angry. "No prisoners!"

I knew that this was rhetoric and bluster, for we had no means to reduce the walls. You do not take a castle with horsemen, and we had no siege engines. The point, however, became irrelevant when Martin led my riders, who had been watching the far side of the castle, in at a gallop. I saw that some of my men sported wounds.

Martin shouted to me, "Captain, there are askari heading this way. There must be a thousand of them!"

Lord Edward had heard, and he took charge instantly. "Captain, put your men on the roofs to protect us. Knights, I want three lines. It seems our work is not yet finished."

While the knights shuffled into lines, I shouted, "Get the wounded to the rear, Richard get your men on the rooftops. All of you, keep their fighting platform clear!" I chose not to join my archers, for I wanted to be more mobile and besides, I still had my Mongolian bow.

The Mamluk askari who had come to the aid of the Turcoman warriors were fast, well-led and the equal of our knights. I hoped that we had enough bodkin arrows, for askari wore mail. I positioned myself behind the last rank of knights. I recognised a couple from Evesham, Godefroi of Waus and John of Parker.

I was just forty paces from Lord Edward, for the knights would keep a gap between the three ranks. I heard Richard and Will Yew Tree shout out their orders and arrows began to fall upon the walls of Qaqun. The askari were too far away to be a target and by the time the knights engaged, it would be impossible for the archers to successfully decide if the target was friend or foe.

The hastily-assembled three lines meant that our horsemen did not present a continuous front and there were gaps. I exploited them and rode between Godefroi of Waus and John of Parker. They turned to look at me but, recognising me, allowed me to stay there. It meant that I was much closer to Lord Edward and could use my bow.

Sir John Malton and Lord Edmund, holding their banners, were behind Lord Edward and so I had a clear line of sight. I pulled back when I saw the emir who led the askari charge towards Lord Edward. I had now used the bow enough to understand how best to employ it. Eleanor was made for this sort of work, for she did not rise and fall as much as some other horses. Using the saddle to steady myself, I released, and my arrow flew into the shoulder of the emir. He was not wearing a ventail, and my arrow slammed into his shoulder a heartbeat before Lord Edward swept his sword into the side of the emir's head. My second arrow had more success, and it struck the askari behind the emir in the head. The effect of two arrows was astounding, for Lord Edward and the commanders of the Templars and Teutonic Knights were able to plough into the heart of the Muslims. I had to use my left hand to rein in Eleanor and allow Godefroi of Waus and John of Parker to close with the standards.

By now, the two lines had locked and I reined in and stopped. Standing in my saddle, I sent arrow after arrow into all those who tried to get at either Lord Edward or the standards. My standing position and my still horse meant that I was more accurate; I did not miss. The danger was that I would run out of the longer Mongolian arrows.

Another danger came from the archers on the walls, who began to send arrows at me. The duel between them and my archers was being won by our side, but when the Turcoman archers in the castle saw the effect I was having, then arrows came at me. I was lucky, for the one that hit me and stuck in, drawing blood, was in my thigh and the dribble of blood told me that it was not serious. I saw the archer who hit me, but I did not waste an arrow on him. I used my penultimate arrow on a second emir, who was bringing men from the flanks. As he fell, I saw two archers pitch from the walls. I saved my last arrow, and when I saw two askari riding at Sir John, who was hampered by holding the standard and a shield, I killed one and then dug my heels into Eleanor's flanks.

She leapt forward and I shifted my Mongolian bow into my left hand as I drew my Mamluk sword with my right. Had Eleanor not been such a good and well-trained horse, then this would have been impossible. I brought my sword down across the left shoulder of the askari. As I had learned long ago, fighting alongside Hugh of Rhuddlan, archers may not be the most skilled of swordsmen, but they are the strongest. My new sword shattered mail and broke his shoulder. Bright blood sprayed and Sir John nodded his thanks.

It was then that Lord Edward saw more riders appearing, and he was wise enough to know that we risked being outflanked. "Fall back to the village, where the archers can protect us!"

I turned and galloped back to the safety of my archers. I saw the concerned faces of Alan and Richard. William of Matlac jumped down from the roof when I approached. William was the nearest thing we had to a healer and even as I dismounted, he had gathered what he needed.

"Captain, that was mighty brave but as foolish an act as I have ever seen! Archers do not fight alongside knights!"

I laughed, although the pain from the arrow was severe. "Sometimes you have no choice."

"The leather breeks have saved you and the arrow was stopped. I can pull it out."

Archers knew the effects of arrows better than most, and I trusted his judgement. I nodded. He gave a tug and I winced from the pain as the arrowhead popped out, followed by blood and some flesh. He jammed a vinegar-soaked dressing under the leather breeks and then tied a pair of leather thongs to hold it in place. I knew not what it was called, but I had been taught that tying a price of cord around a wound stopped the bleeding. It just had to be released every now and then.

When he was satisfied, he said, "Don't you move too much, Captain!"

I nodded absent-mindedly, then shouted, "Will, how goes it?" I did not want to risk climbing up on Eleanor's back. The wound would soon seal itself, but these first moments were vital.

"We have made them realise that we are good, Captain. There are some horse archers coming up."

"When they do, concentrate your arrows on them. They can hurt us."

I turned and saw that the knights had formed lines as close to the walls and our archers as they could manage. One or two of the more reckless Templar knights had ridden forth to have individual combats with the Mamluks. More often than not, such combats resulted in death for the Templar; so it proved here. Three died before the commander of the Templars called a halt to the senseless deaths.

I saw Lord Edward calmly conferring with the other leaders. He said something and Sir John detached himself to speak with Richard, his squire. Richard, in turn, rode over to me. "Is the hurt grievous, Captain?"

I shook my head. "I have had worse shaving. What does Lord Edward wish of us?"

"He asks you to take half of your men a mile down the road and prepare an ambush. He intends to disengage but knows that they will pursue. Half of your men will stay here to deter them and then follow when they can."

I shook my head. With the Berber horse archers so close, this was a death warrant for whoever remained.

Richard said quietly, "Sir John said he is sorry."

"Aye, well, such condolences and tuppence will buy a flagon of ale. Robin, son of Richard."

Robin joined me. "Aye, captain?"

"Take the new men and ride a mile or so down the road. Find somewhere with cover and buildings. You are to make an ambush. Lord Edward will bring the knights when you are in position. Have the horn sounded three times."

"And you and the other lads, Captain?"

"Don't worry about us. We will follow when the knights are clear. We might take the coast road if we can, for it is quieter."

Shaking his head, he shouted, "Come on, my lads! We get to leave this place first!"

I said to Will, "Have one in three men act as horse holders. When we leave it will have to be fast."

Looking down from the roof he nodded. "And all that booty we have to leave!"

"So long as we are alive, eh?" He turned and left to give orders. "Will, your hands, I need to mount." He made a cup of his hands and I stepped into it with my good leg. Swinging my wounded leg over the saddle was agony. When I had my foot in my stirrup I said, "Before you leave, pick up as many of the Arab arrows as you can." He gave me a questioning look. "I can use them with the Mongolian bow."

He found me six. It was not a huge number, but it increased the chances of our survival. Richard the squire rode back to me. "Lord Edward is ready."

Just then, I heard the three notes of the horn in the distance. The enemy would know that something was afoot, but they would not know what.

"And the ambush is ready. God speed, Master Richard!"

"And may he watch over you, too, Captain."

As soon as Richard rejoined Sir John, the two standards were raised and lowered, and a line of Lord Edward's knights rode at the askari. At the same time, the rest of the horsemen turned and fled.

I shouted, "Loose!"

We had far fewer men, but there were not as many of our own men in range and at risk of our arrows. The sudden charge and our arrow shower worked in our favour, and the enemy were taken by surprise. Some knights paid the price. I only saw one killed, for he landed awkwardly with a bloody wound, but others were captured. I saw one askari raise his mace to finish off a young and idealistic knight from the north of England, Sir Thomas of Yarum, and I brought up the Mongolian bow and sent an arrow into the askari. Sir Thomas, although wounded, needed no further urging and he wheeled his courser to flee the battle. I suspected some of his idealism evaporated with the arrival of the wound.

I then nocked, but did not release, an arrow. My remaining arrows would be saved until my men were mounted. They would not be able to loose arrows, but I would. I had just over a third of archers dismounted and able to use their bows, but these were the best and my men made up a sizeable portion of their number. They picked off leaders and the riders who rode the best horses.

Then, I saw the Berber horse archers. They were being sent to finish us off. All but a handful of knights were now heading down the road and I decided not to follow them.

"Archers, mount and follow me! We head west!".

I decided to take them down the coast road we had used, as this would mean splitting the enemy. They would have a choice of following archers or going after the richer prize of knights, and I gambled that the promise of booty would be greater than the honour of defeating English archers.

I had an arrow nocked already and was the only archer facing the fifty or so Berbers who rode towards me. My men were mounting their horses and so I took aim at the flamboyantly-dressed horse archer who led them. He had his bow ready, but I saw that his horse's head was rising and falling too much as they passed over the dead. I waited until he had loosed and then sent my arrow back at him.

He was not as good as Ahmed and the Mongols, but he was skilled, and despite his bouncing horse, the arrow he sent at me almost skimmed my helmet. Mine did not miss and threw him from the saddle. Nocking another arrow, I whipped Eleanor's head around as the archer and his horse caused those following to baulk. I could use the bow, but I could not do as the Berbers and the Mongols could; I could not turn and loose an arrow behind me. However, Eleanor was a bigger and stronger horse than those following.

I waved my men to pass me and I shouted, "Keep going until I order otherwise!"

Will Yew Tree and my own men merely passed me and then slowed. They glanced behind to make certain that I was not doing anything foolish. It was then I remembered I had, in my saddlebag, a dozen or so caltrops. I had had them made and issued to every archer, but we had not needed them. I reached in and began to toss them behind me. It did not matter which way they landed; a spike would always be sticking up.

I shouted, "Throw your caltrops behind you." It was unlikely that any other than my men would hear me, and they would throw them to the side, widening the deadly trail through which the enemy would have to pass. I heard a horse scream behind me and knew that I had at least one victim. Our trap would make the Berbers look down, rather than at me. A man cannot look down and use a bow.

Glancing under my arm, I saw that we were increasing our lead and losing them. I saw the men ahead of my men slowing and I knew why. We were approaching the place we had turned east.

I shouted, "Tell them to head north!" and heard the command repeated as those at the fore began to turn. It was when I looked at Tom's horse just ahead that I realised our horses were tiring. Eleanor was the exception, but she was the best horse that we had. We could not keep up this speed, for our horses were not Mongolian. The Berbers could have had a short ride and I dared not gamble that they would be as tired. I would not gamble, I would use the turn to help us as the buildings would shield us from those behind.

"Will, stop our men! Dismount and ready your bows!"

Will shouted, "Yarpole, halt and dismount!"

It says much for my men's loyalty and trust in me that there was not a question. The rest of the men carried on north, up the coast road.

Wheeling Eleanor, I drew back with the bow and the first Berber who turned the corner of the building was knocked sideways from his saddle by my arrow. He had been just forty paces from me. Two more followed, and I hit one at the corner and the second as he raised his bow, four strides later.

I was running out of arrows and had just one left. I heard the creaking of yew bows behind me and sent my last arrow a heartbeat before theirs. It coincided with the bulk of the horse archers turning the corner. My arrow hit as did those of my men and confusion reigned, for men fell and horses with dying riders on their backs careered out of line. I hung the bow from one of the horns on the saddle and drew my sword.

"Will, mount and leave. I will follow!"

227

I waited until I heard, "Aye, Captain. Mount!" then I dug my heels into Eleanor's flank and rode at the disorganized archers who had been cut in two by our arrows. I bowled Eleanor into the lighter horses and slashed sideways with my sword. I connected with both strikes, but I did not push my luck and I wheeled Eleanor and sped after my men who, I was pleased to see, had obeyed me and were well down the road. No matter what happened to me, I had saved the bulk of my archers and my best archers had a chance to escape.

I lay low over the saddle to make as small a target as I could, and I kept close to the mud buildings to my right. Some had low wooden roofs, and any shelter from the Berber arrows I anticipated would help me. I felt a smack in my back and knew that at least one arrow had hit. I moved Eleanor slightly to the left and then immediately back to the right and was rewarded with a couple of arrows flying past my left side. My almost prone position allowed me to see under my arm and I saw just four men following me. If I had more arrows for the Mongolian bow, I could have thinned their numbers further, but instead, this would be a race.

I had not had time to count the mile markers, but I knew that it would not be long before we were at the fork in the road where we had parted from Lord Edward. My own men, led by Will Yew Tree, were on tiring horses and just twenty paces from me when I saw familiar buildings. We were close to the fork.

It was as we neared it, I heard Robin, son of Richard, say, "Draw! Release!"

I saw the shower of arrows soar overhead and heard them as they struck the four horse archers who had pursued us. I reined Eleanor in as I saw that Robin had organised the rest of my archers.

"Well done, Robin! I thought you would be with your father."

He jumped down from the roof where he had commanded my archers. "Aye, Captain, but while we waited at the ambush, he sent me here, for he said that you would not follow the knights but lead some this way. When I saw our archers coming down the road, I ordered them to dismount and set up an ambush. Most obeyed."

I nodded, for not all would have heeded orders from such a young archer, but Robin had helped his father to organise the disparate group of archers and enough had obeyed to save us. "Good. William, take four men and see what the dead Berber archers yield. Fetch me their arrow sheaths."

"Aye, Captain and their bows too – for your Mongolian bow saved us this day."

I patted the khan's gift. "Aye, it did."

I saw that the four horses had stayed by the dead archers. My men and I would have some reward for our action. As I had learned to my cost, you could never count on Lord Edward to do the right thing.

I turned to Will. "I think I was hit by an arrow in the back. I feel no pain, but it is better to check."

He examined my back and I felt a little prick, then he proffered the arrowhead and broken shaft. "Your leather and padding saved you, Captain. The shaft broke off." He handed it to me. "You can reuse it, Captain!"

Nothing was wasted this far from home. My men now had four Berber bows and whilst not as good as the Mongolian ones, I knew that they would come in handy – for this crusade was not yet over.

It was getting dark when the weary Christian army finally joined us. I allowed Lord Edward, his brother, Sir John, the English knights and the military orders pass us before we mounted. I knew, without any orders, that we would be with the rearguard. Robin, son of Richard, led the survivors. More than half of the archers were now bodies draped over the backs of horses. Richard was, mercifully, wound free. The surviving archers all saluted me as they passed. They, at least, knew and acknowledged our achievements. My men were the last Christians to ride down the road.

"What happened, Richard?"

He looked at his son and smiled. "I am glad that Robin was able to help you, Captain." He sighed. "We found a good ambush site and I had half on the rooftops as at Qaqun and the other half lining the road. Lord Edward and the knights passed us, but some of those at the rear were engaged with the enemy and we could not clear the road. That was our undoing, Captain, for we saved the knights but their horse archers and askari cut us up. If we had fled, then you would be speaking with ghosts and so we fought them until they saw the knights had escaped and they withdrew." He nodded proudly. "We showed them that English yeomen do not flee barbarians. We brought the dead and some of the horses as well as weapons. It is little compensation for so many dead archers, but…"

I nodded. "But the knights who brought those archers with them will think it is a good trade." I shook my head and said, to no one in particular, "I hope that Lord Edward has learned his lesson. We need to have foot soldiers if we are to reduce his castles and we need a larger army than the one he now leads."

We ended up walking our horses for the last two miles to Acre. We passed horses that had fallen because their riders had pushed them too hard. We had kept a good watch on the road behind and knew that we were not pursued. We were the last through the gates of the city.

I was the only one of the archers housed in the castle itself, and so I let Will Yew Tree organise my men.

"Captain, do not forget to have the leg and the wound in your back looked at. This country is unhealthy!"

"Aye, I will."

I had not said anything, but the stiffening leg had been agony while we had walked our horses. Had the arrow penetrated any deeper, then I do not think that I would have made it back – such are the margins between life and death. I knew I had been lucky and since Mary had come into my life, I had more purpose.

Life was more precious than it had been. I did not wish to die in this land – for I truly believed it was not worth dying for.

Chapter 14

Before I even thought about my own wounds, I had to see to Eleanor. I led her to the stable. I had the lowliest stall, but the stables were well lit and Eleanor would be comfortable. I took my weapons from my saddle and then removed the saddle and her reins. I used the horse blanket to wipe her down as she gratefully drank from the bucket of water and as I did so, I examined her for wounds. She had been injured in the battle, but all wounds were minor. However, in the heat of this land, even minor wounds could prove fatal if not treated and so I watered down some vinegar and cleansed her scratches and scrapes. When I was satisfied that all had been attended to, I brushed her, before giving her oats. I had spent an hour with her, but it was time well spent. Her strength and courage had saved my life. She had outrun the Muslim horse archers.

I stroked her mane and rubbed her muzzle. "Well, I hope I shall not need you again in a hurry! If Ahmed and the Mongolian army can do what we did not, then we shall be able to go home."

When Eleanor neighed and nodded her head, I left. My horse could see what Lord Edward could not. This was not a war we could win.

Encumbered by my bows and weapons, for they were too valuable to abandon in the stable, I made my way to the hospital. There were many healers. The time I had spent with Eleanor meant that most had either been tended to or were almost ready to leave.

One of the healers, an Englishman, waved me over and asked me to lie down on the bed. "Where are you wounded, Captain?"

"My leg is the more serious wound, but I was also struck in the back by an arrow."

"I will tend to your back first and then you will be able to lie down. Let us remove all of your clothes." Another healer joined him and, as I stood naked, they probed my back. "You are lucky the arrowhead was not poisoned and did not penetrate. The wound is clean and shallow."

The second healer handed me a beaker. "Drink this, Captain."

Even as I swallowed the ale, I felt the sharp shock of vinegar as they cleaned the wound, and then they wrapped a bandage around it. That done, they had me lie on the bed while they saw to the more serious injury. Perhaps there was a potion in the ale, for I fell asleep and that is remarkable as they had to clean the wound and remove fibres, which had become embedded in my leg.

I knew not how long I lay there but eventually, the healer's voice said, "You can awake now, Captain." The healer was wiping his bloody hands on a cloth. "You lost more blood than was good for you. Eat and then get you to bed. I had to stitch the wound. I will take them out in ten days." He saw the expression on my face. "You have removed stitches before?"

"Once the itching lessens, then the stitches will be ready to come out and the wound cleaned with vinegar and dressed with honey."

He laughed. "I would that nobles had such knowledge."

As the two of them helped me to dress, I asked, "The leg, will there be permanent damage?"

He shook his head. "No, but you are acquiring some serious scars" He pointed to my face.

I nodded. "It comes with the job."

"You are a hard man, Captain. You never stirred, even when we probed and poked."

"It is only the dead who feel no pain. I thank you." I handed him a coin.

"There is no need."

"There is, healer, for I will now heal and one day, go back to England – and that is thanks to you."

I did not relish going to the hall, where the knights would be eating, and so I went to the kitchens. My nightly duty in the antechamber meant that I frequently ate at odd times and the kitchen staff knew me well. I had learned as a young archer that making such connections in any new hall or castle was vital.

As I walked in, the head cook beamed at me. "So, Gerald War Bow, you survived another battle although, from your limp, I can see that you are not completely unscathed."

"Ironically, Gaston, it was an arrow."

He laughed. "Sit, there is food left." He waved over one of his helpers. "A bowl of food for the archer and some of the good bread." He shook his head. "We did not have much notice of the return and I daresay Lord Edward will be less than happy with the quality of the food we served. It is just bread and stew."

"I think that Lord Edward has too much to think about to worry about food. We lost knights today, and he did not achieve that which he intended."

Gaston tasted the food in the pot. "Between the two of us, Gerald, I intend to head back to France soon. I came here with the hope that King Louis and Lord Edward would, between them, make this land safe for Christians. The disaster in North Africa has ended that dream.

One day, the Muslims will take Acre and that will be the end of the Christian east."

"Perhaps. Good stew!"

He laughed. "Do not let the lords hear you call it that. I give it a fancy name and they think that the name makes the food taste better. They are fools!"

I had just mopped up the last of the stew and was finishing my ale when Richard, Sir John's squire, and Mary burst into the kitchen. Richard grinned. "There, Mistress Mary, I told you he was not dead and would be filling his face! I shall have to return to Sir John."

She strode up to me and poked me hard in the shoulder. "I was worried sick about you! I heard that you were wounded and thought you had succumbed to your wound! The healer said you had left already." She lowered her voice. "I feared the assassins had ended your life."

I stood and pain coursed down my leg. "I am sorry, but I was hungry. Let me escort you back to your room." I turned to Gaston. "Thank you for the food. I will send someone for my war gear later."

"It will be safe here until you do." He winked. "Enjoy yourself!"

I shook my head; Gaston was a good man and a fine cook, but he had a mind that rarely left the cesspit.

As I led Mary up the narrow stairs to the upper chambers, she chattered on like a magpie and rarely waited for an answer from me. "The knights were all talking of the battle today and how you saved Lord Edward and Sir John's lives, and that you and your men took on ten times your numbers of archers. Is that true? And that you slew a great Muslim prince. Is all of this true? Did you? Why will you not answer?"

We had reached the main floor of the hall and my leg was aching. I took the opportunity to rest and I smiled. "If I could squeeze a word in, then I would. I did what I was supposed to, and I slew warriors who were about to kill our men. I know not if I killed a prince, but I did slay some well-dressed warriors. I did not manage to recover their fine mail. As for the numbers, a man who has time to count his enemies is not fighting hard enough!"

She saw my face. "Do your wounds hurt? I heard you had an arrow in the leg and one in the back!"

I nodded and headed towards the stairs, which led to her chamber. "Aye, but the pain will lessen, and a good night of sleep will help."

I allowed her to ascend first.

She had been listening to my words, for she said, "Knights do not recover mail, why do you?"

"Knights have a good income and I do not. Yarpole is a fine village, but my men and I need to make coin while we are here."

We stopped at the next floor, which was the feasting hall. I heard the noise from within and I could tell that they had consumed much wine.

"Does not Lord Edward pay you?"

"Sometimes he does, and sometimes he forgets."

"That is not right."

As we began to ascend the last flight of stairs, I said, "You of all people should know that folk like us only have the rights that our masters remember to give us. Lady Maria thought that she was a kind mistress, but she still used you for her own purposes, did she not?"

"I suppose you are right, but when I look back, that Mary seems a different person to who I am now."

"That is true of me, too, but one thing is certain, we can never go back."

We had reached our floor and I could not have climbed one more step. I leaned against the wall to steady myself.

Lady Maud and Lady Eleanor were coming from the garderobe and when she saw me, Lady Eleanor frowned. "Gerald War Bow, this is reckless behaviour. Will you undo all the healers' work?"

I smiled, a little wanly it must be admitted. "I have escorted Lady Mary to her room and now I will go to the antechamber and prepare my bed for my duty."

"You will do no such thing!"

"Then I shall descend the stairs, leave the castle and find my men, where there will be a bed waiting for me. That cannot take me much above an hour!"

I saw Mary smile and as I turned, Lady Eleanor put her hand on my arm. "You are not only brave, but you have wit, too! Sleep in the chamber but not across the door this night. My husband will be late to bed and in his cups. We will have to hope the assassins have forgotten you – and my husband!"

"Somehow, as much as I might wish that, Lady Eleanor, I do not think that it will be." I turned to Lady Mary and kissed the back of her hand. "Thank you for your concern, Lady Mary, I am touched that you thought of me."

She shook her head and said to Lady Eleanor, "Is Gerald the only man who is a goose?"

Lady Eleanor laughed. "No, Mary, it seems they are all cut from the same cloth. Perhaps it is the drugs the healers gave to him. Goodnight, Gerald War Bow, and thank you for keeping my husband alive. I appreciate it, even if he sometimes forgets what you have done for him."

It may have been discourteous but a mixture of the food, the ale and my wound made me feel a little lightheaded and I slipped into the antechamber and placed my sleeping fur so that the door could easily be opened. By the time I had laid down and closed my eyes, I was asleep, and that sleep was deep and dreamless.

Then, the ale wore off and the pain in my leg woke me, and I rose in the middle of the night. The sentry outside the door smiled when he saw me limp. He did not speak for fear of waking Lord Edward.

I went to the pot at the end of the corridor and made water. As I limped back, the sentry offered me his wineskin. I took advantage and then, after nodding good night, entered the antechamber, placed my bed behind the door and tried to sleep once more. As I tried to rejoin the sleep I had left, I thought of the sentry. If any tried to enter the chamber, then the sentry would be dead. I wondered if he knew that. He had been told that I was a nightly bodyguard and would have heard of the threat of the assassin, but would he have thought that through? With that in my head, I slept.

By the time Lord Edward was awake, I was up and dressed. I waited until he emerged from the bed chamber and, after nodding my greetings, went down to fetch my war gear from the kitchen. My conversation with Mary had driven it from my mind. Such distractions were unwelcome. I was a warrior and my war gear was all!

If I thought we would have time for me to recover from my wound, then I was to be disappointed. By noon, riders were galloping into the fortress along with Christian refugees. As I was showing the men who now had the Asian bow how to use it to the best effect, we heard that Baibars was coming from Egypt and with a powerful army, too. The mighty horn of Acre was sounded, and my men and I ran to our position, although my run was a limping one.

We had been allocated an important position to defend, the gate of St Antony, which was close to the castle and next to the tower of the Countess of Blois. The city walls ran from sea to sea and with almost twenty towers and a double wall it would be hard to take – but an enemy would come, for the gate of St Antony was the only gate into the city. An attack anywhere else would require tunnelling and mining. If Baibars wanted a swift victory, then he would attack the gate.

The double wall had many towers along its length. The other towers close to us were the tower of the Countess of Blois and the tower of the English and to the north-west lay the twin Hospitaller towers. As well as the double wall, there were three other castles apart from the main castle. The three military orders each had their own castle and the Templars' was the last refuge at the south-west corner of the town, overlooking the harbour and the quarters of the Venetians, Genoans and Pisans.

We hurried to the two towers on the top of the outer wall at the gate of St Anthony. The English archers would be spread around the walls and the towers. I just had my Yarpole men to command. As we hurried to the walls, donning war gear as we went, Tom and Peter helped me to carry spare sheaves of arrows and my Mongolian bow. It was just as well, for my leg slowed me up.

The men of the regular garrison made way for us. Our prowess was well known. I saw men at arms, crossbowmen and archers already filling the fighting platform on the outer wall which lay a little below us. I knew the knights would take longer to arrive, for they had more mail to don than we.

As we waited and watched the refugees flooding in, Will Yew Tree said, "What about the Mongols, Captain? Are they not coming?"

I shrugged. "We know that they are here because of the Muslim refugees but I think our raid has angered Baibars and he comes to punish us on his way north to deal with the Mongols." I would not openly criticise Lord Edward, but in my view, he should have waited until the Mongols had attracted the attention of the Mamluks and then attacked their rear. Of course, had he done that, then it would be seen as less than honourable and glorious.

The knight in command of our tower was Sir Reginald Rossel. He was a good knight, who had fought at Evesham. He brought with him twenty men at arms. We had enough men to man the wall and Sir William had five spares in case of injuries and wounds.

Sir Reginald nodded as he arrived. "Well, War Bow, I hope you have plenty of arrows."

"That we do, my lord, and we even have spare bows taken from the heathens."

He laughed. "So we can send them to hell with their own weapons. You are a good fellow, Gerald!"

That first day, we saw no signs of the Mamluk warband until late, when we saw the first of their horse archers. The mighty gates below us were slammed shut. There were many houses and homes outside the town and all the Christian ones were emptied. The first Mamluks sacked the houses and looted them.

I was under orders to wait before I sent any arrows in the direction of the enemy. I looked at Sir Reginald Rossel; he knew what I was thinking, but he said nothing. Lord Edward was in the English tower and he would signal when we were to attack.

When night fell and they had still not attacked, we knew we would have to stand a watch at night. The knights would go to the refectories and eat, but we would be served on the walls and that was where we would sleep.

As Sir Reginald Rossel descended the stairs when the bell sounded for food, and I sent Martin and Tom for our rations, Will Yew Tree asked, "Will you not be needed to sleep in Lord Edward's antechamber this night?"

I shook my head. "Tonight he will be as safe as any of us, for he will sleep in the English tower. We divide our men into three watches. You and Richard of Culcheth will command one each and I the third. Let Richard have the first watch, I will take the second and as you are younger, you can have the dawn watch."

"Do you think they will come at night?"

"It matters not what any of us think. We have to plan as though they will attack. I dare say that Sir Reginald Rossel will organise the men at arms, but I have done my duty and I know that if they do try our defences this night, then we will give them a bloody nose. We had better have a brazier brought here and lit. See to it."

"It is not that cold at night, Captain."

I laughed. "And it is not for comfort! If they try to bring a ram, a tower or ladders, then we burn the bastards."

Siege warfare was unforgiving.

Our knight would not stand a watch, but he was in command of our tower over the gate. Before he retired to his bed in the room below the fighting platform, he said, "Your men will wake me, eh, War Bow?"

I nodded. "They know their business, my lord."

In the end, it was two more days before Baibars began his attack. It was heralded by two hundred camels bearing drums with their riders banging the deafening instruments. The sound they made was deafening and Tom asked, somewhat nervously, "Are they trying to knock the walls down with drums, Captain?"

"No, Tom, they are trying to frighten us." I saw that others were affected, and I said to Sir Reginald, "We could upset their animals if you like, my lord. It might stop some of the men becoming so nervous." I nodded toward some of the men at arms.

"We have had no orders yet, War Bow."

"And we haven't tested the range yet, my lord."

He smiled. "Then a few volleys to test the range might be in order."

I turned to my eager archers. "Let us test these new bows and those with the longbow use them just to keep your eye in! Let us try to silence the drums, eh?"

There was nothing my men loved more than a contest, and each eagerly picked up their bow of choice. I nocked a long Mamluk arrow. All of my Mongolian arrows had been used and while these were not quite as good, they would have to do. "Draw!"

The Asian bows did not creak, and that was something I would have to get used to if I was going to use this bow more frequently.

"Release!"

Eleven arrows flew straight and true; nine drummers and two camels were struck. The effect of the hits on the camels was dramatic. It maddened them. You would have thought the drumming would have had that effect, but the smell of blood drove them wild. After three more volleys, the drumming had ceased and the men on the walls cheered.

It heralded the beginning of the attack. The bodies of five camels and more than a dozen men lay between us and the attackers. The Mamluks would have to clear them first. The horn in the English tower sounded three times and that meant we had permission to use our bows.

"Target the men shifting the bodies. If we can make them leave them before us, then they are at a disadvantage!"

It was not noble, but it was effective and we each chose our targets so that the pile of bodies did not diminish, but grow. As the rest of the attack did not have bodies with which to contend, the walls further along were assaulted. The tower of King Hugh was on a corner and could be attacked from two sides. Long before the first ladders were placed against our walls, the fighting there was intense. The Mamluks gave up on shifting the dead and used huge shields, behind which they advanced.

"Save your arrows for the sight of a man. Those shields will waste your arrow."

My men were good, and they were poised for any mistake. When a Mamluk behind a pavise tripped on a body, William of Matlac sent an arrow into his head. Thus, their progress towards us was slow. I glanced now and then towards the tower of King Hugh and saw that the Mamluks had ladders against the battlements and both sides were losing men. If we lost one tower, then the integrity of the defences was in danger.

I forced my attention back to our wall. Sir Reginald had his and Sir William's men at arms ready. He had them in two lines, set to strike at any ladder that made contact with the walls. My men and I would split into two groups when that happened and kill the men trying to climb.

A warrior can only protect himself from one side at a time. When the ladder carriers came, they were vulnerable and after we had killed the carriers of four ladders, their leader took to sending twenty men with each ladder. We still killed men, but the ladders reached the walls and there, the men could hide behind their shields. We needed patience.

There were large rocks on the fighting platform and Sir Reginald picked the first up himself. As he lumbered towards the crenulations, I said, "Watch for archers!" He would be exposed when he raised the rock above his head. Three archers levelled their bows as they saw his helmet approach the walls, but eight arrows ended their lives, and Sir Reginald dropped the huge stone to smash into the skull of a climbing warrior, knocking him and two others to the ground.

Worse for the enemy was that the ladder was also knocked to the ground, and they had to begin again. It was the same story all the way around the walls, but while we had better numbers, then Baibars would lose more men than we. It was obvious that he had that advantage, but with a Mongol army close by, he could not afford to haemorrhage on the walls of Acre.

By nightfall, the attack had petered out. I sent for more arrows from the armoury and for food and drink. Our supply of rocks was half gone, but our tower had suffered not a single casualty, not even a scratch. When my men returned with the food, we heard that six knights and ten men at arms had been lost at the Tower of King Hugh.

That night they attempted a night assault. Perhaps they thought that our bows would be ineffective or that we would be tired. Whatever the reason, it took place during the first watch, when Richard of Culcheth shouted, "Alarm! We are under attack!"

Fully dressed, we rose and hurried to the walls. I turned to Alan. "Fetch brands! Let us see if their ladders will burn."

"Aye, Captain."

Sir Reginald said to his chosen man, "Sergeant, see if you can lay your hands on some oil!" Grinning, the English man at arms hurried off. We did not know it, but ours was the only tower that had prepared fire. We were still able to use our bows, but the darkness made them less effective. We could only hit them when we could see them, and that was normally when they were at the bottom of the ladder!

We slowed them down and then the fire and the oil arrived. We placed the amphorae next to the brazier to heat it up. When the men lifted it, they would have to use their cloaks to protect their hands from the heat. The sergeant kept an eye on the oil to ensure that it did not ignite.

I said, "Let them fill the ladder up. Will, you and Tom be ready to clear the top of the ladder."

I nodded to Sir Reginald, who commanded, "Lift the amphora."

If the darkness limited our archers, it totally disarmed the Muslim ones, who could see nothing. The two men hoisted the amphora and awaited the orders from Sir Reginald who peered over the side. When he was happy, he nodded at me and then said, "Now!"

As the heated, viscous oil slithered down the ladder, soaking it and the men who were climbing, Alan and I threw two lighted brands. He threw his halfway down and mine was sent a third of the way down. The Muslims screamed as they knew what was coming. Those who might have escaped were towards the bottom, but the oil had yet to find them. When the two brands ignited the oil, four soaked men and the ladder lit up the night sky. The flames rose so high that, had I not jerked back my head, I would have singed my beard. In England, I had not worn a beard, but the journey to the khan meant I had allowed it to grow and now I almost came to regret it.

My archers were not needed and all those on the ladder perished. Even worse, from a Mamluk perspective, was that the falling, burning bodies and ladder fell upon men waiting to ascend, as well as the spare ladders. Although we were the only tower to use fire, the effect was to make the men on other towers retreat down their ladders. The human, screaming torches had demoralised them.

When, the next morning, we viewed the battlefield before the walls, we were greeted with the smell of charred flesh. Few wished to eat that morning. We should all have eaten, for they attacked again – and this time, they had vengeance on their minds. In addition, they knew that their archers could target any men attempting to use fire. That was a weapon for the night.

This time, the Mamluks actually made the top of the ladder. My arm burned as I sent arrow after arrow into the flood of men climbing and attempting to reach the top of the gatehouse. That none did was down to the skill and strength of my archers and the mail and shields of the men at arms. We had our first wound; one of the men at arms had a cut on his face.

That night, we waited for a night attack again, but it never materialised.

The next day, the Mamluk army began to head north. We did not discover the reason for a couple of days, and then we heard that the Mongols were close to Aleppo. Lord Edward's strategy appeared to have worked – and we had allies!

Chapter 15

We went back to our normal routine and that meant I spent the night in the antechamber once more. I quite liked the ritual, for it meant I got to see Mary each night. The sentries outside the two chambers were quite sympathetic. My actions at the gate had been discussed amongst the garrison and the real soldiers recognised what we had done at St Antony's gate.

Mary had also heard the stories and had been able to watch from within the castle. The castle was close to the gate and she and Lady Eleanor were spectators. I wondered if the presence of Lady Eleanor had been a factor in my reward, for a day after it became obvious that the Mamluks had headed north, I was summoned to Lord Edward's rooms and rewarded with a purse of gold.

"It seems you have the luck and, perhaps, the judgement of a good warrior. Despite ignoring my orders, your attack in the drums helped us and your decision to use a brazier was quite brilliant. It is a pity that you did not think to mention it to me, for then men's lives would have been saved." He smiled a silky smile. "Still, you are not a noble and for an archer, you have good instincts."

If he had thought to insult me, then he did not know me. His wife, the wise Lady Eleanor, knew me better. I was able to give my men one gold coin each and I still had nine left for me. When we cleared the battlefield, my men and I had also reaped the reward. The grisly remains of the Mamluk dead had needed a strong stomach but as we had slain them, we took their treasures and we were all richer.

We waited for two weeks to see if the Mongolian attack had succeeded. Had they defeated Baibars? In the end, the news was something of an anti-climax. It had been a bloody draw. Both sides lost heavily but there was no victor, and Baibars still held the Holy Land. I never knew what happened to Ahmed and his general, Samagar. I hoped my friend lived, but I knew from my short time with him that the Mongols viewed death in battle differently from Christians.

I am not certain what would have happened, had not Leo of Armenia and King Hugh suggested a meeting with Baibars. Lord Edward, in theory, was the lowliest of the three, but I knew that he would lead the negotiations. It was his way. A meeting was arranged in Nablus and we were given guarantees for our safety. Hostages were exchanged and a healthy escort was chosen.

I was included in the party, which surprised me. It was Lady Eleanor who told me why. As I was speaking with Mary one night, prior to my nocturnal duty, she approached us. She gave us both a knowing smile and put her hands on ours. It was almost as though we were receiving a blessing – and yet her action was nothing to do with us. She needed to speak with me, and she trusted Mary completely. Since Mary had joined the ladies of Lady Eleanor, she had become an integral part of the circle and I feared that I would lose her when we left the Holy Land. When we returned to England, she would surely choose the court over Yarpole!

"I have asked my husband to take you when he visits Baibars. He says he has knights and that he is guaranteed his safety, but I love my husband and do not trust these heathens. You have something knights do not have, Gerald, you have common sense and, more than that, from what I had seen, you have a good sense of survival. The stories I have heard tell me that few men survive one assassin attack, let alone two. I pray you watch over my husband in case there are those who wish him harm."

"Of course, Lady Eleanor."

She looked relieved and she put my hand on Mary's. "And show common sense by keeping hold of this one. The two of you are meant for each other and it is rare for that to happen. Do not jeopardise it because neither of you has the words!"

When she had gone, I know I was blushing, and Mary laughed. "Lady Eleanor is a wise woman. I would have been happy to be her slave! You are open and honest, and she is right, but I fear that, until we take ship away from here, I will never truly believe that I am free. I think I know how you feel, but I would ask you to be patient. Once we set foot in France and head north to England, then ask me again but for now, you watch out for yourself as well as Lord Edward."

Once again, she kissed me, and I slept happily that night with pleasant dreams and a hope of peace.

Lord Edward sent for me the next morning. "You will come with me tomorrow to this meeting. You will be the only one who is not a knight, but I need you, for you seem to be one of the few men not terrified by these killers from the mountains. You will be my shadow and stand behind me. To that end, I wish you to wear this mail beneath your top." He handed me a short byrnie. "You will not need your bow, and this will stop a knife ending your life before you can save me."

To be fair to Lord Edward, he was honest with me.

"Of course, my lord."

"And when I survive there will be a reward for you." I nodded. He said, suddenly, "Are you like that turncoat, l'Estrange? Do you wish spurs?"

I was able to smile and to answer honestly. "I need no spurs, my lord, I like being my own man."

For some reason, that seemed to make him inordinately happy. "You are a good man and all the better for never having changed! Would that all men were like you!"

The next day, we headed towards Nablus. The military orders were noticeable by their absence, for the Mamluks mistrusted them all, even the Hospitallers. We were escorted by twenty knights. Of course, if there was treachery then we would all die, but Baibars, I came to learn, was no fool. The murder in such a public place of the future King of England would rouse the whole of Europe into a crusade that even Baibars might lose.

Despite the guarantees, no one on either side was willing to risk entering a building to negotiate and, accordingly, a huge open-sided tent had been erected. The Mamluks were there already. The other two Christian negotiators – King Hugh and Leo of Armenia – also had body-guards but in their cases, mailed knights. I looked like an afterthought in comparison with their fine helmets, livery, greaves, mailed mittens and long swords, but I think I must have looked imposing enough, as my broad chest and mighty arms showed my strength. As the six of us and the Bishop of Jerusalem walked towards the shade of the tent and the table with four chairs on each side, I do not think that it was arrogance that made me aware that Baibars was staring at me. I knew him, for he was in the centre of the four Mamluks.

All the nobles sat down and I stood behind Lord Edward. I studied the men opposite. Baibars had wrested the Holy Land, piece by piece, back from the Christians and his face was like Lord Edward's; it was a face with the lines of experience and eyes that could read an opponent. One of the other three was a younger man than Baibars, while the other two were of an age with the Mamluk leader.

It was the young man who spoke, and he spoke in French. During the negotiations, the translator constantly referred back to Baibars. Thanks to my journey to the khan's yurt and my interactions in Acre, I knew a few more Arabic words and although I could not follow all of the conversation between Baibars and his translator, I picked out enough to augment the few French words I knew.

It soon became clear that the Mamluks thought Lord Edward's attempt to invoke a Mongolian invasion had failed and they wanted Acre. The purpose of my presence also became clear, for I heard my name used, first by Lord Edward and later when the translator used the Arabic for war bow. It was confirmed when Baibars' eyes focussed on me and narrowed. I deduced that Lord Edward was using me as a threat. He was suggesting that he might send me back for more of my Mongolian friends.

King Hugh and Leo of Armenia said little in the early discussions, but once they came to talk of a truce they were more vocal. In light of later events, I think that King Hugh had already given up on the Holy Land, for as soon as we returned to Acre, he took ship for Cyprus and never set foot in Acre again. Leo of Armenia was merely trying to ensure that his borders were safe and when the Mongolian threat was mentioned, I saw him shift uncomfortably in his seat. The Belen Pass was now back in Mongolian hands and very close to his borders. Lord Edward's allies might have failed to defeat the Mamluks, but Leo knew that ten thousand Mongolians could easily take Armenia!

It took some hours, but eventually, a ten-year truce was agreed.

Neither Baibars nor Lord Edward was happy about that. I was not versed in political matters, but even I could recognise the disquiet in raised voices and the angry faces of men forced to compromise. Lord Edward did not live here and he would be leaving for England at some time. He had to accede to the demands of King Hugh and Leo of Armenia. Baibars, for his part, thought that he could take Acre, but the trouble in Egypt and the threat from the Mongols forced his hand. There was no handshake, but there was a promise of documents to be exchanged. It was clear that they would mean nothing. The truce would only last as long as Baibars chose.

I rode behind Lord Edward and his brother, Edmund. Sir John, carrying the English standard, rode next to me. Not a word had been spoken to King Hugh and Leo of Armenia and it was obvious to all that the ninth crusade was over. While my mind prepared for a journey home, I caught drifts of conversation from Lord Edward and his brother. It was obvious that Lord Edward wished to stay and finish the job. His brother argued that, as their father was ill, Lord Edward's duty was back in England. They compromised, and it was agreed that Lord Edmund would return to England and support the clerk who was running the king's council.

My heart sank when I heard that decision. I had hoped that we would return to Acre and begin preparations to head home. In hindsight, I suppose I could have asked Lord Edward's permission to sail with his brother, but I was too loyal. I never thought of myself. Since I began to follow Lord Edward's banner, I had obeyed every request and order he had ever given to me. Even when Lord Edward was incarcerated after Lewes, I had worked to free him. I would stay until he left and then sail home.

News of the truce had reached Acre before we did, and already there were knights who were pre-empting a command to return home and ships were being hired. My archers had heard the news and when I had stabled Eleanor and joined them, they assaulted me with questions. I had to disappoint them.

"Lord Edward remains in Acre and I know not how long for. We will return to Yarpole as swiftly as we can, but I cannot say when that will be."

Some of the men were philosophical about the whole thing. Acre was an interesting city and they now knew their way around it. Most had heeded my advice about purchasing goods to take back to England to make them even richer but some, like William of Matlac and Richard of Culcheth, felt that they had been crusaders and having thus guaranteed their entry into heaven, could go home and restart their lives. I knew that his capture in the forests close to Yarpole had changed his Richard's life, and he wanted his son to marry so that he could have grandchildren.

The second evening back, I was invited to dine in the hall used by Lord Edward. It was a farewell meal for Lord Edmund, and I was slightly honoured to be invited. I say slightly, for I always felt that such invitations were an afterthought.

I realised as I entered – richly dressed in my Mongolian robes – that Lady Eleanor had invited me, for there was a seat next to Lady Mary, as she was now addressed. The knowing smile on Lady Eleanor's face showed me the conspiracy.

Lord Edward looked up from where he had his head bowed next to his brother to give me a nod. Lord Edmund was being given instructions about the realm. If his father succumbed to his illness, then Lord Edmund would ensure that it would still be there for Lord Edward to inherit.

Mary fingered the fine cloth of the Mongolian garb and smiled. "Each time I see this, I think back to my time with Lady Maria."

"Then I will have it burned, for I would not have you endure sad memories on my account."

She laughed and shook her head. "My time as a slave was not all bad. This garb reminds me of the fine clothes I wore when Lady Maria dressed me as her twin. I grew used to such clothes."

"And when we reach England, then you shall have the finest of clothes – so that all will have to shade their eyes from the vision of loveliness that is Mary!"

She rolled her eyes. "The attention I seek is that of your eyes and not others'. I have been the centre of attention and I like it not. I would have thought that you, of all people, would have understood that."

I did not understand. "What do you mean?"

She sighed and lowered her voice. Nodding towards Lord Edward with her head, she said, "Your men, the archers who follow you, are safer than you, for you are the one chosen to be with Lord Edward and in danger. Even when he does not choose to place you there, you put yourself in harm's way. Do you not wish for a quiet life in this house in Yarpole? Do you not wish to be simply Gerald, landowner?"

I had not thought about it. Then, as I looked into her eyes, I saw that she was pleading with me to speak and I found myself in an area I did not know. Women were a mystery to me.

Suddenly, Lady Eleanor leaned into me, for I was seated next to her, and said, "Gerald, think with your heart and not your head. A woman needs honesty. What are you afraid of?"

I turned and said, equally quietly, "And if I am laughed at? How can I face anyone?"

She smiled. "This is the man who can face a horde of Mamluk archers and not turn a hair. This is the man who can fight and kill the deadliest of killers and yet, he is afraid of words! It will not happen but if it did, so what? At least if you give voice to that which lies within you, then you will have an answer and you will be able to get on with life at Yarpole." She nodded towards Mary.

I sighed. Lady Eleanor was right, and so I spoke. "You once said that you would wait until we stepped on to French soil before you gave me an answer. I suspect that something has changed and so I will risk a question. Could you be happy as mistress of Yarpole? I have little to offer you, save a love that will never die."

She shook her head and I saw a tear appear in the corner of her eye. She wiped it away and said, "You are a goose! You are the man who risked all to rescue me. I owe you my life, but you are right. That is not enough to commit me to a life with you. Since my rescue, I have seen you with the high and the mighty and with your men. You are the same with all and there is none who will speak a word against you. And as for me, I find you make me laugh even though you do not always mean to and I love that as strong a man as you are, you are also gentle with those around you." She sipped her wine. "But you should know all that there is about me. I am not young and my treatment at the hands of Salar and his men…" she shuddered, "well, I am not certain that I can enjoy laying with a man. The only men who have known me, took me. Do you understand?" I nodded. "It may well be that I can never have children. If you wish to reconsider your kind offer, then I will understand, for Lady Eleanor has promised me a place at court."

My mouth must have dropped open for she closed it with an elegant finger. "You would choose the life with a peasant over a place at court?"

"In a heartbeat." To emphasise her words, she put her hand on my heart.

"Then we shall return to Yarpole and you shall be a lady there. I may not wish a title for me, but Lord Edward owes me a title for you."

She shook her head. "No, I would be happy to be Mistress Mary, wife of Gerald War Bow."

Lady Eleanor had obviously been listening to us rather than her husband and brother-in-law, for she leaned over and said, "And you may have rejected spurs, but I will have Lord Edward make you a gentleman and all that it entails. Would you be wed here in Acre?"

I looked at Mary, who shook her head, and I said, "I think not, Lady Eleanor, for I still have my nightly duties to perform."

"Nonsense! There is a truce and you are no longer needed."

"Nonetheless, until we leave these shores then I will do my duty and besides, I have a lovely church in Yarpole and there are men there who have followed my bow. With all due respect, Lady Eleanor, I would rather they attended the wedding than all of these lords!"

I suddenly realised what I had said, and I burst out, "I am sorry, I meant no offence!"

She laughed and shook her head. "You are Gerald War Bow and true to yourself. I am glad that my husband has you close to him, for you are like the roots of a mighty oak tree, which hold it to the ground. As much as I would love to attend your wedding, I would rather you had those around you whom you respect – and my opinion of you is higher and not lower!"

And that one dinner changed my life. Had Lady Eleanor not urged me to be honest, then I might not have spoken, and Mary would have enjoyed life at court while I would have been a bachelor to the end of my days. However, the decision made by Lord Edward to stay in Acre also had ramifications. Those dark clouds were on the horizon as I went to bed that night, as happy as I had ever been.

Chapter 16

A week later, we watched Lord Edmund and most of the English crusaders head for home. King Hugh and his knights had already left, and the castle had the deserted air of a plague-ridden city. The knights and men who remained all wished to return home too but were compelled to stay with Lord Edward.

The sight of the fleets of ships heading for Sicily and Cyprus made all of us depressed, especially Lady Eleanor who wished to see her children. Lord Edward was still planning something, but I could not deduce why he remained. Luckily, I was not needed, apart from my night-time duties, and Lady Eleanor was able to send Mary on many errands which necessitated a bodyguard of me and my archers. They all knew of my plans and that made them happy, for it confirmed that we would be going home, sometime.

We came to know the markets and bazaars of Acre well and we all used our coin wisely. We sold the weapons and treasure we had collected and converted the proceeds into fine cloth and spices. I also had teak and cedar chests made to transport the goods safely home. Mary had asked me about the house, and I realised how mean and poor it would be. I was honest with Mary, so she knew what to expect and we spoke of the home she would like to have. We purchased wood, which we would take home and have made into furniture. We had a month of such expeditions. It was as we walked in the markets and passed the fine houses that we spoke of the hall and furnishings as they might be. It was then I realised I would have to build a new hall – and in stone. That would mean finding more money!

It was June, and the weather was becoming unbearably hot. Mary and I now had a regular routine where I would spend half an hour outside her room, enabling us to hold hands and enjoy a chaste kiss before I retired. The sentries outside Lord Edward's room changed each night, but they all knew of our lovers' meeting and smiled knowingly as I went to perform my duty in the antechamber. Apart from the one night when I had been wounded, it had never changed. I would lay my fur on the floor behind the door and place my Mamluk sword and dagger close to hand. I always slept in a pair of sleeping breeks, for if I was called into action, I did not want my nakedness to offend Lady Eleanor. Then, after my prayers, I would lie down to sleep. Since the truce talks, my thoughts, before I drifted off to sleep, had been filled with Mary's face and images of Yarpole.

That night in June was no different from any other except that it was very hot. The weather had grown oppressively hot and those who had lived in Acre for many years predicted a thunderstorm. I had always found the nights too hot in this land, but that night it was particularly so. Added to that, I had eaten some seafood that had not agreed with me and so I had had to rise, in the middle of the night, and go to the garderobe at the end of the corridor.

The sentry, Ralph, nodded as I gestured towards the chamber. He would stand in the door until I returned. That too had evolved over the months that I had performed this duty. The night was so hot that I stayed longer than I needed to, just to take advantage of the slight breeze coming up the garderobe. Eventually, the smell from below made me move.

Ralph smiled as I approached him. "It is hot tonight, Captain, and no mistake! I know not how these heathens stand it. I shall be glad to get back to cooler climes. We might complain about the winters, but at least a man can sleep in the summer."

"Aye, you have the right of it. You never know, Lord Edward may decide to return home soon."

Ralph lowered his voice. "Between the two of us, Captain, I know not why we are still here. We have not enough men left to fight a battle and we have a truce." He shook his head. "And the ale is poor!"

I could not say what was in my mind – that Lord Edward hoped the Mongols might return in greater numbers and conquer the whole of the Holy Land. "Goodnight, Ralph."

I entered the room and placed my sleeping fur on the ground. I was about to bar the door when I decided to wait a while for the door was ajar and the cooler breeze made the room more comfortable. I would let the breeze cool it down slightly before I closed the door and entered the steam room that was my bedchamber.

The prickly heat made me reluctant to lie down and that single pause was enough. As I stood and listened to Ralph's footsteps as he moved down the corridor towards the arrow slit which gave some air, I thought I heard a noise from within the chamber. That was not unusual and, in the months that I had been doing this, I had grown accustomed to the noises the royal couple made.

This one was different and some thought in my head, for which I could not account, told me to investigate.

I picked up my sword and, slowly and quietly, opened the door to the bedchamber. The couple were rich enough to keep a candle burning at night. I knew that Lord Edward liked to use the night pot and it was as I entered that I saw the figure, unlikely though it was, hanging like a human spider from the window.

It was an assassin and he was squeezing through the arrow slit.

"Awake!"

I was fast but the lithe little figure was faster. Even as I took the two strides across the room, he had leapt towards the bed. Lord Edward was also gifted with quick reactions and he rose to face whatever threat it was. Lady Eleanor woke and seeing the naked assassin, screamed. I heard Ralph pushing open the door to my antechamber and shouting, "Captain!"

Lord Edward saw the assassin and he stood, raising his hand to fend off the blow which was coming his way. He partially succeeded, but the razor-sharp knife laid open his left arm. By that time, I was close enough to swing my sword and I backhanded hard across the assassin's neck. My sword was kept sharp at all times and the assassin's head flew from his shoulders.

Ralph entered and I shouted, "Send a man to the bailey. The killer climbed the wall and there may be another with him. Call out the guard and fetch Sir John Malton!" At times like these, I needed to know that I could depend on the men who came to aid me.

"Aye, Captain!"

Lady Eleanor had got over her fright and was bandaging Lord Edward's arm. I lifted the dagger the assassin had used and, picking it up by the handle, sniffed it. Wolfsbane! I ran to my room and brought the phial I had been given by the Mongols.

Opening it, I said urgently, "Lord Edward, drink this!" I could see his eyes were wide and his pupils were dilating. The poison was working. "Lady Eleanor, it is wolfsbane on the dagger, and this is the antidote. We have moments to save the next King of England!"

She grabbed the phial from me. "Hold back his head and pinch his nose!"

I did not think of what I was doing. It was only later that I realised I had laid hands on my future king! As his mouth opened, Lady Eleanor poured the liquid down his throat and then held his jaws shut. I changed my grip so that I held his shoulders as he began to thrash. Had I not been so strong, then he might have hurt himself, but between us, we held him.

Sir John and the other household knights ran in with drawn swords. The tableau that met their eyes must have seemed like some kind of weird nightmare. Lord Edward lay on the bed with a bloody bandage around his arm and he was unconscious. Lady Eleanor and I still cradled his head and body, and the headless body of the would-be killer lay in an ever-widening pool of blood.

I shouted, "Sir John, the assassin climbed in through the arrow slit and there may be another!"

"Impossible!"

I shook my head. "Then explain the dead killer there, for he did not pass me nor Ralph!"

He went to guard the window with a drawn sword.

Lady Eleanor shouted, "Fetch a healer, for my husband has been stabbed and poisoned." I think speaking those words drove her over the edge. She had been in control until then and now she began to weep and sob. "My husband, do not die! I beg you to live! Dear Lord, save this man who came to wrest your land from the heathen."

Just then a physician appeared; he was English and looked nervous. "Give me light and give me space."

He looked pointedly at me and I shook my head. "I stay with him until he wakes, doctor. There has been one attempt on his life, and I will ensure that there is not another!"

"But I am a physician and I heal!"

"Perhaps." I turned. "Sir John, you stay here with us, the rest leave but guard the door and have the castle sealed and searched, for there may be other killers."

Sir John Vesci said, "I do not take orders from an archer!"

Lady Eleanor's voice was as cold and commanding as I had ever heard and she snapped, "Then obey me, for until he recovers, Gerald War Bow decides who has access to Lord Edward! If it was not for him then Lord Edward would be already dead!"

That worked.

By dawn, the wound had been cleaned and stitched. To all intents and purposes, we seemed to have healed Lord Edward. The physician had left us, complaining about English peasants. That began the longest two days of my life. Lady Eleanor, Sir John and I slept in the bedchamber of Lord Edward. Four knights guarded the door and the three ladies, Anne, Maud and Mary, saw to our food and drink. On the third day, Lord Edward had not fully woken and he fitfully became conscious and then unconscious. When he was conscious, we gave him wine and tried to give him broth. His arm blackened and began to stink and when we summoned the physician, he seemed at a loss with how to proceed.

For the first time since the attack, Lady Eleanor erupted. "Get from here, leech, and hie you back to England for you are a poor apology for a physician!" He ran from the room and had not the situation been so serious, then I might have laughed at the speed of his departure.

Lady Eleanor began to sob on Lady Maud's arm; the two ladies were close.

Mary looked at me and then said, "Lady Eleanor, there are some good physicians in the Venetian quarter. They are Greek and know their business. Since the truce, many have been trying to take a ship home. I can speak Greek; would you like me to fetch one?"

The relief on Lady Eleanor's face almost broke my heart. This lady loved Lord Edward. "I would give half my husband's kingdom if he could be saved."

"I do not think that it will come to that. I shall go now."

Lady Eleanor said, "The Venetian Quarter is closer to the harbour. Gerald, guard her and make certain that she and the doctor are safe." I looked at the others in the room. "Sir John is just a knight, but I think he can keep you safe with four knights outside the door!"

I nodded and I donned my cloak, while Mary went to fetch her own. There was a high degree of security, but my name and my face guaranteed that none would stand in our way or stop us. To make certain, I ran with drawn Mamluk sword.

We passed the hall and castle of the Teutonic Knights and I spied the masts of the ships in the harbour. With no tide to speak of, ships were leaving and entering at all hours of the day. The fact that it was late afternoon made no difference. I was suddenly aware that England's fate lay in the hands of a former Greek slave. If Lord Edward died, then Edmund would become king and as much as I liked him, he did not possess one-tenth of his brother's ability. Edmund would make a good commander of knights on a battlefield, but ask him to direct them and the battle would be lost.

Mary knew exactly where to go, for she had been on errands for Lady Eleanor and visited the harbour, although it had been in broad daylight and she had been heavily escorted. She went directly to an inn. It was on the waterfront and had tables outside. I recognised the physicians and healers by the tools of their trade, which they proffered in hope of employment. These were waiting for a ship and either had not enough money or were hoping for a master who would guarantee pay. I sheathed my sword to lessen their fears of this wild Englishman.

Mary did not stand on ceremony. She stood with her hands on her hips and rattled out Greek. I saw the wisdom of her strategy. Those who were not Greek looked bemused, while the ones she sought looked attentive. One spoke, and then another. She asked them more questions. I knew that they were questions, for each man answered her. She nodded and pointed at one who picked up his bags. "Basil is the one for us."

Others began to clamour for employment. I did not speak Greek, but I knew how to impress upon others. I turned and half drew my sword. "We have made our choice – now back off or be prepared to heal yourselves!"

Mary smiled. "I can see that you will be a good husband who knows how to talk to tradesmen – but never make the mistake of speaking to me in that tone!"

We hurried back through darkening and ever-threatening streets. We had just passed the castle of the Teutonic Knights when three men stepped out from the shadows. Almost without thinking, I drew my sword and my dagger. I knew, from their garb, that they were English – and I knew their story. Their lord had either died or left them, and that told me their worth. If they were good men, they would not have been left and if their lord had died, they would have found employment elsewhere.

They were a mob and I spoke quietly but with authority. "Back away or you will die. There is nought for you here."

The leader – I knew who it was because he spoke to me – was a man almost as big as me but running to fat. He had been a man at arms and had a faded livery but no mail. That was often the first thing a man would sell. His sword had not been sharpened and he stank of ale. His two companions flanked him. They were equally intoxicated and had weapons that showed they had not cared for them.

"Friend, there are three of us. You and the perfumed one with you can leave, but that wench looks like she can earn a few coins for us and, at the very least, can give us pleasure. Back off and you shall live."

I was coldly angry. Mary had suffered enough at the hands of men like these, but they were Englishmen and I gave them one last chance. I used my name. "I am Captain Gerald War Bow and I know how to fight. Go now and you shall live. This is the last warning I shall give."

To be fair to the man's two companions, they hesitated and looked at each other, for they recognised my name. But their leader made the decision for them. I saw his eyes flicker and was ready when he swung his long sword at me. I blocked it with my own and after ramming my dagger under his ribs, brought my sword sideways into the side of the second man's head. As the two men fell, I inclined my head to one side. "You really wish to die?"

The third man turned and fled. Mary stood on her toes and kissed me. "You are always saving my honour. When we are wed you shall earn your reward! Now, physician, we run – for Lord Edward's life is in danger."

We were admitted to the castle quickly and we whisked the physician up the stairs. He was breathless as he looked at the body. He sniffed. "The wound is putrefying!"

Mary snapped, "As I told you! You said you were the best, now if you are to prove it, you need to save the life of Lord Edward." She lowered her voice. "Failure could be fatal for you!" My wife-to-be had a hard side to her.

He looked shocked. Lady Eleanor said, "Physician, do your best. If you must take the arm, then so be it, but he must live. England shall need him."

He nodded. "Then I shall do my best. I need hot water and vinegar."
Lady Eleanor said, "Ladies, see to his needs."

Sir John and Richard, his squire, had been dozing in their chairs and now they rose. Doctor Basil said, "I will need you three men to hold him." I nodded as he began to cut away the bloody and stinking bandages.

The wound was worse than it had been. I feared that Lord Edward would lose his arm. The physician, however, sniffed, poked and then nodded. He unwrapped his roll of tools as boiling water was fetched by servants and the ladies brought the rest of his requests. He dumped his tools in the boiling water – all except for a pair of tongs.

He turned to Lady Eleanor. "Lady, I need to cut away all of this blackened flesh. It will leave a hole, which might appear to be as deep as the Dead Sea, but it is the only way to save his arm. It is good that it is his left and not as much use as his right. There will be blood and he may cry out, but what I do may save his life."

"Will he have a hole in his arm?" There was genuine fear in Lady Eleanor's voice.

Doctor Basil smiled. "The human body is remarkable and the flesh – or some of it – will regrow and I will not touch the muscle. He was lucky when the knife struck, for it damaged just flesh." He hesitated. "Was this an attack by an assassin?" Lady Eleanor nodded. "Then he is indeed lucky, for whoever gave him the antidote has saved his life. Now, we begin. You three hold him. Squire, you shall hold the head. Archer, you are strong; hold his left arm for that must be still. I dare not nick a vein or artery. You, sir knight, hold his right. If you – Lady Mary and Lady Eleanor – would sit on his legs, then I shall begin!"

The two ladies had their backs to the operation and they could avert their eyes, but the three men had no such option. When the operation began, Lord Edward was, mercifully, unconscious – but he did not remain that way. The doctor placed a piece of smoothed wood between Lord Edward's teeth. I saw the bite marks, which showed where other patients had bitten down. He put a tourniquet around Lord Edward's upper left arm, and he tightened it. Satisfied with his preparations, he took the tongs and extracted a long thin blade from the boiling water. It had a metal handle and must have burned when he touched it, but he showed no sign of distress.

Then, he made a swift incision. I was the closest to the blade and I saw that he cut into healthy flesh. He sliced all the way around the blackened flesh. It reminded me of the way I had seen a bishop once cut a bruise from an apple, delicately. There was blood, but the leather thong around Lord Edward's upper arm prevented a deluge.

The doctor then began the gory but necessary work of slicing away the blackened dead flesh. The more he cut, the worse was the smell. I wondered just how much flesh would need to be removed. As he neared the healthier flesh, so Lord Edward felt the pain and I was aware of movement. I held on tightly, so that the doctor's hand was not jarred. Lord Edward's eyes opened, and he stared at me. The wood in his mouth prevented words. He was trying to rise but, between us, we held him down. As the doctor cut away another piece of black flesh, Lord Edward's eyes closed, and he was still.

"We are almost finished. That was well done by all of you, but do not relax now. There is still a piece of dead flesh, which I must remove."

I saw pink, healthy flesh when the last blackened piece had been removed. The arm looked strangely deformed and I wondered if Lord Edward would ever be able to use it. The doctor dropped the blade into the boiling water and took the white wine he had brought with him. He poured it into the wound. Then, he took honey and smeared that over the flesh. I was in more familiar territory now, for we archers knew that honey stopped bleeding and seemed to aid the healing process.

He covered the wound with a strong-smelling salve from a jar and then he loosened the tourniquet to let blood flow into the arm. There was a little seepage of blood and the doctor applied more honey and salve to those areas. Satisfied, he began to bandage the arm.

"Ladies you may stand and you two gentlemen may release his lordship. Archer, maintain your hold if you please."

Lady Eleanor came around to hold her husband's right hand. She held it to her mouth and kissed it. Mary came behind me and held me around the waist. She looked at the dish with the blackened putrefied flesh and shook her head. "All of that from one cut!"

"It was a poisoned blade." I sounded matter of fact, but I was thinking that I had had three encounters with assassins. I had been lucky, but that sort of luck cannot last. I would head home as soon as time allowed.

The physician put his instruments and salves back in his bag. Lady Eleanor asked, "What next?"

"He should begin to heal. The flesh will grow back, as will the skin, but there will be a permanent scar and mark there. In the fullness of time, he will recover the use of his arm and he will be almost as he was before, but he will know that the arm is weaker."

Lady Eleanor handed him a purse of coins. "I would not have you leave Acre, Doctor Basil, until my husband can thank you." Lady Eleanor was a strong woman and there was a threat in her words.

The doctor nodded. "I will call again tomorrow." He looked at me. "Archer, I have to cross to the Venetian Quarter and…"

"And you fear that you may be attacked." He nodded. "Then I will escort you, and tomorrow I will send four of my archers to bring you back here."

"How will I know they are your men?"

I shook my head. "They are English archers! Trust me, you will know them."

Mary said as I left, "Be careful!"

"I shall."

Epilogue

Lord Edward was a strong man and by the third day after the operation, he was walking about the castle. He had three shadows with him, for Lady Eleanor feared another attack and so Sir John, Richard and I walked with him. Lord Edward had been in and out of consciousness since the attempt on his life and I took him through all of the events. He shook his head in disbelief when I told him that the killer had climbed the walls to enter. "And once again I owe you my life, Gerald War Bow. What reward would you have now?"

I did not mention that Lady Eleanor had promised me the title of gentleman. It was mine already and I was content with that. Instead, I said, as one man to another, "Lord Edward, let us go home. There is nothing more for us here. The assassins do not forget, and I fear that they may be the end of me yet. I am just an archer, but you are England's hope. Let us go home."

He nodded. "As plain spoken as ever, Gerald, and I will heed your advice. The crusade is bleeding away men daily. We will sail as soon as I can organise ships."

Sir John was on his other side and he said, "Lady Eleanor has already organised that, Lord Edward. We can sail at any time you decide."

He smiled. "I can see a conspiracy here, but one of which I approve, for you conspire to keep me alive! We leave in three days then. Sir John, let all those who need to know, know."

"Aye, Lord Edward."

He and Richard hurried off and with the two of us alone and looking out to the west, Lord Edward said, "My wife has told me that she has promised you the title of Gentleman."

"She has, Lord Edward, but, as you know, I was granted that title when you gave me Yarpole…"

He shook his head. "It is just that I do not think it was enough."

"It is, and now that Mary has agreed to be my wife, I can perhaps enjoy a life of peace."

"You and I will never know *that*, Gerald, but you are due some time with your bride-to-be and I need time to recover for, as you know, the attack took much out of me." He looked at his left arm in a sling and shook his head wryly. "Quite literally! However, I can give you more than just the title. You shall have hunting and timber gathering rights in the woods and forests of Yarpole and the surrounding countryside. I shall write to the baron and inform him."

As with our outward voyage, Lord Edward insisted upon my men sailing on his ship. This time, we were not attacked by pirates, but we avoided the African coast and sailed, instead, directly to Sicily.

As we sailed, I noticed a change come over Mary. The further west we sailed, the happier she became. The khanate and Byzantium were bad memories for her and although she had done well out of the experiences, she was glad to be leaving them behind. The days heading west were joyous ones, for we sailed with other ships and there was no danger.

When we reached Sicily, we were greeted with the news that King

Henry had died and when we heard that, we all dropped to one knee as Sir John shouted, "The king is dead! Long live the king!"

King Henry had been ill for some time and he and his sons were not close, but when a man's father dies, it makes him realise his own mortality so there was little celebration. Charles of Anjou ruled Sicily at the time, and we were housed in one of his palaces. The first evening on the island, I was invited, with Sir John and one or two others who were close to King Edward, to dine. Lady Eleanor and the ladies were there, and the new king spoke openly to us.

"I have decided that I will make the journey home through Italy and France. The Queen and I wish to visit with the Pope and give thanks for my life."

Queen Eleanor looked at me and smiled. My heart sank, for that meant an even longer journey to our home in England and it would delay my marriage. I was selfish enough to resent that.

King Edward carried on. "I have asked Sir John and ten of my household knights to accompany me. I will be safe in Italy and the Duke of Anjou has promised me an escort." Smiling, he said, "God, it seems, is as vengeful as me. Simon de Montfort the younger and his brother, Guy, were both taken by a plague, here in Italy. They thought they had escaped vengeance, but they were wrong." He turned to me. "My enemies appear to be dead and you may go directly home, Gerald War Bow. You have earned your time in England."

I did not know what to say, for I was conflicted. As much as I respected Sir John and the knights who would guard the king, they were not my men. I think the king saw the hesitation on my face and he said, "Gerald, let us go to the balcony and take the air."

We left the hall and went to the Moorish balcony that overlooked the courtyard.

"Gerald, I will be safe and in extending this journey, I am being selfish. I have left England in good hands."

"Lord Edmund?"

He laughed. "My brother is loyal and a stout knight, but he cannot rule England. Bishop Robert Burnell has been on the king's council for some time and when my brother returned to England, he took a letter with instructions for the bishop, so you see, I do not need you. Not for a while, anyway."

"Then I will obey you, and gladly. I will get to England as soon as I can."

He nodded and, putting his arm around my shoulders, led me back into the feasting hall. "Know this, that when I am crowned and when England needs you, I shall call upon you and your bow once more."

"And I will ever be there."

We parted the next day, for the ships that had brought us were still in the harbour. The parting between Mary and the queen was tearful, but the tears were tinged with joy.

Sir John and I had grown slightly apart for a time, but the assassin's attack had drawn us closer together. "It is now you who will have to watch the king's back, Sir John!"

"Aye, well, I have had a good teacher. Enjoy your time in England, Gerald War Bow."

With that, we set sail for France. The journey across the sea was not a quick one and took a month. After we had landed, we spent a further month and a half riding north to Calais, and I reflected that we were not the same men who had left on crusade two years earlier. I had spent almost five months travelling in the desert and two months at sea. We had fought in battles and sieges, but we had profited from our time away from home. My entire company of archers now rode horses that were the envy of knights, and each had a good sword made by the finest weaponsmiths in Acre. Our clothes marked us as men of means. The tanned faces and the crosses on our tunics marked us as crusaders and our journey north was accompanied by welcomes, even in France.

Once we landed in England we rode directly to Canterbury, where we all prayed at the place St Thomas was murdered and kissed the ground, for we were back in England. For Mary, the chilly and damp weather was something new but for my men, it was welcome, and they sang their way north and west.

I halted our caravan on the hill outside the village and waved a hand. I had first viewed Yarpole after Evesham and yet I had spent bare months there.

"Well, Mary, this is what I have brought you to. There is no castle and the hall is not what you are used to, but it is all mine."

She reached over and touched my hand. "And I do not care. I have lived in palaces, but this is better than any palace. Let us hurry and speak to your priest, for I would have the banns read and be wed just as soon as we can! My life begins the day we are joined."

I laughed. "You are a wanton! Let us ride. Master Gerald War Bow comes home to Yarpole with his bride-to-be!"

My men all cheered, and we galloped into the village. Life was good!

Historical Note

My story is that of Gerald War Bow, the archer. The kings and lords are incidental. It is the archers of England and Wales that I celebrate in this series of books.

The inspiration for this book came from the discovery that Lord Edward sent three men through enemy territory to persuade the Mongla Khan to attack the Mamluks. That they did so with alacrity is interesting. As history will attest, the Mongolian attack did not succeed. Lord Edward did negotiate a ten-year truce but Baibars, the Mamluk leader, sent an assassin to kill Lord Edward. The blackened flesh and its removal by a Greek doctor are recorded.

The strange story of the uniquely-named Hamo l'Estrange is a true one. He was one of the men who went on crusade with Lord Edward, and he married the Lady of Beirut. In my novel, it is a story of love – and I have to think it was as she made him Lord of Beirut and, on his deathbed, he willed it to Baibars so that his wife would be looked after – and she was.

The de Montfort brothers did murder Henry Almain in Germany, but they did not enjoy their revenge for very long. Simon died of Toscana virus at Siena, and his epitaph was "cursed by God, a wanderer and a fugitive".

When Lord Edward reached Sicily, he discovered that his father was dead and he was King of England, but he took two years to reach home. Unusually for England, this was a time of peace and the new king and queen enjoyed a grand tour.

Books used in the research:

The Normans, David Nicolle

The Knight in History, Francis Gies

The Norman Achievement, Richard F Cassady

Knights, Constance Brittain Bouchard

Feudal England: Historical Studies on the Eleventh and Twelfth Centuries, JH Round

Peveril Castle, English Heritage

The Longbow, Mike Loades

Norman Knight AD 950–1204, Christopher Gravett

English Medieval Knight 1200–1300, Christopher Gravett

English Medieval Knight 1300–1400, Christopher Gravett

The Scottish and Welsh Wars 1250–1400, Christopher Rothero

English Longbowman 1330–1515, Bartlett and Embleton

Lewes and Evesham 1264–65, Richard Brooks

A Great and Terrible King – Edward 1, Marc Morris

Glossary

Battle – a medieval formation of soldiers.

Burghers – Ordinary citizens of a town.

Caltrops – A weapon thrown to the ground to hurt horses. It was so made that whichever way it landed, there was a point sticking up.

Chevauchée – A raid by mounted horsemen.

Gammer – Mother, used as a term of affection for any older woman.

Garderobe – Toilet (basically, a seat above a hole which led outside a castle).

Hie you to – Get you to.

Hospitallers – A charitable religious order, such as the Knights Hospitaller.

Pursuivant – The rank below a herald.

Lightning Source UK Ltd.
Milton Keynes UK
UKHW011239191120
373690UK00002B/439

9 781839 012150